# THE DARK FREEZE

# THE DARK FREEZE

PETER GREGORY

Copyright © 2019 Peter Gregory

The moral right of the author has been asserted.

Apart from any fair dealing for the purposes of research or private study, or criticism or review, as permitted under the Copyright, Designs and Patents Act 1988, this publication may only be reproduced, stored or transmitted, in any form or by any means, with the prior permission in writing of the publishers, or in the case of reprographic reproduction in accordance with the terms of licences issued by the Copyright Licensing Agency. Enquiries concerning reproduction outside those terms should be sent to the publishers.

This is a work of fiction. Names, characters, businesses, places, events and incidents are either the products of the author's imagination or used in a fictitious manner. Any resemblance to actual persons, living or dead, or actual events is purely coincidental.

Matador
9 Priory Business Park,
Wistow Road, Kibworth Beauchamp,
Leicestershire. LE8 0RX
Tel: 0116 279 2299
Email: books@troubador.co.uk
Web: www.troubador.co.uk/matador
Twitter: @matadorbooks

ISBN 978 1838591 151

British Library Cataloguing in Publication Data.
A catalogue record for this book is available from the British Library.

Printed and bound in Great Britain by 4edge Limited
Typeset in 10.5pt Adobe Garamond Pro by Troubador Publishing Ltd, Leicester, UK

Matador is an imprint of Troubador Publishing Ltd

*For Andrew and Michael*

> Good science fiction is
> better than bad science
>
> Professor Martin Rees
> Astronomer Royal

# CONTENTS

## PART 1
## STRANGE HAPPENINGS

| | | |
|---|---|---|
| 1 | Impact | 3 |
| 2 | One Month Earlier | 6 |
| 3 | Liz Conway | 14 |
| 4 | Meteor Showers | 25 |
| 5 | Shock Wave | 35 |

## PART 2
## STRANGE FINDS

| | | |
|---|---|---|
| 6 | Meteorite Hunters | 41 |
| 7 | The Find | 51 |
| 8 | Analysis | 60 |
| 9 | Confirmation | 66 |
| 10 | Decisions | 74 |
| 11 | Leaks | 80 |
| 12 | Going Public | 89 |
| 13 | Religion Refuted | 97 |
| 14 | A Lull | 103 |

## PART 3
## COLLISION COURSE

| | | |
|---|---|---|
| 15 | Asteroid | 111 |
| 16 | Collision Course | 120 |
| 17 | Black Deflection | 126 |
| 18 | Illicit Love | 132 |
| 19 | A Surprise | 137 |

## PART 4
## DARK DAYS

| 20 | Earth Orbit | 141 |
| 21 | Nuclear Winter | 147 |
| 22 | Alien Life | 157 |
| 23 | Plans | 166 |
| 24 | Life at the Edge | 175 |
| 25 | The Dark Freeze | 184 |
| 26 | Activity | 195 |

## PART 5
## END GAME

| 27 | Scouting Mission | 199 |
| 28 | First Glimpse | 203 |
| 29 | Origins | 208 |
| 30 | Asteroid Belts | 213 |
| 31 | Desperation | 220 |
| 32 | Options | 223 |
| 33 | Drones | 232 |
| 34 | Samples | 237 |
| 35 | Superbugs | 241 |
| 36 | Whispers | 246 |
| 37 | Decision Time | 249 |
| 38 | Success | 251 |
| 39 | Reunion | 254 |
| 40 | A New Beginning | 256 |
| 41 | An Unlikely Coupling | 258 |

| Epilogue | 259 |
| Acknowledgements | 261 |

Part 1

· · ·

# STRANGE HAPPENINGS

All our science, measured against
reality, is primitive and childlike –
and yet it is the most precious thing
we have

Albert Einstein

# 1
# IMPACT

They watched the asteroid on the flickering screen in silent fascination. The giant lump of extraterrestrial rock that was hurtling towards them at 70,000 miles per hour, 20 times faster than a speeding bullet. The giant lump of extraterrestrial rock that measured over 500 miles in diameter. The giant lump of extraterrestrial rock that would, in less than one hour, smash into the Earth with a force of over a trillion hydrogen bombs. The giant lump of extraterrestrial rock that would extinguish all life. Everything. Forever. Plants, animals, birds, fish, insects, even bacteria and viruses. And, of course, humans. Nothing would survive.

They'd known for a while that it was only a matter of time before a giant asteroid would collide with Earth. It was a simple matter of probabilities. Given enough time, the probability was one that such an event would occur. In other words, it was an absolute certainty. The only question was when? And now that question had been answered. The answer was NOW.

Over its 4.5 billion year existence planet Earth has been bombarded with asteroids countless times, some big, most small. The last really big asteroid to collide with planet Earth, in what is now Chicxulub on Mexico's Yucatan peninsular, happened around 65 million years ago, an event that blasted billions of tons of dust and debris into the atmosphere. Dust and debris that spread around the globe, blocking out the sun's life-giving rays for years. A nuclear winter that not only caused the extinction of the dinosaurs, but also caused the extinction of 70 per cent of all life on Earth. A mass extinction. But that asteroid was a mere tiddler compared to the one that was hurtling towards them now, just a piece of intergalactic dust compared to the monster coming to destroy them all.

The scientists watched in hushed silence as the asteroid hit the Earth's atmosphere. Watched as it glowed first red, then blue and finally white. A white hot piece of rock the size of a small moon hurtling towards its final destination. THEM!

Without taking her eyes off the screen, Liz whispered to the man sat to her right, 'How long to impact?'

'Five minutes, ten seconds,' answered Professor Cecil Vivian Shawcross, the leader of the small British team involved in the early detection of 'Near Earth Objects', the team tasked with keeping a lookout for rogue asteroids. 'In just 310 seconds, the whole of the USA will be completely obliterated, vaporised. Soon after, the rest of the world will suffer the same fate.'

Liz said nothing, her eyes glued to the flickering screen. It was horrific, yet compelling, viewing. The static caused by the approaching asteroid made the picture on the screen almost unviewable, as if she was viewing it through a snowstorm, but she could still make out the shape of the massive white hot piece of rock as it hurtled inexorably towards its final destination.

'Thirty seconds to impact,' a voice said in the darkened room. To Liz, the voice sounded disembodied, unreal, as if it was coming out of thin air rather than a human mouth. 'Why is it,' she thought, 'that humans always count down to an event. Counting down to major events, such as the launch of a space rocket or the start of a New Year, was fine, but counting down to trivial events like the end of a rugby match, or the start of a race, or the start of a stupid game on a stupid reality show, or… Well, it was just silly. A silly human trait.'

'Five, four, three…' the floating voice said in a calm, emotionless manner.

'How can anyone be so calm at a time like this?' thought Liz.

'Two, one – **IMPACT**.' The screen showed a massive explosion, then went dead.

# 2

# ONE MONTH EARLIER

The shooting star sped across the night sky like a supersonic bullet, leaving a wispy white trail of stardust in its wake. The weather forecaster had said there'd be a meteor shower, and he wasn't wrong. This was the seventieth one she'd seen in the last 30 minutes. Granted, it was a cool, clear night. A night ideal for spotting shooting stars. But seventy in just half-an-hour, this was the most that Liz had ever seen.

The weather forecaster's prediction had spurred Liz into action. She gulped down her tea, grabbed a thick sweater, woolly hat and walking boots, and dashed to her car. She dumped them in the boot, checked that her prized binoculars were there, closed the lid and hurried to the driver's door. As she was inserting the key into the ignition, she paused, opened the door and dashed back to the house. Moments later, she returned clutching a plastic bag full of nuts, placed them carefully on the front passenger seat and sped off towards her destination.

It took Liz no more than 20 minutes to drive the short distance from her home in Southport to Freshfields. As a member, she normally parked on the National Trust car park adjacent to the beach. Tonight, that wasn't an option – Formby Point Nature Reserve closed at dusk. Instead, she parked on the road leading to the entrance, the road of expensive million pound plus properties, some of which were the residencies of famous footballers from nearby Liverpool and Everton. Quickly, she put on her walking boots, sweater and woolly hat, placed her binoculars around her neck and put the packet of nuts in her pocket. Satisfied that she had everything, she strode purposefully towards the entrance.

Liz knew this place like the back of her hand. The National Trust's Formby Point Nature Reserve was one of her favourite places. Nestling between the pleasant village of Formby and the Irish Sea, it was an idyllic spot. Pine woods flanked the road that ran through the Reserve, the tarmac road that Liz was hurrying down towards the beach, tall pines that sprung from the undulating sandy floor. Numerous man-made paths traversed the woods, especially those to her left, paths designed to allow visitors close access to the Reserve's main attraction. Red squirrels.

As she strode towards the beach, Liz thought how beautiful this place was at night. No people, no cars, no noise. None of the sounds of civilisation. Just the peace and tranquillity of nature. The stillness. The serenity. The solitude. The only sound was the gentle rustling of the trees caressed by the soft breeze, punctuated with the occasional hoot of an owl as it called to its mate. Toowit, toowoo. And the smells. She loved the smells of autumn. The smell of decaying leaves, of cut grass and hay, and the crisp, fresh 'after-the-rain' smell so pronounced in autumn. Liz also loved the autumnal colours. The golden yellows, the rustic reds and the russet browns. They delighted her. Fulfilled her. Nourished her soul. But tonight, the only colours were grey. A million shades of grey. And black. The black of the night sky, a black dome speckled with dazzling dots of brilliant white.

After about half-a-mile, the pine trees petered out, replaced by a flat, sandy expanse of grass. At the far side of the flat expanse lay the deserted car park. Immediately beyond the car park, about a quarter-of-a-mile ahead, large sand dunes rose into the sky. Hidden, at the other side of the sand dunes, was the beach, the large sandy beach that stretched for miles and miles. Her destination.

On reaching the beach, Liz paused and gazed up at the sky. She couldn't help herself. It was something she'd done since childhood. Gaze up at the night sky. On a windy night she'd face into the wind, look up at the clouds scudding overhead, and imagine she was piloting Spaceship Earth as it sped on its fantastic journey through the galaxy.

Elizabeth Conway had been fascinated by the night sky since childhood. Fascinated by the big black dome with twinkling lights. The 6,000 twinkling lights visible to the naked eye and, sometimes, a big white ball too. Or a white banana. In her mind, she likened it to a big black tea cosy studded with sparkling diamonds. A big black tea cosy that appeared every night to keep her warm. As she grew older and her knowledge increased, the reality of the Cosmos, with its billions of stars and galaxies, proved infinitely more fascinating than her childhood perception. She was hooked. The Universe intrigued her. Fascinated her. Captivated her. She wanted to know more. To learn how it got here. How it works. To understand it, unlock its secrets. But what intrigued her most of all was a simple, childlike question. Was there life out there? Intelligent life. Life that we could communicate with. Interact with. She fervently hoped so. Because of her passion for the Cosmos, it surprised no one when Elizabeth Conway became an astrobiologist.

Liz loved her moonlight rambles along Freshfield beach. Along the wide stretch of sand illuminated with second-hand sunlight from the moon. It relaxed her. Helped her unwind. The noise of the waves lapping gently on the sandy shore soothed her. Calmed her. As did the moonlit sea, the vast, shimmering, silvery expanse of water that stretched to the distant horizon. And she loved the feel of wet sand beneath her feet: it was much softer than walking on tarmac, or concrete. Much kinder to her tender feet. The beach had one other big advantage too. It was away from the bright lights of the towns and cities. Bright lights that interfered with stargazing. Or spotting shooting stars.

Although the clouds were beginning to roll in, most of the sky remained clear. And dark. Alone on the beach, Liz scanned the heavens with her binoculars. Wow! That one was a beauty. A large one. Definitely large enough to reach the Earth's surface before burning up in the atmosphere. A meteorite.

Minutes later, another shooting star streaked across the night sky, disappearing behind a cloud before reappearing at the other side. This one was smaller: it would probably burn up before it reached the Earth's surface. A meteor.

Liz spotted several more shooting stars before realising how cold she was. The increasing cloud cover had caused a change in the weather. The temperature had dropped considerably, imparting an icy chill to the wind. Exposed and alone on the cold, dark, windswept beach, she suddenly felt vulnerable. Instinctively, she pulled the woolly hat down over her ears, lifted the collar of her sweater to protect her neck, and hunched her shoulders to make herself a smaller target. Then she headed for the shelter of the sand hills.

Huddled in the sand hills away from the chilling wind, Liz continued scanning the night sky. The clouds were scudding across the sky at an ever increasing pace, black ominous rain clouds that cast weird, shifting shadows as they flitted across the face of the moon. Weird, shape-shifting shadows that raced across the deserted beach. Rain was in the air. She could sense it. And it was windy and cold. Time to retreat to the relative safety, and warmth, of her car. Anyway, the increasing cloud cover made further stargazing impossible. But she'd had a good night. In just over half-an-hour, she'd spotted 70 shooting stars, the most she'd ever seen. A record.

As she arose from her sheltered position, a strong gust of wind blew sand into her face. Instinctively, she rubbed her eyes. Why was it always windy at the seaside? She'd wondered that from being a toddler splashing in the sea. Even on hot, sunny, summer days, the wind on her wet skin always made her feel cold. Now, as a 29-year-old astrobiologist, she knew the answer. It was rudimentary 'O-level' physics. During the day, the sun heats the land to a higher temperature than the sea (it has a lower heat capacity), warming the air above it. The warm air rises, drawing in cooler air from the sea. A cool onshore breeze. At night, the reverse happens. The sea retains its heat better than the land, causing the wind to blow from the land to the sea, an offshore breeze.

The wind was really cold now and she felt the first drops of rain on her face. A flash of lightning lit up the night sky, followed by the distant rumble of thunder. A storm was on its way. Liz quickened her pace, hurrying to reach the shelter of the pine trees before the storm broke. Her face and hands felt really cold. 'Why didn't you bring your gloves, you stupid fool?' she said to herself. 'It's autumn now, not summer.' Stuffing her hands into her pockets, her right hand encountered the bag of nuts. The bag of nuts she'd forgotten about. Forgotten about completely. The bag of nuts she'd brought with her to feed the squirrels.

She faced a dilemma. On the one hand she wanted desperately to feed the squirrels. It was something she did every time she visited the Reserve. She knew it was silly but she thought they'd come to expect her to feed them. In fact, it was more than an expectation. Liz thought the squirrels *depended* on her feeding them and, if she didn't, they would starve. On the other hand, a storm was approaching and she was still half-a-mile away from her car. All these thoughts flashed through her head as the road left the flat expanse of the car park and entered the wood.

Her heart implored her to feed the squirrels but her head told her to hurry back to the car. Fast! She could see the path that led into the wood: it was about 50 yards ahead on her right. 'Never shelter under trees in a thunderstorm. It's dangerous. You could be killed by a lightning strike.' The warning drummed into her by her parents swirled around her head. A lightning flash lit up the sky for the second time, followed by a sharp crack of thunder. The storm was getting closer.

Before she knew it, Liz felt the soft feel of pine needles beneath her feet. Without realising it, she'd left the tarmac road and taken the path leading into the wood. The narrow sandy path covered with a thick layer of pine needles. She felt like she was walking on a cushion of air. Her decision made, she walked even faster, indeed almost ran, to reach the spot where she fed the squirrels.

As she hurried towards her feeding spot Liz reflected on the plight of one of Britain's most endearing mammals, the red squirrel, our own native red squirrel which was fighting a losing battle against that ubiquitous foreign invader, the North American grey squirrel. Although she would never harm a grey squirrel, Liz despised the Victorians for deliberately introducing them to Britain in the nineteenth century just to satisfy their penchant for novelty. Adaptable, tough and hardy, these foreign invaders thrived, causing a catastrophic decline of our own native red squirrel. The grey was able to out-compete the red in every phase of its life cycle. Furthermore, it is more resistant to disease, another factor that helped it spread like wildfire. Liz knew that the main hope of survival for the red squirrel was isolated conifer habitats like Formby Point, where the grey squirrel does not so easily out-compete the red. Here, in one of the few remaining strongholds of the red squirrel, Liz did all she possibly could to ensure the survival of her favourite animal.

On reaching her feeding spot, Liz emitted a low whistle followed by, 'I'm here. I'm here.' She scoured the forest floor for signs of life. Nothing. And the trees. Nothing. She whistled and called again. Nothing. Perhaps the thunder and lightning had scared them. Made them too afraid to come down. She tried for a third time. Still no luck. Just as she was about to leave, she heard a faint rustling on the forest floor. From the corner of her eye, she saw movement. Was it a squirrel or… It was! It came running to her feet, stopped, and sat up like a dog. Begging. Begging for some nuts. Placing one between her thumb and forefinger, Liz offered the treat to her visitor. Gently, it accepted the gift and moved a few feet away to consume its food.

By now, a few more had gathered. Liz fed them all. But her favourite wasn't here. The one without a tail. Squirrel NOTAIL. How it came to have no tail she didn't know. Was it lost in a fight? Or was it born without one? She didn't know. What she did know was that NOTAIL was friendlier and bolder than all the other squirrels. And cute. She felt sorry for him. But why wasn't he here? He hadn't been… No. Surely not. Not NOTAIL.

The rain was getting heavier so, reluctantly, Liz bade farewell to her furry friends and set off towards her car, disappointed at NOTAIL's no show. As she hurried along the path, she felt something tug ever so slightly on the bottom of her leg. And again. She stopped and turned around, expecting to see a twig that had snagged on her trouser bottoms but, to her immense surprise and delight, it wasn't a twig, it was NOTAIL! She'd known he wouldn't let her down. Not NOTAIL. Her best friend. Her Manx squirrel. The squirrel without a tail. Kneeling down, she said, 'Hello NOTAIL. Do you want some nuts?' Then, as if he understood, NOTAIL stood on his hind legs, begging. As she'd done many times before, Liz gave him a nut. Gently, he placed it in his mouth but stayed where he was. 'One not enough, eh?' said Liz, offering him a second nut. He positioned this in his mouth too, next to the first, and waited. 'Really hungry tonight, eh,' said Liz, handing him a third nut. Sat up with three nuts in his mouth he looked so comical. And cute. 'Sorry fella. That's your lot for tonight,' said Liz getting up from her kneeling position. Realising that feeding time was over, NOTAIL dropped down from his haunches and ambled off into the wood.

Stood there, in the pouring rain, Liz was amazed how wet and cold she was. She'd been so absorbed, so engrossed, in feeding the squirrels, she hadn't realised how hard it was raining. It was pelting down. And the wind was howling too. She was thankful she was in the wood rather than out in the open. At least the trees offered some protection.

She hurried along the path as fast as she could and was grateful when the tarmac road came into view. The entrance was only 100 yards ahead. Not far to go now. Just as she was about to start running, a jagged bolt of lightning lit up the sky followed immediately by the loudest thunderclap she'd ever heard. The storm was directly overhead. At the same time – everything seemed to happen in a blur – an old pine tree in front of her split in two and came crashing down across the path. Startled, she instinctively jumped backwards, avoiding the falling tree by a matter of feet. Shocked and surprised, she ran to her right, clambered over the split trunk and sprinted to her car.

Sat in the car cold, wet and soaked to the skin, Liz realised just how lucky she'd been. The lightning had struck the tree ahead of her on her right. If it had happened just a few seconds later, the falling tree would have almost certainly crushed her to death. Although Liz Conway would never admit it, she'd deemed feeding the squirrels more important than her own safety.

# 3

# LIZ CONWAY

A hot bath had never felt so good. The water enveloped her cold body like a warm blanket. However, even though the bath water was piping hot, it took a full five minutes for Liz to warm up. To thaw out. To restore some feeling to her frozen extremities; her feet and her hands. As she soaked herself in the hot, soapy water, Liz let her mind wander. To freewheel. But her thoughts always returned to the meteor showers. The unprecedented number of meteor showers currently lighting up the night skies around the world. And about the important meeting she had tomorrow to discuss them.

Refreshed and warmed after her relaxing hot bath, Liz put on her robe, went down to the kitchen and made herself a mug of steaming hot coffee. Coffee was one of her favourite drinks. Not only did it taste good, it smelled good too. She loved the aroma of freshly made coffee. Clasping the mug in both hands, she lifted it to her nose and took a deep sniff of the black liquid before taking her first sip. It tasted so good, and warm, as it slid smoothly down her throat. She knew that drinking coffee just before bedtime, especially strong, black coffee, was wrong. The caffeine would keep her awake, making sleep difficult. But what the hell. She liked it, so why not indulge herself? Anyway, tonight she had an excuse. She needed something hot to warm her up – the driving rain had chilled her to the bone. If it did prevent her from sleeping, well… she'd just do some work. Some work on the puzzling meteor showers currently drenching the planet. With her mug of coffee in one hand and a chocolate biscuit in the other, Liz walked into the lounge, sat in her favourite armchair and turned off the lights. Safe and snug in her comfy chair, she sipped her coffee, nibbled her biscuit and closed her eyes. She thought about her family.

Elizabeth Esme Conway was the eldest of two girls born to her parents, John and Mary Conway. It wasn't a name she was particularly fond of. Elizabeth. In her eyes, it was too old-fashioned. Too staid. A name used by royalty. But it was better than the names some of her classmates at school had called her, Betty and Beth. She hated Beth and, if at all possible, never acknowledged anyone who called her by that name. Betty wasn't as bad but the name she preferred was Liz. Liz was okay. It was cool, crisp and modern. It slipped easily off the tongue. And so Liz was how she was known. The name that everyone called her. Her family, friends and colleagues. The name used by everyone who knew her. Everyone that is, except one. Rupert Templeton-Smythe. He always called her Beth.

Liz often wondered if her parents had a wicked sense of humour by giving her the middle name Esme. It's not that she didn't like the relatively uncommon name, it was the effect it had on her initials. EEC. Not just Elizabeth Esme Conway but also the European Economic Community, the forerunner of the European Union. Perhaps it had been an oversight by her parents but then again, perhaps not, because her little sister had inherited a similar problem.

Beatrice Blu Conway was six years younger than Liz. Her parents were fervent Everton supporters and hoped their second child would be a boy. It wasn't to be but, from the day she was born, they always called Liz's little sister Baby Blu. Baby Blu after their team's colour and the boy they never had. It was a name that stuck. A name they made official in the Christening ceremony. A name that has been used ever since. But it presented Beatrice with a problem even worse than Liz's. BBC. Beatrice Blu Conway aka the British Broadcasting Corporation. Perhaps her parents had been mischievous after all.

Liz's grandparents lived in Toxteth, a rough place with a history of riots. Jack and Edith Conway did their best to provide a decent living for themselves and their only son, John. Jack Conway was a welder, a welder who found work easy to come by in the thriving dockyards of Liverpool in the 1950s and 1960s. A welder who began to earn enough money to enable them to consider moving out of their council house and buy a house of their own. A house away from Toxteth. His wife had always hankered for a house across the Mersey, a terraced house with a view over the river to Liverpool. Just as they were on the brink of making their dream a reality, Jack Conway was crushed to death. A metal plate he was welding on to the hull of a new cruise liner suddenly broke free and crushed him, killing him instantly. He was 52.

The sudden and untimely death of her husband made Jack's widow even more determined to move out of their council house and buy one of her own. She couldn't stay there anyway. It held too many memories. So, using the money they'd managed to save, plus the compensation she received for Jack's death, Edith Conway bought one of the terraced houses she'd always fancied. It wasn't in affluent New Brighton – the houses there were out of her reach – but in the poorer area of New Ferry in Bromborough. It was where she lived until her death.

By the time her son, John Conway, Liz's father, was ready for work, the dockyards were in decline. They had no future. So he took an apprenticeship at the giant General Motors plant in nearby Ellesmere Port, working on the car assembly line. It was here that he met, and later married, Mary, a local girl from New Brighton.

Neither John nor Mary settled at General Motors. They didn't like the repetitive nature of the work or the culture, especially the dominance and belligerence of the unions. And they certainly didn't like the strikes. They hated going on strike, the industrial disease of the seventies and eighties. Eventually, they could stand it no more and both left. John got a job at Unilever whilst Mary trained to become a teacher. By studying part-time for seven long years at Liverpool John Moores University, her father got himself a BSc (Bachelor of Science) degree in chemistry.

Because both her parents had steady, well paid jobs – her mother became a primary school teacher – Liz's family were never poor. They were never rich either, just comfortable. When her grandmother died, Liz's father used the inheritance from selling her terraced house to help buy a nice semi-detached house in New Brighton, a house in a pleasant residential area. A house that her grandparents could only have dreamed of.

Her devoted parents ensured that both her and Baby Blu had a wonderful childhood. They took them to the seaside, for walks in the country, teaching them to respect and love nature, to National Trust properties – Formby Point was always their favourite – to museums and to the cinema. Both Liz and Baby Blu loved the little fairground at the bottom of the Marine Drive in Southport – it's now a MacDonalds. They'd clap and cheer when her father parked on the car park, paid the attendant and received a free book of tickets to use on the fairground rides. She and Baby Blu would race each other to the little train, their tongues hanging out in eager anticipation, to see who would reach it first; the little train with the red engine that went over humps and bumps and through a dark tunnel. Later, they'd frolic around in the paddling pool, laughing and giggling as they splashed each other with water. Then, they'd have a meal, all four of them, sat outside their favourite cafe in the sunshine. (It always seemed to be good weather then.) Finally, an ice cream would round off a perfect day.

Liz also remembered the time two bullies tried to steal Baby Blu's ice cream, pushing and shoving her and making her cry. Even though they were older and bigger than her, Liz ran at them full pelt, crashing into them with such force that she knocked both of them to the ground. Standing over them like a conquering hero, she yelled at them so loud that the terrified bullies scrambled to their feet and fled for their lives. No one treated her precious Baby Blu that way. No one.

Everything was fine and dandy until the day she arrived home from school to find her mother waiting for her at the front door, something she never did. She looked upset. Very upset. 'What's the matter, mummy?' Her mother didn't answer. Instead, she flung her arms around her eldest daughter, hugged her tighter than she'd ever done before, and burst into tears. Without knowing why, Liz burst into tears too. 'Mummy, what's the matter,' she repeated, becoming frightened by her mother's sobbing.

'Darling. Oh, my little darling. I've got some terrible news.'

Although she was only 12, Liz knew what 'terrible news' meant. They'd said that when her grandmother died and she feared the worst.

'It's your daddy,' continued her mother, 'he's…'

'NO!' screamed Liz. 'No, NO, **NO**! He can't be. He can't be dead!'

Her mother knelt down so that her face was level with Liz's. 'No darling. He's not dead but he's got a very serious illness. He's been diagnosed with muscular atrophy.'

Liz burst into tears and sobbed uncontrollably, holding on to her mother as though her life depended on it. 'There, there, dear,' said her mother, regaining a little composure. 'Don't worry. It'll be alright.'

Liz didn't know whether her daddy would be alright or not because she didn't understand what muscular atrophy was. But her mother knew. She knew that progressive muscular atrophy, a form of motor neurone disease, blocked signals from the brain which affected the nerves and muscles, causing weight-loss and impairing speech. It was a debilitating, untreatable, pernicious disease that is, ultimately, fatal. A death sentence. But a delayed death sentence. A death sentence that had struck down her husband, her beloved husband, at 39. Struck him down in the prime of his life. Struck him down when his daughters were a mere 12 and six-years-old.

Her father's illness sent her mother off the rails. She couldn't cope. Although she tried her best, the realisation of what was to come, coupled with the strain of looking after her sick husband and two young daughters, proved too much. She suffered a nervous breakdown.

The doctors advised Mary to go into hospital for specialist treatment, but she refused point blank, fearing that if she did, her husband might be unable to cope, resulting in her two young daughters being taken into care. That was the last thing she wanted. Instead, both she and her husband managed to persuade the authorities to allow them to receive medical care at home, arguing that it was better to keep the family together than split it up. It was a close run thing but, eventually, the authorities agreed. Because her father was in the early stages of the disease, he was still physically mobile and fully *compos mentis*. It was this, Liz believed, that edged the decision their way. In practice, the decision to look after the family at home placed most of the burden on Liz's young shoulders, a heavy burden for a 12-year-old child to bear. The Social Services helped too, but they weren't there 24 hours a day, not like her and Baby Blu.

For all her good intentions, as time passed her mother became withdrawn and far away, as if she was in another world. She took to drinking to blot out the harsh reality of their situation. Even the simple tasks were too much for her and she spent most of her time alone in her bedroom, either asleep or drunk. Or both. It was Liz, with the help of her little sister, who attended to most of the family chores.

Watching her beloved father waste away before her very eyes broke Liz's heart. Broke her heart watching his body wither and die and his mental faculties diminish. Little by little. Bit by bit. Every day. Unrelenting. As she helped him eat his food in the evening, they'd reminisce about the past. About the great times they'd had. It cheered them both up. Occasionally, very occasionally, she'd catch a glimpse of the man he used to be. A caring, devoted father and loving husband. He wasn't rich or famous. Or a top sportsman or celebrity. He was none of those. But he gave them something far more precious than money or fame. He gave them the gift of his time. His time to play games with them, to comfort them, to make them happy when they were sad. He taught them to believe in themselves, never to accept anything at face value, always to think about it, evaluate it and, if necessary, to challenge it, even if it meant flying in the face of accepted dogma. It was the best thing he taught them: how to think for themselves. To thank him for all of this, Liz always ended the evening by squeezing his hand and kissing his forehead. It was the least she could do.

Time is a great healer. Liz had heard her parents say this after bad things had happened. Bad things like the death of her grandmother. Like any desperate child, she hoped that time would heal her parents. In her heart, she knew it wouldn't heal her father. Nothing could do that. But she hoped it would heal her mother. Help her revert to the mother she used to be. Gradually, time worked its magic. As the weeks turned into months and the months into years, her mother improved. She took more interest in Liz, and Baby Blu, and even helped with the daily chores; the shopping, cooking, washing, ironing and cleaning. In fact, she was almost back to normal. As her health improved, the doctors reduced the dosage of drugs; the tranquillisers, anti-depressants, pain killers and sleeping pills she'd come to rely on. Their mother did her bit too by cutting down on the drinking, the drinking to which she'd resorted to blot out the world. Liz and Baby Blu had their real mother back. Almost.

The burden of caring for both parents at such a young age would have affected the education of most children, but not Liz. The desire that burned fiercely within her chest to become an astrobiologist drove her on. She knew she needed a good education with good qualifications at the end of it and worked really hard to ensure that she got them. Her GCSE (General Certificate of Secondary Education) results were excellent. She got A and A* grades in three of the most difficult GCE (General Certificate of Education) 'A' level subjects – mathematics, physics and biology – and graduated from Liverpool John Moores University with a BSc honours degree in astronomy.

Her graduation at Liverpool's Anglican Cathedral was one of the proudest moments of not only hers, but also her family's life. Being the first girl in their family to obtain a degree made the occasion even more special. The only downside was the health of her father. The nine long years since he'd been diagnosed with the deadly disease had taken their toll. Now aged 48, he was frail and weak. Unable to walk and confined to a wheelchair, he was nothing more than skin and bone. A skeleton. The doctors were surprised he'd lasted so long. But his family, and especially Liz, weren't. They knew he'd hung on to see his eldest daughter graduate. The daughter he'd nurtured and taught. And loved. He wasn't going to die without seeing her graduate.

The choice of who should attend the ceremony had been a difficult one for Liz. Only two guests were allowed, so Liz had taken the diplomatic option and opted for her father and mother. She'd have liked to have Baby Blu there too, of course she would, but that wasn't possible. Her mother was having none of it; she gave her place to Baby Blu. 'I want your father and his two daughters present today. Hopefully, I'll be around to see Blu graduate,' she said, knowing it was something her husband would never see.

Sat in his wheelchair, her father was so proud as his daughter walked on to the stage. So proud as she received her degree. Even though he was terminally ill, tears rolled down his wizened, grey face, a face bursting with pride. As Liz descended the steps and hurried back to her father, tears welled up in her eyes. She kissed him tenderly on his wrinkled forehead and whispered, 'I did it for you, dad. I did it for you.' Then she burst into tears.

A few days later, her father died. He'd fought bravely for nine long years but to no avail. The disease won. It always did. As she stood beside his open coffin and studied his face, a face that was now at peace, Liz thought back to the time about a year earlier, a time when he still had some control of his mental faculties, when he begged her to end his life. Implored her to administer an overdose of tablets, or even the garden weedkiller, Weedol, to end his suffering and let him slip away with a modicum of dignity. Liz was torn between conflicting emotions; on the one hand she hated seeing her father suffer, but there was no way she could have a hand in hastening his death. No way at all.

Her father's death proved to be the last straw for her mother. It crushed her. Devastated her. She lost the will to live, to carry on, even though she had two beautiful daughters. Two beautiful daughters she adored. She became withdrawn and introverted again, like a zombie, and shut herself off from the world. A recluse.

It was a difficult time for the whole family, particularly Baby Blu – she was only 15 – but, despite the difficulties, Liz still managed to obtain a PhD (Doctor of Philosophy) in astrobiology from Bangor University and a job at Jodrell Bank. Her little sister followed in her mother's footsteps and became a teacher at a local primary school, fell in love with a fellow teacher and got pregnant.

Blu's pregnancy seemed to instil a new lease of life in their mother. Invigorate her. Give her something to look forward to, something joyous and happy instead of the sadness and despair she'd had to endure. She was really looking forward to the birth of her first grandchild when tragedy once again reared its ugly head. Blu tripped and fell down the stairs, causing the baby to miscarry at six months.

It was one tragedy too many for their mother. One evening, Blu came home from school to find her mother on the floor: a packet of sleeping pills and an empty gin bottle lay beside her. She wasn't dead, although death might have been a better outcome. She'd suffered a massive stroke that left her severely brain damaged. A vegetable who'd spend the rest of her life in hospital. Two years later, she died.

Liz and Baby Blu sold the family home. Liz bought a modest semi-detached house in Southport, a place where houses are surprisingly inexpensive, whilst Blu and her teacher boyfriend bought an apartment near Chester. Both of them wanted a new beginning.

Dong, dong, dong… chimed the clock on the wall. The noise startled Liz, snapped her out of her reverie. She sat up abruptly and glanced at the time. Midnight. Good God! Had she reminisced for so long? Despite the coffee, she felt drowsy. It was time for bed. After making sure that everything was switched off, she climbed the stairs to her bedroom, took off her robe and snuggled under the duvet.

As she was dozing off, her thoughts returned to the recent glut of meteor showers. There was nothing unusual about meteor showers. They were a natural occurrence. But there was something different about these. Something that wasn't quite right. She couldn't put her finger on what it was, not yet, but maybe she'd have a better understanding after the meeting tomorrow. Suddenly, a bright light startled her. Made her sit up. It was coming from the bedroom window and getting brighter by the second. She jumped out of bed, dashed to the window and flung back the curtains. It was a shooting star. A meteorite. And it was heading straight for her!

## 4

# METEOR SHOWERS

Liz had never moved so fast in her entire life. She flung herself away from the window, away from the white hot piece of rock hurtling towards her, landing in a heap on the bedroom floor. Almost simultaneously – everything happened so fast – she heard a bang, like a dull explosion, as the meteorite thudded into the wall. The bedroom shuddered and, just for an instant, Liz feared it would collapse on top of her, crushing her to death just like her grandfather. It didn't, but it left her shaking all over. Shaking with fear at her close encounter with a meteorite. She was scared, very scared, but also excited at the same time. She realised what a great opportunity it was. Would there be any fragments from the meteorite? Even the intact meteorite itself? Any clues as to its origin? Recovering her composure, she put on her robe and dashed downstairs.

The 'explosion' had woken her neighbours. People were milling about in pyjamas and nightgowns wondering what the hell had happened. Confused, bewildered, frightened people. Explosions simply didn't happen in their street.

Liz ignored them and made a beeline to the side of the house where her bedroom was located. What she saw surprised her. She'd expected to see a gaping hole but what met her eyes was… just a circle of damaged bricks no more than a foot in diameter. A circle of badly damaged bricks and dust. Dust that spread out from the damaged bricks and dust on the floor. Lots of it.

Liz examined the damaged bricks more closely. In the centre, where the meteorite had struck, the damage was more extensive but even here, the meteorite hadn't penetrated the wall. She was puzzled. It had seemed so large as it hurtled towards her, a white hot missile as big as a football. But it couldn't have been. A meteorite that size would have demolished not just the wall but the entire house. It must have been smaller, much smaller, probably the size of a pea or, at most, a golf ball. And yet… and then it dawned on her. Even a meteorite the size of a pea left a trail of white hot gas larger than a football. That was it! It had appeared large but in reality it wasn't.

A wave of excitement swept over her. A meteorite that small explained everything. Atmospheric friction has little effect on the velocity of large objects such as asteroids, but it quickly slows the speed of small objects like meteorites from tens of thousands of miles per hour to just a few hundred. Not only did that explain the minimal amount of damage to her house, it also meant that the meteorite should still be intact. At that speed, it shouldn't have disintegrated on impact. It should be around somewhere. She looked at the drive under the impact point but couldn't see anything other than fragments of bricks and dust. The drive sloped down towards the road so it could have rolled on to the road. But it wasn't there either.

By now, a crowd of curious onlookers had gathered, wondering what all the commotion was about. The man from next door approached her. 'What's happened, Liz?' he asked.

'I think a meteorite hit the house,' replied Liz. 'It's a good job it was only a small one.' Secretly, she wished they'd all leave so she could continue searching for the meteorite. Realising there was nothing much to see, the crowd dispersed, slowly at first then more quickly, leaving Liz free to resume her search. Perhaps they'd read her thoughts.

If it wasn't on the drive, it could only mean one thing. Unless it had defied the laws of physics, it must have rolled into the front garden. The garden was wet and muddy from the storm and all she had on her feet were bedroom slippers. Clean, white, fluffy bedroom slippers. 'What the hell,' she thought, stepping into a muddy puddle – she didn't want to waste time changing her footwear. In her haste, she slipped and would have fallen had she not grabbed the branch of a silver birch tree. She stopped and looked around. A sodium vapour street light cast a pale yellow glow over the small garden, imparting a strange hue to the grass and the shrubs. There was no meteorite on the lawn. As she turned towards the shrubs at the side of the drive, a faint hissing noise caught her attention. It seemed to be coming from under the hydrangea bush. As she moved closer, she noticed wisps of steam curling up into the cold night air. They too emanated from the hydrangea bush. Liz thought it looked, and sounded, eerie. Like an invisible snake hissing its steamy breath into the night sky. Carefully, she parted the branches with her hand. There, under the bush, was a red hot piece of extraterrestrial rock the size of a golf ball, a meteorite, lying in a puddle of water.

'Don't be bloody stupid,' snapped the young man sat across the table from Liz. 'It's just a natural event. Yes, there are some irregularities, some differences, between these meteor bursts and previous ones, and yes, there are a lot more meteorites than usual, but that's because the Earth is passing through the debris from the collision of the comet with the asteroid.'

'Have you finished? Have you quite finished, you...?' She was about to say jumped-up, toffee-nosed, supercilious prat, but corrected herself and said, instead, 'blinkered idiot'. Both were very apt but the latter was more relevant to the current discussion.

'Your closed mind "I'm always right" attitude just pisses me off,' she spat.

'It isn't that, is it Beth?' he replied in his calm, superior manner, deliberately drawing out the word 'Beth'. Drawing it out because he knew how much she hated being called by that name. 'You just can't stand being proved wrong.'

'No one's proved me wrong,' she hissed. 'Certainly not you.'

Professor Cecil Vivian Shawcross, the leader of the small Near Earth Object (NEO) team, glanced at his counterpart, Professor Frank Rogers, the leader of the equally small 'Astrophysics' team, and sighed. The two young protagonists were at it again, arguing like cat and dog trying to get the better of each other. Liz Conway, his star protégé and Rupert Templeton-Smythe, Frank Rogers' bright young man. He'd yet to attend a meeting without the two of them going at it hammer and tongs. 'Look,' he said, defusing the situation, 'let's all calm down. At this stage no one's right and no one's wrong. We just don't have sufficient data to make an informed judgement. Let's move on. And,' he continued, glancing at Rupert and Liz, 'let's behave like adults, not unruly, spoilt children.'

'I think it's a good idea if we review the facts,' said Frank Rogers, doing his bit to calm the situation. 'As we all know, a meteor shower happens when streams of debris, usually from the tail of a passing comet, enter the Earth's atmosphere at extremely high velocities. Most are smaller than a grain of sand and burn up before reaching the Earth's surface. However, a few do make it to the surface, but not many. Intense meteor showers, meteor storms, like the kind we are experiencing now, can produce over a thousand meteors per hour.

'What has been unusual,' he continued, 'is the number of meteorites in the meteor showers. Normally, there are none, or very few. But, as someone mentioned earlier,' he didn't mention Rupert's name, 'that's because of the debris from the collision of the comet and the asteroid.'

'With respect, sir, ...'

'Oh please, call me Frank.'

'With respect, Frank,' continued Liz, 'what you've said is true as far as it goes, but it doesn't explain everything.'

'What doesn't it explain, Liz?' said Frank in a fatherly way to the young woman he admired. The young woman who wasn't afraid to challenge existing dogma.

'Well, it doesn't explain the fact that these meteor showers don't originate from a single point in the sky, like normal meteor showers do. And...'

'That's perfectly true, Liz,' interjected Frank, knowing full well that he hadn't explained everything. 'But again, it's probably because of the debris from the comet and the asteroid. Such a collision is a very rare event so we don't really know what to expect.'

'I suppose that could be the explanation,' replied Liz slowly, although it was obvious she wasn't fully convinced. She had her own ideas.

'But the really interesting thing,' continued Liz, 'is the distribution of the meteorites.'

'What do you mean?' queried Frank. This was new information to him.

Liz glanced at Zak Rhodes, a newly qualified PhD and the third and final member of the NEO team. An expert in probability theory, it was Zak who'd plotted, predicted might be a better word, the likely distribution of the meteorites. He nodded for her to carry on.

'Well,' continued Liz thoughtfully, 'the majority of the meteorites landed in the sea, which isn't surprising given that 70 per cent of our planet is covered with water. However, what is surprising,' she paused for effect, scanning the faces of the people in the room, 'is the distribution of the meteorites that didn't end up in the sea.'

'And what distribution is that, Liz?' asked Frank, becoming more and more interested.

'What's surprising about their distribution,' said Liz, 'is that an unusually large proportion of the meteorites landed in the coldest regions of the planet. The Arctic, the Antarctic, Siberia, Alaska and the Himalayas.'

'Beth,' said Rupert somewhat resignedly, 'that's because of the tilt of the Earth. The Northern Hemisphere is pointing towards the debris, so it's perfectly natural that more of them will fall in the Northern Hemisphere.'

Rupert's confident, superior manner irritated Liz. She was about to respond when someone beat her to it.

'That explains the higher incidence of impacts in the Arctic, Alaska, the Himalayas and Siberia,' chimed a nervous voice from the back of the room, 'but it doesn't explain the high level of impacts in the Antarctic. That's in the Southern Hemisphere.' It was precisely the same point that Liz was about to make but one of the young PhD students stood at the back of the room had said it first.

'Good for you,' thought Liz, turning around to look at the young man who'd plucked up enough courage to speak. 'Even young students can spot flaws in your pronouncements.'

Rupert shrugged his shoulders. 'Just another quirk of nature,' he said nonchalantly.

'You self-opinionated, smug, know-it-all bastard,' seethed Liz to herself. 'When you don't know the answer, you just shrug it off as "just another quirk of nature." ' She could have hit him. But she'd get him. Expose him for what he was. Starting right now.

'Then why is it?' said Liz, looking him straight in the eye, 'that the meteor showers are spread randomly around the globe whilst the meteorites aren't?' She had him now. That's what Zak's data had shown.

'It's puzzling,' chimed in Frank.

Liz continued looking straight at Rupert. 'Rupert?'

'I agree with Frank,' he said. 'It's puzzling, but I'm sure I'll come up with an explanation.'

'You smug bastard,' she thought. 'You have a bloody answer for everything.'

'What do you think, Liz?' asked Professor Cecil Vivian Shawcross, her team leader and boss.

'What do I think!' said Liz, still seething with rage at Rupert's comments. 'I think that intelligent extraterrestrial beings are using the meteor showers as cover to either contact us or as a prelude to invading and conquering us.'

Rupert burst out laughing. 'Not the "Little Green Men" scenario again,' he smirked. 'You know there's no intelligent life on Mars.'

Liz was furious at his facetiousness. 'You know very well that I don't mean Mars,' she snapped. 'There are 200 billion stars in our galaxy and 100 billion galaxies in the Universe. Billions of these stars will have planets and millions of them will be suitable for life to have evolved. Intelligent life. And, given the age of the Universe, many civilisations will be far more advanced than ours.'

'Then why is it they haven't contacted us?' sneered Rupert.

'You know as well as I do that the main reason there hasn't been any contact is because of the vast distances involved,' retorted Liz. 'The vast interstellar distances which even light, the fastest thing in the Universe, travelling at 186,000 miles per second, takes billions of years to reach us. That, and the fact that civilisations may have existed at different times. Come and gone. After all, we've only had the technology to search for extraterrestrial life for less than a hundred years, which is nothing compared to the 13.7 billion year history of the Universe. Just the blink of an eye.'

'Surely they'd have made contact using radio waves or some other form of electromagnetic radiation?' said Frank. 'Not a physical object which only travels at a fraction of the speed of light.'

'But using radio waves would betray their presence,' replied Liz. 'Maybe they want to keep themselves hidden.'

'So what's your theory, Liz?' asked Frank.

'My theory is that some of the meteorites are probes from an advanced alien civilisation. Probes to obtain information about Earth.'

'For what purpose, Liz?' asked her boss.

Rupert Templeton-Smythe could contain his anger no longer. 'For Christ's sake!' he shouted, thumping the table with his fist, 'stop pandering to this woman's deluded fantasies. We're here to discuss science, not science fiction.' His outburst over, Rupert Templeton-Smythe got up from his chair and stormed out of the meeting.

'They're going to make contact some time. WHY NOT NOW!' shouted Liz to the man striding out of the room.

'I'm sorry about that,' said Frank apologetically. 'He can be difficult at times.'

'Too bloody right he can,' thought Liz. 'Just another example of his closed mind mentality.'

'Well everyone, I think that's enough for today,' said Professor Cecil Vivian Shawcross. 'We'll know more about the meteorites when the search teams bring some back to the lab for analysis.'

As the people began filing out of the room her boss walked over to where she was standing, placed his hand on her shoulder and said, in a fatherly sort of way, 'Are you sure you're alright? Last night must have been frightening.'

Liz had mentioned her encounter with the meteorite to her boss just before the meeting, then forgotten about it. Dismissed it from her mind. His comments brought the whole experience flooding back.

'I'm fine,' she replied. 'It was scary yet exciting too,' she continued. 'And I've got a meteorite as a souvenir. But thanks for asking.'

'Okay,' said her boss, 'but take a few days off if you want.'

'Thanks, but no thanks,' said Liz. 'I'd rather be at work.'

'Fine. Then I'll see you tomorrow,' said Professor Cecil Vivian Shawcross, striding out of the room. On reaching the door, he paused, turned around and said, 'Liz, if it's any comfort I think there's extraterrestrial life too. I know we haven't found any yet, but I think we will in the next couple of decades. If this is the only place, even in our galaxy, where there's not just life, but life that's fairly clever, that makes us a miracle and after looking at 500 years of astronomical history, I'm disinclined to believe in miracles.'

'Thanks for that,' said Liz. 'I'm glad that someone else believes in extraterrestrial life.'

Liz respected her 49-year-old boss. The six foot five inches tall lanky Lancastrian with square-framed spectacles and an infectious chuckle. Professor Cecil Vivian Shawcross came from a modest, middle-class family in Blackley, North Manchester. He began his studies at a local comprehensive school and achieved such outstanding grades in his GCE 'O' levels that he was awarded a scholarship at the prestigious Manchester Grammar School. After obtaining excellent grades in his GCE 'A' levels, he went on to study astronomy at Manchester University, graduating with a first class honours degree. Being something of a home bird, he stayed at the same university to get a PhD in astrophysics, followed by a job at the Jodrell Bank Observatory. His curious, inquisitive mind, allied with his pragmatism, served him well, enabling him to rise to his current position as leader of the NEO team. He was a good, well-liked leader. A leader who always listened to everyone's views before making a decision.

Professor Cecil Vivian Shawcross loved his parents but hated the names they'd lumbered him with. Cecil and Vivian. He thought such old-fashioned names had disappeared with the Ark. But they were the names of his two grandads, his dearly beloved grandads, and that's why his parents had chosen them. He wasn't particularly fond of either name, especially Cecil, and considered having them changed, but decided against it. It would upset his parents. Over time, he got used to Viv. Viv wasn't too bad. As a cricket lover, his favourite batsman was Viv Richards, one of the finest batsmen the West Indies had ever produced. So he'd left well enough alone and let people call him Viv.

Alone in the meeting room, Liz wondered why the majority of the meteorites had landed on the coldest, most inhospitable parts of the planet. And, just for an instant, she wondered if the meteorite that had hit her house the previous night had been deliberately sent to kill her.

# 5

# SHOCK WAVE

They waited in silence for the shock wave to strike. The shock wave that would almost certainly destroy them all.

As astronomers, they knew the devastation an asteroid impact caused. They knew the one that gouged out the massive Meteor Crater in Arizona was just a mere 50 yards across. And they knew that if it hit today, the Meteor Crater asteroid would destroy an entire city. As it approached at eight miles per second, heat from the ball of fire would sear the surface, vaporising any organic life unfortunate enough to be in the vicinity, but most damage would occur after impact. The asteroid would be obliterated, blasting rocks and debris into the air for miles around, rocks and debris that would demolish buildings and homes. The mighty shock wave from the impact would generate winds six times more powerful than the fiercest hurricane. Yet the Meteor Crater asteroid was small – there are millions of much larger asteroids that would destroy not just cities, but entire countries, even whole worlds.

The asteroid that wiped out the dinosaurs and 70 per cent of all life on Earth 65 million years ago was much bigger than the Meteor Crater asteroid. Some seven miles across, it crashed into the Earth with a force equivalent to five billion Hiroshima atomic bombs. But even that was just a piece of galactic dust compared to the 500 mile wide monster that had just vaporised America and, very soon, would destroy the entire planet.

The shock wave arrived quicker than expected. The whole building shook and shuddered, creaked and groaned, as the shock wave hit, but it didn't collapse. They were still alive! Suddenly, bright light flooded the room, harsh light from the overhead fluorescent tubes. The power had returned. A buzz of excited conversation filled the air, replacing the eerie silence, as if someone had flicked a switch.

'Right, ladies and gentlemen,' said Professor Cecil Vivian Shawcross, having to raise his voice to make himself heard above the noise, 'that was pretty realistic, eh. I think we should congratulate the tech boys on a job well done.' Polite applause spread around the room. 'Time to get back to work,' he continued, 'and thanks for attending.'

He didn't know what to make of these simulations. They'd never had them when he was young but then again, they'd never had many other things either. They simply hadn't been invented. Technology advanced so rapidly. He remembered his family being one of the few privileged enough to have a telephone. Now, they were virtually obsolete. Everyone had a mobile phone. Or an iPad. Or both.

Set in a secret underground location in the North West of England, the hi-tech Simulation Chamber also doubled-up as a nuclear shelter. It was built after comet Shoemaker Levy smashed into Jupiter in July 1994, an event too close to home for comfort. Normally, the simulations were held once a year but, because of the recent, unprecedented meteor activity, the frequency had increased to three times a year. Meteor showers and asteroid activity were probably unconnected but they were taking no chances. The stakes were too high.

The simulations were designed to see how their team would respond if a large, rogue asteroid was detected. To test the procedures they had in place should such an event actually occur. Procedures to calculate whether or not it would hit the Earth and, if it would, the procedures needed to deflect it. To knock it off course. In previous simulations, they'd successfully managed to deflect the asteroid. But not this time. Everything they'd tried had failed. The asteroid was just too big. So they'd had to watch the consequences of failure. To watch what would happen if ever a giant asteroid did hit the Earth. To watch the apocalypse. Watch the end of the world. The end of all life.

In a way, it was similar to the simulation of a nuclear explosion at the Secret Bunker in Hack Green near Nantwich, Cheshire, a vast, underground blast-proof complex built to house the regional government in the event of a nuclear war. Similar, but much more technologically advanced. And realistic. It was a way to hone their skills. To keep them on their toes. To make them realise the catastrophic consequences of failure. To make the simulations more interesting, they competed with their counterparts in the USA, with Professor Carl Ryan's NEO team at NASA (National Aeronautics and Space Administration), to see which team, if any, could deflect the asteroid. This time, both teams had failed miserably.

Rather than working together in sweetness and harmony, the two teams had a history of discord and disagreement, a history that stretched back to their conflicting views on the trajectory of a rogue asteroid three years earlier. The US team, led by Carl, a strong-willed, self-opinionated individual who was never wrong and loved to be in the limelight, predicted the asteroid had a 50:50 chance of colliding with the Earth, a prediction that not only caused great anxiety but also ensured that he was the centre of media attention for weeks on end. Viv's team predicted, correctly, that the asteroid would miss the Earth by at least 100,000 miles, a near miss in astronomical terms but safe enough. Viv often wondered if Carl's team also knew that the asteroid would miss the Earth – after all, they had the same data and Carl was no fool – and that he did it just to hog the limelight. He wouldn't put it past him. Ever since, there had been an intense rivalry between the two teams, a fierce competition, with each team trying to outdo the other. It would have been unbearable for the losers if one team had succeeded in deflecting the asteroid.

'It's scary,' said Liz, turning to the man beside her as they filed out of the top secret Simulation Chamber, 'to think that something lurking in the vastness of deep space could destroy everything. Wipe out thousands of years of civilisation and seven billion people. In an instant. And, despite our best technologies, there's nothing we can do to prevent it.'

'You're right,' replied Frank. 'Let's hope it never happens.'

'But it will,' thought Liz. 'It's just a matter of time.'

# PART 2

· · ·

# STRANGE FINDS

> In the deepest sense, the
> search for extraterrestrial
> life is a search for ourselves
>
> Carl Sagan

# 6
# METEORITE HUNTERS

KARUMPH! The dull thud of the explosion penetrated the stillness of the Arctic night like a knife through butter. Kurt Andersson sprang up from his sleeping bag, grabbed his rifle, poked it through the flap of the tent and peered cautiously into the greyness of the night. At first, all he saw was the snow covered landscape and the dark Arctic sky. Then, as his eyes adjusted to the darkness, he saw it. The large white shape of a polar bear bounding away on all fours. A polar bear that had tripped the perimeter wire and set off the explosive charge, frightening it away. Its keen nose must have detected the smell of meat from their evening meal and, like any predator, it had followed the scent trail looking for an easy meal. The long Arctic winter was a lean time for hungry polar bears and they would take any food on offer, including humans.

Satisfied that it was safe to venture outside, Kurt left the relative warmth of his tent to reset the perimeter wire. If one polar bear was sniffing around, there might be others. He discarded the spent charge and replaced it with a fresh one. He wasn't taking any chances.

As a former member of the Norwegian Special Forces, Kurt Andersson was a specialist in Arctic conditions. He knew the terrain, the weather and what it took to survive in this most inhospitable of places. He'd trained elite Special Forces teams, including the SAS, in cold weather survival techniques, and successfully led several missions to the North Pole on behalf of the Norwegian government.

Born in Bergen, Norway's second city, Kurt Andersson had always been a bit of a daredevil, a thrill seeker, a risk taker. It was in his blood. As a teenager, he'd spend all his school holidays alternating between the Norwegian fjords and Norway's rugged, snow-capped mountains, climbing, skiing and abseiling with his best friend, Henrik Larsson. He too shared similar interests and it came as no surprise when, at the age of 18, both Kurt and Henrik joined the Norwegian army.

As he turned to walk back towards the tent, the tent with a welcoming yellow glow from the solitary oil lamp, Henrik was standing at the entrance, scanning the snowy waste with night vision goggles. 'What set it off, Kurt?' he asked, continuing to scan the snow covered terrain for any signs of movement.

'A polar bear. It must have caught the scent of our evening meal and came to investigate.'

'I didn't know there were polar bears so far from the sea ice,' replied Henrik. 'We'll have to be more careful in future.'

At the entrance to the other tent two women stood huddled together. Kurt and Henrik walked over to them.

'What was that bang?' asked Helga Hoffstadter, a 35-year-old German astrophysicist of some repute from the renowned Max Planck Institute. 'It sounded like an explosion.'

'It was an explosion,' said Kurt. 'A polar bear tripped the perimeter wire and set off the explosive charge. The resulting explosion scared it off.'

'But I thought you said there weren't any polar bears in this area,' said Helga, failing to hide the concern and fear in her voice.

'I did, and normally there aren't. But it's the Arctic winter and if food is scarce, they forage further afield.'

'Are there likely to be any more?' asked Helga, still sounding a little apprehensive.

'There may be,' replied Kurt, 'but it's unlikely. Polar bears are solitary animals. Anyway, I've reset the perimeter wire just in case.'

'Out here, you can't afford to be careless,' interjected Henrik. 'This year alone several people have been killed by hungry polar bears. Killed because they didn't take the necessary precautions. Forgetting to arm, or even worse, not setting up a perimeter wire, can be fatal.'

'It's normally inexperienced foreigners who take chances,' said Kurt. 'School trips are the worst. The children, and sometimes the teachers too, think polar bears are harmless, cuddly creatures. They're not! They're cunning, calculating, vicious killers that aren't averse to the taste of human flesh.'

Kurt Andersson, Henrik Larsson, Helga Hoffstadter and Liz Conway made up the meteorite search team for the Arctic. Governments around the world had collaborated to send search teams to the areas with the most meteorite activity. A USA and Canadian team to Alaska; a Russian team to Siberia; a Chinese team to the Himalayas; an international team to the Antarctic and a European team to the Arctic. Each team comprised four people: a guide who knew the local area; a specialist in cold weather survival techniques – usually an ex-Special Forces soldier – and two scientists.

The appointment of the guide and the cold weather specialist was out of his hands, but Professor Cecil Vivian Shawcross had been the person charged with the unenviable task of selecting the British scientist for the Arctic team. Dozens had approached him but most were easy to reject: they didn't have the relevant skills or qualifications. In the end, it came down to a straight choice between Liz Conway and Rupert Templeton-Smythe. His own protégé and Frank Rogers' bright young star. Both were really keen to go – Liz had been on at him for weeks, imploring, pleading, begging to be chosen. He thought she had the edge, not because she was his protégé, but because an astrobiologist was better suited for the mission than an astrophysicist. Anyway, they already had one astrophysicist on the team. He saw no point in sending two. Before making his decision, Viv explained his reasoning to Rupert's boss, Frank Rogers. He didn't want to be accused of nepotism. 'You're absolutely right,' said Frank. 'Liz is the one who should go.'

Orbiting satellites had monitored the meteor showers for weeks and pinpointed the areas where most meteorites had fallen. As per Sod's Law, they weren't in easy to reach locations, but in remote, impenetrable, hard to reach areas. Despite their difficult locations, these were the areas they'd search first.

In the Arctic, the area with the highest density of meteorites was a treacherous, uneven region of rubble ice surrounded by a pressure ridge, a jagged ridge of ice caused by the collision of two ice sheets. In a way, it's a miniature version of what happens when tectonic plates collide to form mountain ranges, like the Himalayas, only on a much smaller, and infinitely faster, scale. Although they only rise about 5 to 10 feet above the sea ice, their sharp, jagged, irregular shape makes pressure ridges extremely difficult to traverse. Many an explorer has suffered a broken leg crossing a pressure ridge. If crossing one alone is dangerous, crossing one hauling a heavily laden sled requires a feat of Herculean proportions. But it was an obstacle they'd have to overcome. Ideally, it would have been preferable if the helicopter had dropped them at the epicentre of the meteorite zone, but the uneven terrain and bad weather made that an impossibility. It was far too risky.

The harsh Arctic weather didn't help their search either. It was the beginning of the long polar winter, six months of continual darkness coupled with sub-zero temperatures and bitterly cold, icy winds. Blizzards were a frequent hazard, as were the whiteouts, snowfalls so dense that visibility was zero. The snowfalls caused another problem too; they covered up the meteorites, making finding them by eye virtually impossible. Specialist detection equipment was needed, equipment to detect iridium.

Iridium is the smoking gun for the detection of meteorites or meteorite impacts. It is one of the rarest elements on Earth – the Earth's crust contains just one part per billion of iridium – yet meteorites contain over 500 times this amount. This dichotomy in its distribution makes iridium the DNA (deoxyribonucleic acid) of astronomy. An 'iridium spike' is the unequivocal, tell-tale sign of a meteorite or meteorite impact. Indeed, it was the iridium-rich sedimentary layer around the crater at Chicxulub that provided compelling evidence for the impact of the massive asteroid that wiped out the dinosaurs some 65 million years ago.

Liz peered out of her tent bleary-eyed. She hadn't slept well. The morning sky was no different to the night sky. It was just as black. Perhaps that's why she wasn't sleeping well. There was nothing to distinguish night from day. Nothing to tell her body clock when to sleep and when to wake. Kurt and Henrik had already loaded the supplies on to the two sleds and were busy making the final preparations to leave, fastening the harnesses from the sleds around their waist. After last night's scare, both men had their rifles slung over their shoulders, just in case they encountered any more polar bears.

'Right,' shouted Kurt. 'Is everyone ready?' Three heads nodded simultaneously. Three heads completely covered except for the eyes, nose and mouth. Covered to protect them from the bitterly cold, Arctic temperature. And the biting, icy wind. They were ready to go.

Dressed in colourful hi-tech clothing, they stood out like beacons in the night. Four brightly coloured, fluorescent figures in a world of white. Kurt in bright red, Henrik in blue, Liz in yellow and Helga in orange. Brightly coloured gear to make them easier to spot in the case of an emergency. 'And,' thought Liz, 'easy for a polar bear to spot too.'

Both Liz and Helga felt sorry for Kurt and Henrik. Negotiating their way through the rubble ice, the jumble of ice fragments covering the polar ice cap, was bad enough, but having to haul a heavily laden sled as well must be murder. Progress was painfully slow. Every so often they'd pause to give Kurt and Henrik some respite and allow her and Helga to take readings from the iridium detectors. The signals were still weak. They weren't there yet.

Ahead, a jagged ridge of ice blocked their way. A pressure ridge. Although it was no higher than 10 feet, it may as well have been a thousand. To Liz, it looked impassable. 'How on earth do we cross that?' she asked Kurt.

Kurt had encountered pressure ridges many times. He knew exactly what to do. 'First, we have to unload all the supplies from the sleds. Everything. Then Henrik and I will haul the empty sleds behind us as we clamber over the ridge. Finally, we have to carry the supplies over by hand.'

It was the only way to do it. After unloading the two sleds, Kurt and Henrik clambered carefully over the ridge, dragging the empty sleds behind them. Liz and Helga watched in hushed silence, keeping a sharp lookout for any stray polar bears. One slip on the jagged ice could mean a broken leg, not something you wanted in a place as hostile as this. After one or two stumbles and a lot of cursing and swearing, the two sleds sat firmly at the other side of the ridge. Liz and Helga were glad that Kurt and Henrik were with them. There was no way they could have got the sleds over the ridge.

With the sleds safely on the other side, Kurt and Henrik began the tedious task of repeating the same procedure with the supplies. 'Do you want us to help?' asked Helga, realising that Kurt and Henrik would have to make several forays across the treacherous ridge.

'No,' replied Kurt firmly. 'It's too dangerous. You might slip and injure yourselves. Leave it to us. We've done it many times.'

'I've done it before too,' thought Helga and, ignoring Kurt's advice, slung a heavy rucksack over her shoulders and started to ascend the ridge. All was going well until her foot slipped on an icy slab and, as her body twisted to compensate, the rucksack swung around, shifting her centre of gravity and causing her to overbalance. She screamed as she slid backwards, only stopping when her leg jammed in a crevice. Kurt and Henrik were there in an instant. Gently, like a mother with a child, they eased her out of the crevice, taking extra care with her jammed leg. Kurt pinched her ankle. Hard. 'Ouch. That hurts,' winced Helga.

'Not as much as if you'd broken your leg,' he barked, clearly angry that Helga had disobeyed his instructions.

'I was only trying to help,' she said, in a muted, apologetic tone. 'To speed things up.'

'Well don't,' said Kurt rather brusquely. 'Leave things like that to us.'

He ran his hand up and down her leg, feeling for any signs of a break. 'You've been lucky this time,' he said. 'There's no break. But next time I give you instructions, obey them. Okay.' This was his soldier's voice. His leader's voice. A commanding voice. A voice used to being obeyed.

'Okay,' said Helga sheepishly. 'I'm sorry. I won't do it again.'

When all the supplies had been reloaded on to the sleds, Henrik spoke. 'We need to move on. I don't want to make camp near a pressure ridge. It's too dangerous. We'll move to somewhere safer.'

During their training in Norway's Special Forces, both he and Kurt had been told about the early Arctic explorers who wouldn't sleep near a pressure ridge for fear of drowning in case a lead suddenly opened up while they slept. The Arctic Ocean is up to three miles deep and the strong ocean currents cause the surface ice sheets to shift and move constantly. This incessant movement pulls sections of the sheets apart, creating open channels of water called 'leads'. Fast flowing deep water at temperatures as low as minus 40°C. Anyone unfortunate enough to fall into a lead would either drown or quickly freeze to death.

They made camp about two hours later in a flat section of rubble ice, exhausted after crossing the pressure ridge. This time, they were more careful with the evening meal. They didn't want to attract any unwelcome visitors. Although still relatively weak, the iridium signals were getting stronger. They were definitely heading in the right direction.

After a light breakfast, they set off towards the epicentre of the meteorite cluster. The signal strength was increasing. Not far to go now. Suddenly, without any warning, Henrik, who was leading the way, stopped. He motioned for them to follow suit. The 'day' was still and quiet. The wind of the previous few days had abated, resulting in a stillness that bordered on the eerie. Henrik removed his headgear and cupped his large hands behind his ears. Listening. Initially, he heard nothing. Just the stillness of the Arctic winter. Then he heard it. Heard what he was listening for. A faint groaning and creaking coming from the ice. 'Get back! GET BACK NOW!' he barked, turning on his heels and running as fast as he could towards them, the heavy sled trailing in his wake. Liz, Helga and Kurt followed his lead, turning around and running back the way they'd come as fast as they could.

Suddenly, an almighty crack shattered the Arctic silence as the ice where he had been standing just a few seconds earlier split asunder, opening up a channel of fast flowing water. A lead.

'Shit, that's the last thing we need,' spat Kurt. 'A bloody lead.'

Everyone stood looking at the torrent of freezing water that had appeared out of nowhere. A torrent that was getting wider by the minute. It was already five feet wide, too wide for them to jump. 'We'll have to wait until it settles down,' said Kurt, obviously disappointed at having this formidable obstacle thrust upon them at the last minute. 'We may as well rest and eat lunch.'

After about four hours, the lead seemed to have settled down. It's width had increased to 15 feet. 'It's far too wide to jump and too wide to straddle with the sleds,' said Kurt, considering his options. 'We'll have to use the dinghy.'

It was something he'd hoped they wouldn't have to use. The small dinghy had to be inflated and could only carry one person, necessitating at least six crossings; four for the people and two for the sleds.

'I'll go first,' said Kurt, clambering into the flimsy craft carrying a coil of rope, a hammer and a metal spike. Even though the lead was only 15 feet wide, the strong current made the crossing extremely difficult. It took all Kurt's strength and skill to reach the other side. Although he paddled furiously, because of the strong current he reached the far side a good 10 yards downstream. After clambering ashore, he hauled the dinghy out of the water and walked back until he was directly opposite them on the other side of the lead. Then, he did what Henrik had already started doing: he hammered the metal spike into the ice.

Having checked it was secure, he tied one end of the rope to the spike, threaded the other end through the eyelet of the dinghy and threw the rest of the coiled rope across the lead to Henrik. Henrik pulled it taught and secured it to his spike. Kurt slid the dinghy back into the water and began pushing it away from the ice with his walking pole. As it reached the middle of the lead, Henrik took over, pulling it to their side of the lead with his walking pole.

'I think we should send the sleds across first,' said Kurt. 'To make sure it's safe.'

'Affirmative,' replied Henrik, sliding one of the sleds on the dinghy. Both sleds were transported across the lead without incident.

'Right. Which one of you ladies wants to go first?' Henrik said to Liz and Helga.

'I'll go,' said Helga, ruefully rubbing her badly bruised leg. 'Standing here in the cold is making my leg ache.'

'Okay,' said Henrik, holding the dinghy as steady as he could. 'Step aboard.'

'Right, pull her over,' he shouted to Kurt. Less than a minute later, Kurt was helping Helga clamber out of the dinghy.

'Two down and two to go,' shouted Kurt, pushing the dinghy back towards Henrik.

'Your turn, Liz,' said Henrik. Gingerly, Liz stepped into the dinghy and squatted down. The lead was only 15 feet wide but she was dreading the crossing. She hated water. She'd never been a swimmer or a sailor.

'Okay Kurt, she's all yours,' shouted Henrik. 'Pull her over.' Liz grabbed the sides of the dinghy for dear life as the flimsy craft moved slowly away from the edge of the ice. She could feel the current trying to tear it free from the rope. She was just about to close her eyes – something she did when she was frightened – when a dark shape in the water caught her eye. Something upstream that was coming towards her. Fast. At first, she couldn't make out what it was, but as it closed in, she knew exactly what it was. A black fin. The fin of a shark!

She panicked. 'SHARK!' she screamed, standing up and pointing to the black fin rushing towards her. It was a mistake. She lost her balance and toppled into the fast flowing, freezing water.

# 7

# THE FIND

Kurt's training kicked in immediately. He assessed the situation in a flash. Liz was in the middle of a lead of fast flowing water being swept along by the strong current. There was no way he could drag her out from the middle of the lead: she was too far away. She had to be close to the edge of the ice for him to reach her. He had to act fast. She wouldn't survive for long in water at minus 40°C.

He scanned the lead for any sharp bends or turns. They were in luck. About 50 yards ahead, the lead swung sharply to the right. At that point, the current would sweep her close to the edge of the ice. He had to get there before she did, or she would die. It was their only chance.

Kurt also knew that a fast flowing lead meant only one thing. The water was heading for a massive hole in the ice, a hole that could be miles deep, a hole where the water would plunge into the Arctic Ocean, taking Liz with it. A spectacular Arctic waterfall.

All these thoughts flashed through his head in an instant and he started running the moment he spotted the bend in the lead. He ran like he'd never ran before, knelt down at the point of the bend and dug his knees and the toes of his snow shoes into the hard snow, making himself as secure as possible. He didn't want the impact of Liz's body to drag him into the lead. Then, he discarded his gloves. He needed uncluttered, bare hands to haul her out of the water.

As she came rushing by, he plunged both his hands into the icy water – the pain was instant and excruciating – grabbed her under both armpits and yanked her to the edge of the ice. The force of the water and the weight of her body almost caused him to topple in. It took all his strength and years of training to prevent the water from tearing her from his grip. His muscles and sinews were stretched to breaking point. He could feel his grip start to loosen as numbness began to creep along his hands. He couldn't hold on much longer.

It seemed like he'd been in this position for ages – in reality it was no more than 30 seconds – when he felt a figure loom over him and grab Liz's arms. 'Okay Kurt. Let's pull her out,' said Henrik.

Henrik had assessed the situation too and crossed the lead as fast as he could, sprinting the 50 yards to where Kurt was holding on to Liz. Together, they hauled her from the freezing water. She was barely conscious and in a state of shock as they laid her gently on the snow. Her clothes were wet through and she was shivering uncontrollably.

'We have to get her wet clothes off NOW!' yelled Henrik. 'Helga, you take off her clothes and wrap her in foil. I'll erect the tent and fire up the stove.' And, looking at his friend's hands, he said, 'Kurt, put your gloves back on.'

As Liz and Kurt thawed out by the stove, Henrik examined Liz for signs of frostbite. The skin on her extremities, her fingers, nose, ears and toes, was white and cold. He didn't want to disturb her to ask if they felt numb, but he was sure they would. She was exhibiting the early stage of frostbite – frostnip. Of more concern was the hardness. If it persisted, she could have the intermediate stage of frostbite, but they wouldn't know that for another day or two.

Kurt was less of a worry. Only his hands had been exposed to the freezing water, and for less time. He should be fine. At best he wouldn't have any frostbite. At worst, just mild frostnip.

For their evening meal, Helga prepared a pot of steaming hot tea and a bowl of warm broth. She stroked Liz's cheek. 'Wake up, Liz,' she whispered. 'I've got a mug of hot tea and a bowl of broth to warm you up.'

Liz's eyelids flickered, then opened. Slowly. She looked confused. It was the first time she'd regained consciousness since being pulled from the water. 'What... what happened? Did I fall into the lead?'

'I'm afraid you did,' replied Helga softly. 'You stood up, shouted "shark" and then fell in.'

It all came flooding back. 'I... I remember now,' she said. 'I saw a fin. A dark fin. I thought it was a shark. Was it a shark?' she asked.

Henrik looked at Kurt and smiled. 'No, Liz. It wasn't a shark. It was a baluga whale. Probably a young one that got separated from its pod. Adult ones are white. It was probably lost.'

'Or injured,' interjected Kurt. 'If you saw a fin the whale must have been on its side. Balugas don't have dorsal fins. Anyway, it wasn't a shark.'

'Then I needn't have...' She was about to say 'panicked', but decided against it.

'It's okay,' said Henrik, seeing her distress. 'It was a natural reaction.'

Liz felt foolish. Foolish and childish. She'd panicked and almost died. And, worst still, she'd put the lives of her colleagues in danger.

'Who pulled me out?' she asked.

'Kurt,' replied Helga. 'He acted so fast and was so brave, plunging his bare hands into the...'

'It's what I'm trained to do,' interrupted Kurt. 'Just part of my job. And it wasn't just me. I couldn't have done it without Henrik's help.'

'That's enough talking for now,' said Helga. 'Let's get some tea and broth into you.'

For the next two days they rested, allowing Liz to get over her ordeal and regain her strength. And to allow Henrik to assess the extent of the frostbite. As he feared, it had progressed beyond frostnip: she was displaying the signs of superficial frostbite. Her nose, ears and fingers had turned red and blistered. But it wasn't too bad, just the top layer of skin. She should be fine in a few days. Thankfully, her toes were okay. At least she'd be able to walk.

The first meteorite they found was the size of a cricket ball. Helga's keen eyes spotted the irregular shaped greyish-black lump of extraterrestrial rock from outer space lying on a bare sheet of ice where the fierce Arctic wind had blown away the snow. It was one of the few meteorites they found that was visible to the naked eye. Most were buried beneath the snow and had to be located by the iridium detectors.

They came in all shapes and sizes. The smaller ones, those less than the size of a golf ball, resembled smooth nuggets. The larger meteorites were less smooth and more irregular shaped, in part because fragments had broken off the surface on impact.

All the ones they'd found seemed normal, natural meteorites. Just lumps of extraterrestrial rock. None showed any sign of intelligent, alien design. Liz was disappointed. Perhaps Rupert was right. Perhaps she was a deluded young woman.

The following day, Liz detected a strong signal. It was emanating from a depression in the snow. Excitedly, she scraped away the snow to expose the bare ice, but there was no sign of any meteorite. She checked the detector. The signal was still strong. Puzzled, she scraped away more snow, exposing an area of ice about 12 feet in diameter. But still she found nothing. No meteorite, no signs of a meteorite impact. No fragments. Nothing. But lots of iridium. Strange. Panting from scraping away the snow, she squatted on her haunches and called to Helga.

'Helga, can you come and check my readings with your detector? I'm getting a strange result.'

Helga knelt beside Liz and switched on her detector. The signal was very strong. 'Where's the meteorite?' she said to Liz. 'It should be here.'

Kurt and Henrik strolled over to the two women sat on the circle of ice. 'Is there a problem?' asked Kurt.

'Not exactly a problem,' said Liz. 'But it's puzzling.'

'What is?' asked Henrik.

'Well,' said Liz, glancing at Helga, 'our iridium detectors are receiving strong signals from this area, but there's no sign of a meteorite or a meteorite impact. I've shifted the snow to extend the search area,' she continued, pointing to the 12 foot diameter circle of ice with her hand, 'and still found nothing. It's strange.'

Kurt and Henrik rubbed the ice with their gloves until it shone like polished glass and examined the surface with expert eyes. It didn't take long for them to spot what they were looking for. A patch of roughly circular ice that had melted and refrozen. Unless you knew what to look for, it would never be noticed. Just a barely perceptible, irregular shaped ridge where the reformed ice met the existing ice. To the untrained eye, it was invisible.

'This patch of ice has melted and refrozen,' said Kurt, tracing out a shape approximately three feet in diameter with his gloved finger. 'The meteorite must be buried in the ice.'

Helga looked perplexed. 'For a meteorite to penetrate the ice,' she said, as if speaking to herself, 'it must have been travelling very fast. And to have been travelling very fast, it must have been fairly large. And if it had been fairly large, it should have made a large impact crater, one much bigger than this,' she said, pointing to the three foot diameter circle of refrozen ice. 'It's strange.'

'Strange or not,' said Liz, 'it must be in the ice. The question is: how do we get it out?'

'We'll have to radio the helicopter to bring in some specialist drilling equipment,' replied Kurt. 'Specialist drilling equipment for drilling through ice.'

'I'll do it now,' said Henrik, getting out his radio. 'But we'll have to wait for a suitable window in the weather. And they'll have to winch it down. It's too dangerous to land.'

'How wide shall we drill the hole?' asked Helga, a novice when it came to drilling through ice.

'About two feet,' replied Henrik. 'Big enough to fit a person and extricate a large meteorite.'

'How deep do you think we'll have to go?' asked Kurt, looking at Liz and Helga.

'Difficult to say,' replied Helga. 'Our instruments aren't sensitive enough to calculate that. However, if we lower one into the hole, the signal should get stronger the closer it gets to the meteorite.'

'Won't the drill destroy the meteorite?' asked Liz. 'Churn it to bits.'

'It shouldn't,' replied Kurt. 'Ice is relatively soft to drill and the drill is designed to cut out automatically if it encounters anything hard, like rock. Or a meteorite.'

But the drill didn't encounter anything hard. It encountered exactly the opposite. Thin air. An empty space. An ice cave about 75 feet down. It wasn't what they were expecting.

Although common in the Antarctic, ice caves were rare in the Arctic. Rare but not unknown.

'Looks like we'll have to go down,' said Kurt, already fixing the rope to his body. 'I'll go first then one of you two ladies can follow. And don't forget to bring a detector.'

The view that met her eyes as she descended into the ice cave took Liz's breath away. It was other-worldly, as though she'd entered another planet. The whole cave was suffused with a stunning silvery-grey glow, the effect of the moonlight filtering down the drill hole. Stalactite spikes of ice hung from the ceiling, some over three feet long. It was a crystal palace draped in a pale silvery-grey ethereal light. It was the most beautiful sight she had ever seen.

Surprisingly, the floor was flat and smooth. Sea ice, probably. She removed her glove and rubbed her finger along the smooth, cold floor and then placed it in her mouth. It tasted salty, salty from the frozen ocean water. She gazed in wonder at the arched ceiling with a neat row of icy stalactites. They reminded her of a shark's mouth. A shark's mouth with a row of razor sharp teeth. She shuddered, thinking about her ordeal at the lead.

'Are you okay?' asked Kurt.

'I'm fine,' replied Liz. 'It's... just so beautiful. So... magical. I've never seen an ice cave before.'

'They're certainly different, aren't they?' said Kurt.

'They certainly are,' replied Liz with a sense of wonderment.

Although beautiful to behold, the silvery-grey glow provided little in the way of illumination. Kurt and Liz scanned the dimly lit cave floor looking for the lump of extraterrestrial rock. There was no sign of any meteorite. Liz switched on the iridium detector. Although the signal was very strong, there was still no sign of a meteorite. Frustrated, she moved slowly around the cave in different directions trying to pinpoint the source of the signal. 'I think it's over there,' she said, pointing to the far side of the cave.

Kurt switched on his powerful flashlight and swept the icy floor with the beam. There, caught in the torch beam at the far side of the cave, lay a lump of grey-black rock.

'There it is!' exclaimed Liz. 'There, by the wall,' she shouted, dashing across to examine it. The meteorite was the size of a large melon but not melon-shaped. It was more pear-shaped, more pointed at one end. It's surface was smooth but uneven. Apart from its odd shape, it seemed just like the other large meteorites.

As she was getting up from the floor with the meteorite in her hands, a dark patch on the cave wall caught Liz's attention. 'Kurt, would you shine your torch on this?' she said, pointing to the green-black patch in the ice. The patch next to where the meteorite lay.

Liz studied the green-black patch intently. As an astrobiologist, she knew immediately what it was. Bacterial life! Even in the dark, icy depths of an Arctic ice cave, life had a foothold. Carefully, she scraped a small sample into a Pyrex glass vial and sealed it securely. 'I'll get it analysed when we return,' she said to Kurt. 'It's probably of terrestrial origin but you never know.'

'Is everything okay down there!' It was Henrik, worried they were taking so long.

'Everything's fine,' shouted back Kurt. 'We're just about finished. Haul us up, Henrik.'

'You've just got to see it,' enthused Liz to Helga. 'You've just got to! It's so beautiful.'

'She's right,' said Kurt. 'You can't leave without seeing it. Both of you.' And they didn't.

The ice cave had the same effect on Helga and Henrik as it had on Liz. Both were overcome by its sheer beauty.

As they prepared to leave, both Liz and Helga were puzzled. Puzzled that a meteorite the size of a melon could penetrate to a depth of 75 feet into the Arctic ice. And puzzled why there was no fragmentation on impact. No debris as it smashed into the ice at great speed. It just didn't make sense.

Kurt called in the helicopter. By a stroke of luck they'd found a relatively flat expanse of ice and the weather had relented. They'd exhausted the highest density impact zone. It was time to relocate to the second site. Here, they found a similar scattering of meteorites, but fewer of them. They also found another pear-shaped meteorite, similar to the one in the ice cave, embedded just a foot below the surface of the ice.

Plans to examine the third and final site had to be abandoned. The weather had taken a turn for the worse. It was time to head for home.

All the meteorites were labelled and packed in special containers. Labelled to show their precise location, whether they were found on the surface or embedded in the ice. Or, in one case, in an ice cave 75 feet below the surface.

On their final night in the Arctic, Kurt, Henrik, Helga and Liz ate a slap-up meal of steak and mashed potatoes washed down with a single bottle of wine to celebrate the end of a successful mission. Then, they went to bed.

During the night, high-pitched, barely audible, bursts of energy emanated from two of the meteorites, but no one heard. They were all fast asleep.

# 8

# ANALYSIS

'How many?' asked Viv.

'Six in total,' replied Frank. 'The American and Canadian team found one; the Russians – they sent four teams to Siberia because of its vast size – found one; the Antarctic team found two, just like the Arctic team; and the Himalayan teams – the Chinese also sent four – found none.'

'Just six pear-shaped meteorites,' said Viv thoughtfully, 'but hundreds of other meteorites, including the one from Liz's house.'

'Have we any results from their analysis?' he asked, glancing at Rupert.

Because they had two presumably similar pear-shaped meteorites, the decision was taken to keep one intact and use the other for analysis. Detailed analysis. But there was a problem. A major problem. Unlike the other meteorites, this one was almost impossible to fragment or crush, it was so hard and dense. Eventually, using specialist equipment, they'd managed to obtain thin slices from different parts of the meteorite, some of which they pulverised into a powder. Both the slices and the pulverised powder were subjected to a whole battery of tests, both physical and chemical. Mass spectrometry, infrared and ultraviolet spectroscopy, nuclear magnetic resonance, X-ray diffraction, electron microscopy, chromatography, gravimetric and volumetric chemical analysis, everything, to unlock any secrets they might hold. But such a rigorous analysis took time.

'Only the preliminary findings,' replied Rupert, who was heading up the analysis team. 'So far, they appear to be no different to the other meteorites, except in one respect. They're harder. More compact, more dense, than the other meteorites. More difficult to chip samples off the surface.'

'Have the Americans or Russians found anything?' asked Liz.

'If they have, they haven't told us,' replied Frank.

As Liz listened to the discussion, her mind began to wander. She was convinced the pear-shaped meteorites were different from the rest. Held some secret they hadn't yet discovered. There were just too many anomalies for them not to be. For instance, why were they only found in the coldest regions of the planet? In the Arctic, why was one found just 12 inches below the ice and one in an ice cave 75 feet underground? Both were the same size and shape. How could 'natural' meteorites behave so differently? It just didn't add up. And why had two been found in both polar regions, the Arctic and Antarctic, but only one in Alaska and Siberia and none at all in the Himalayas? She knew what the counter arguments would be, that the meteorites were easier to find in the Arctic and Antarctic because of the smaller size and relatively flat terrain of the polar regions. And it was a plausible argument: Alaska and Siberia were huge and the Himalayas… Well, the world's highest mountain range was almost impossible to search thoroughly. She wasn't surprised they hadn't found any meteorites at all in the Himalayas.

'What's you view, Liz?' asked Viv, jolting her from her thoughts.

'My view on what?' she said, looking blank.

'On the pear-shaped meteorites,' said Viv.

Liz considered the question carefully before answering. 'The fact that two were found in both the Arctic and Antarctic, the two coldest regions of the planet, could be a coincidence,' she said, 'but I doubt it. I think whoever sent them,' she paused, expecting another outburst from Rupert Templeton-Smythe, but none materialised, 'deliberately sent two to the coldest regions, and just one to the other cold regions.'

'Why?' asked Rupert.

'Here it comes,' thought Liz. 'The interrogation.'

'To obtain as much information as possible about the two coldest regions of our planet,' she replied.

'What for?' asked Rupert.

'I don't know yet, but I'm sure I'll be able to figure it out,' she said, paraphrasing what he'd said at a previous meeting.

'Who do you think sent them?' asked Frank.

Liz thought about answering but just shrugged her shoulders instead.

'Okay,' said Viv, 'let's leave it at that for now. Oh, before we go,' continued Viv, 'have we had the result on the bacterial swab from the cave?' He looked at Liz for an answer.

'Yes, we have,' she answered. 'I'm afraid it's just a terrestrial bacterium, an extremophile that thrives in cold conditions. It's not alien.'

'Ah well,' said Viv, 'I just hoped it might have been an alien life form. Never mind, we'll meet again when Rupert has more results.'

She was just finishing her lunch when the phone rang. 'Great, another bloody example of Sod's Law,' she thought, swallowing her mouthful of food as she picked up the receiver.

'Liz Conway,' she said, making no effort to disguise her annoyance at having her lunch interrupted.

'Liz, get over here! Quick! I've got something really interesting to show you. Hurry!'

Rupert Templeton-Smythe sounded excited. Very excited. There was an urgency to his voice. At that instant, she felt ashamed by the offhand way she'd answered the phone. Although she didn't like him – and the feeling was mutual – she'd been rude. What had prompted the call? He hardly ever rang her, so it must be something important. And there was something else too. He'd called her Liz.

'Here, look at this!' he blurted out, pointing excitedly to the screen of the electron microscope. Liz followed his finger but saw nothing exciting, just a jumbled-up mass of dots.

'What am I looking for?' she asked.

'There!' he said, jabbing the screen with his forefinger. 'There! Can't you see it?'

Liz stared intently at the point where his forefinger had touched the flickering screen. For a few seconds all she saw was an amorphous mixture of jumbled-up dots, molecules she presumed. Then she saw it. Mixed in amongst the mass of molecules – concealed might be a better term – was a regular, crystalline array of atoms, or molecules – she couldn't tell which – in a spheroid shape. No, not spheroid, in a geodesic shape. A miniature, nano-sized geodesic dome.

'Is… is this what I think it is?' gasped Liz.

'Why? What do you think it is, Liz?' asked Rupert expectantly.

'There, he's said it again,' she thought. 'Liz. Why Liz and not Beth?'

'I… I don't think it's natural,' she said, looking at Rupert for any clues. 'It's too precise. Too… designed. Is it something… unnatural? Alien?' she ventured tentatively, remembering Rupert's scathing comments about the meteorites.

His reply shocked her. 'Absolutely!' he shouted, finding it hard to contain his excitement. 'That's exactly what I think!'

Liz was shocked. She'd never seen him so emotional, so pumped-up, so… boyish. He was like a different person.

'Have you told anyone else?'

'No, not yet. I wanted to tell you first.'

'Why?' queried Liz, shooting him a quizzical look. 'Why me?'

'Because I knew you'd be the person most likely to believe it could be an... alien artefact. And,' he continued, averting his eyes, 'because I'm the one who's always ridiculed your views on intelligent, alien life. I thought it only fair that you should be the first to know.'

Liz stood there, dumbfounded. She was completely taken aback. Shocked even. This wasn't the Rupert Templeton-Smythe she knew. The arrogant, condescending, know-it-all who had an answer for everything. The privileged 'posh' boy from a rich family in Berkshire. The privileged 'posh' boy who'd trodden the familiar path from Eton to Cambridge. The privileged 'posh' boy she hated. But this wasn't him. This was a normal, decent human being.

'Have you found anything else unusual?' she asked.

'No. Not yet. I only discovered this... artefact last night. I slept on it just to make sure my mind wasn't playing tricks. This morning I checked and rechecked to be absolutely certain, then called you.'

'What do you think it is?'

'I'm not sure,' replied Rupert. 'I suspect there'll be more of them concealed in the meteorite. Now I know what to look for, I should be able to find them. Having more will give us a better chance of finding out what they are.'

For a few moments they just stood in silence collecting their thoughts. If what he'd found really was an alien artefact, a sign of intelligent alien life, it would be the greatest discovery ever made.

'In the deepest sense,' said Liz, breaking the silence, 'the search for extraterrestrial intelligence is a search for ourselves.' Liz spoke the words softly, abstractedly, as though she was speaking to an invisible presence.

'What was that?' said Rupert.

'It's something Carl Sagan said, that our search for intelligent life in the Universe is a search to find ourselves. It's a quote I've never forgotten.'

'It sounds familiar. I must have heard it somewhere too,' said Rupert.

'Do you think we should tell the others?' asked Liz, changing the subject.

'I've wrestled with that already,' replied Rupert, 'and I think it's best if we keep it secret. At least for the time being. Is that okay?'

'That's fine,' said Liz. 'Let's wait until you're more certain. We, er, don't want to look foolish. But,' she added quickly, 'don't wait too long. I don't want the Americans or Russians to steal your thunder.'

'Our thunder, Liz. Our thunder.'

# 9

# CONFIRMATION

The adrenaline rush kept him going. Stimulated him. Spurred him on. He'd never worked so hard in his entire, privileged life. Thirty-six hours without a break. Day and night. But he wasn't complaining. He was on the brink of the greatest, most momentous, discovery in the history of the human race. The first real sign of extraterrestrial life. The first piece of evidence that we are not alone. That at least one other intelligent life form exists in the vastness of the Universe. If he could prove, beyond any shadow of doubt, that these artefacts were indeed from an advanced, alien civilisation, then his, and Liz's, names would be immortalised. Forever. Dr Rupert Templeton-Smythe and Dr Elizabeth Conway, the people who discovered the first ever signs of intelligent, alien life. Their names would rank alongside that of Neil Armstrong, the first human to step on to another world.

A knock on the door interrupted his thoughts. And his deliberations. He glanced at the clock on the laboratory wall. 3.15 a.m. It could only be one person. 'Come in, Liz,' he shouted. 'The door's unlocked.'

'I couldn't sleep,' she said. 'I'm just too excited.'

'Me too,' replied Rupert. 'I just can't leave the lab.'

'You mean, you haven't been home?' said Liz, flabbergasted by his conscientiousness.

'No. I've been busy locating the artefacts in the meteorite. There are thousands of them when you know where to look. I've managed to separate and extricate most of them,' he said, pointing to two petri dishes full of tiny dark specks.

'When's the last time you had anything to eat, or drink?' asked Liz, noticing his dishevelled, unkempt appearance. It was so out of character to his normal immaculate persona.

'Er, yesterday lunch time,' he replied.

'Good God! I'm surprised you haven't collapsed from hunger, or thirst. I'll nip to the canteen and grab us a sandwich from the freezer cabinet, and a coffee from the machine.'

'Have you had chance to examine the… artefacts?' asked Liz, munching a mouthful of chicken and stuffing sandwich.

'Only briefly,' replied Rupert, biting a large chunk off his beef and onion barm cake.

'And…'

'Well,' he said, trying to chew and talk at the same time, 'their structure and composition are different to the bulk of the meteorite, and to that of the other, er, natural meteorites. They need to be subjected to a more thorough examination using experts in the relevant fields but, as far as I can tell, the artefacts seem to be made of a composite material unlike any I've ever come across – although I'm not an expert in such matters,' he added quickly. 'The engineering and science needed to construct such precise, minute, geodesic domes must be of the highest order. I've never seen anything like them.'

'Have you any idea what they are?' asked Liz, sipping her coffee, her favourite drink.

'Not exactly, but the interesting thing,' he said thoughtfully, 'is that there are two distinct types of artefacts, small ones and larger ones.'

'Is that why there are two petri dishes?' asked Liz.

'Yes, it is,' replied Rupert. 'The larger ones, which have a slightly different shape to the smaller ones, appear to be concentrated at the bottom of the pear-shaped meteorite.'

'The wide end?' asked Liz.

'Yeah,' replied Rupert. 'The wide end. The smaller ones seem to be concentrated in the centre.'

'For protection?' asked Liz. 'Because they're more delicate?'

'Possibly,' replied Rupert, 'but we need to analyse the intact meteorite to determine their precise locations.'

'That's fascinating,' said Liz. 'Do you think they have different functions?'

'Yes, I do,' replied Rupert. 'I can't say for certain but if I had to hazard a guess, I'd say the larger ones were some kind of propulsion device and the smaller ones some kind of sensing and transmitting device, to gather information and transmit it back to… wherever they came from. However, so far, I've not detected any transmissions.'

'But it doesn't mean there aren't any, right?' blurted out Liz.

'I suppose so. It depends *when* they transmit and *how* they transmit,' replied Rupert.

'What do you mean, *how* they transmit? Surely they'd use radio waves or some other form of electromagnetic radiation.'

'That's true,' said Rupert, 'but there are millions of possible frequencies and, if they're an advanced civilisation, millions of ways to encrypt or encode the signal.'

For a while, neither of them spoke. They just sat in silence eating their food and drinking their coffee. It was Rupert who broke the silence. 'First thing tomorrow, I'll have a word with Billy. See what he suggests.'

Neither he nor Liz heard the burst of energy emanating from one of the petri dishes, a sound so high-pitched, so short-lived, that it was barely audible to human ears.

Approaching his 60th birthday, Mr Billy Croston was the epitome of a practical, hands-on experimentalist. What he didn't know about astronomical experimentation wasn't worth knowing. Although only qualified to GCE 'A' level standard, he was an absolute genius when it came to devising and setting up experiments. He was the most talented, experienced, experimental physicist any of them had ever known.

After Rupert explained what they were looking for, Billy knew immediately what to do. 'It's simple,' he said. 'All we have to do is to set up a sensitive detection field around the artefacts and link it to the computer for detecting signals for intelligent alien life from outer space, the SETI (*S*earch for *E*xtra *T*errestrial *I*ntelligence) computer. It's programmed to detect any kind of "intelligent" signal.'

'Brilliant!' exclaimed Rupert. 'How long will it take?'

'Oh,' said Billy looking at the clock on the wall, 'I'll have it done by nightfall.'

Liz exchanged glances with Rupert. 'No sleep tonight then,' she said.

'No,' said Rupert. 'Let's go and stock up on sandwiches and coffee.'

The first night passed without any sign of a signal, as did the following day. 'Do you think we might be wrong?' asked Liz, looking a little forlorn.

'Could be,' replied Rupert, 'but I doubt it. We need to give it more time. Maybe they only transmit at certain predetermined intervals.'

'Or the "batteries" have gone dead,' said Liz.

When no signal was forthcoming over the following day and night, both Liz and Rupert began to have doubts. Serious doubts. Had their imagination run wild? Were they seeing what they wanted to see? Believing what they wanted to believe, rather than being objective and dispassionate scientists? Were they letting personal beliefs cloud their judgement? Either way, both of them were deflated.

'Do you want to stay up again?' Rupert asked a dejected looking Liz.

'Why not,' she replied. 'I've got nothing better to do,' she lied, thinking of sipping a mug of steaming hot coffee and nibbling a chocolate biscuit sat in her favourite, comfy armchair.

'Okay. I'll grab the sandwiches and coffee,' replied Rupert, walking towards the door. 'For the graveyard shift,' he added as he disappeared down the corridor.

Three days and three nights without any proper sleep – all she'd had was the occasional catnap – took their toll on Liz. Her eyelids felt heavy and she struggled to stay awake. Just as she was on the verge of dozing off, it happened. BEEP. BEEP. BEEP. A transmission. A transmission had triggered the detection field. Suddenly, Liz was wide awake. She jumped out of her chair, sprinted to the door and yelled, at the top of her voice, 'RUPERT. GET BACK HERE. **NOW!!!**'

'It's definitely a transmission,' said Rupert, checking the SETI computer. 'An extremely short, intense burst of high frequency radiation, but definitely a transmission.'

Liz couldn't contain her excitement. She jumped up and down like an excited little girl about to receive a coveted present. 'I knew it! I KNEW IT!' she shouted. 'I just knew there was intelligent life out there!' Then, overcome by excitement, Liz did something she never thought she'd do. She flung her arms around the man who, until a few days ago, she'd loathed, and hugged him. Hugged him tight.

Rupert's response surprised himself. Not only did he return Liz's hug, he went one step further. He kissed her on the cheek. Kissed the woman he'd ridiculed at every available opportunity. Ridiculed her for believing in intelligent, alien life and, in one of life's little ironies, it was he, the doubter, who'd proved her right.

When they'd calmed down, Liz and Rupert considered their options. Should they wait for a second transmission to be absolutely sure, or should they tell everyone now? 'We have no idea when the next transmission will be,' said Rupert. 'It could be tomorrow or it could be weeks, or even months, away. We have to tell them now. Anyway, they're becoming suspicious about us spending all this time in the lab, plus they know Billy has connected something to the SETI computer. We have to tell them now.'

'That's tremendous news,' beamed Viv. 'Absolutely tremendous.'

'Earth shattering more like it,' enthused Frank. 'It's the biggest single discovery ever made. Well done to both of you.'

'To the three of us,' chimed in Liz. 'We couldn't have done it without Billy.' Billy shuffled his feet and looked down at the floor. He hated being in the limelight.

'Yes, well done to all three of you,' said Viv, who'd gathered everyone together to hear the news.

The room crackled and fizzed with the buzz of excited conversation, as if it was charged with electricity. People jabbered frantically to their neighbours, to Viv, to Frank, to anyone who would listen. It was a cacophony of uncontrolled noise, of pent-up emotions spilling out after years of frustration. Finally, after decades of wondering, they'd discovered the first real evidence of intelligent, alien life. Intelligent, alien life trying to contact us.

Viv waited for the excitement to subside before addressing the assembled throng. 'Let me reiterate again what a truly momentous discovery this is,' he said. 'The most important discovery ever made. But with such a discovery comes a heavy responsibility. I want each and every one of you to think very deeply about what our next step should be. Think about it and discuss it with your colleagues, but only your colleagues. No one else must know, at least not yet. We'll reconvene at,' he glanced at his watch, '1.00 p.m. sharp. That gives you three hours. Thank you.'

The ensuing discussion was short and sharp. Everyone had spent the previous three hours in frenzied conversations with their colleagues, arguing and debating the various options, and came to the meeting armed with definite views. Each individual was bursting to speak, to contribute, to be part of the greatest discovery ever made. To be part of history.

'Right,' said Viv, settling into his chair at the head of the table. 'Who wants to begin?'

Twenty voices spoke at once. Every single person present wanted to air their views. To be the first to speak. To make their mark. It was chaotic. 'QUIET!' bellowed Viv, raising his hands into the air to quell the racket. 'Quiet,' he reiterated in a softer tone. 'One at a time please.' He waited until the noise died down completely before continuing. 'Seeing it was Rupert and Liz who made the discovery, I think it's only fair they should be the first to speak. Rupert, would you start us off please.'

'It's simple really,' said Rupert, delighted at being the first one to speak. 'Basically, it boils down to two questions. One. Are we sure, absolutely sure, that we really have discovered evidence for the existence of intelligent, alien life? And two, if we have, when do we make it public and who do we tell first?'

As soon as Rupert finished speaking, Viv asked Liz for her views. 'Well, we shouldn't be too hasty,' said Liz. 'We don't want to make fools of ourselves. Remember the excitement when the first pulsar was discovered in 1967: a source from deep space emitting very strong, highly directional, periodic signals? Some scientists were convinced they were signals from an alien civilisation – Jocelyn Bell, a PhD student and her supervisor, Professor Anthony Hewish, even named their discovery LGM-1, for "Little Green Men" – but it turned out the signals were a completely natural phenomenon; regular, intense bursts of directional energy from a rapidly rotating neutron star. We don't want to make the same mistake. Then again,' she added quickly, 'we don't want to wait too long and have the Americans or Russians beat us to it.'

Almost before the last word left her mouth, a dozen other voices filled the room. It was verbal warfare. Each person was so desperate to be the next one to speak.

'This is hopeless,' thought Viv, trying to restore order. He waited as, one by one, the voices fell silent. 'To keep it orderly,' he said, 'I'll ask each one of you in turn to present your views. That way, you'll all get your chance to speak. Okay?'

Although there were some differences, the views put forward from around the table were essentially the same as those of Rupert and Liz. After the last speaker had finished, Viv turned to Frank and nodded.

'Viv and I have discussed it too,' said Frank, 'and it's a bit more complicated than you've made out. For instance, even if we're certain these artefacts represent incontrovertible evidence of an advanced alien civilisation, the decision on whether to make that public knowledge is out of our hands. Such a major decision cannot be made without the approval of the government. Furthermore, we'll have to inform all the other teams: the Americans, the Russians, the Chinese, in fact, the whole scientific community, before going public. But,' he continued, looking at Viv, 'I'm afraid the decision has been made for us. About one hour ago, we received a call from the Americans. They too have discovered the artefacts.'

# 10

# DECISIONS

A stunned silence filled the room as what Frank had said registered in their brains. A silence borne of shock and... and a mixture of frustration, anger and stupidity. Frustration that the Americans had stolen the limelight. Anger that they'd let them. And stupidity at their dilly-dallying and indecisiveness. 'And,' thought Liz, 'if the Americans have discovered the alien artefacts, it won't be long before the Russians, Chinese and the international team discover them too.'

'I'm surprised,' said Viv, breaking the silence. 'Really surprised. I thought it would have taken them longer. After all, they only had one pear-shaped meteorite to work with compared to our two.'

'That's true,' said Frank, 'but they have better equipment.'

Either way, the delay in reporting their findings had cost them dear.

'Have they gone public?' asked Liz.

'No,' said Frank. 'No, they haven't. To their credit, they informed us first.'

'What exactly did they say?' asked Rupert.

'Carl asked how we were getting on with the analysis,' replied Frank.

'And what did you tell him?' said Rupert.

'That we had discovered something interesting. Very interesting,' said Frank.

'And...'

He said, 'Have you? Like what?'

'Bloody hell!' exclaimed Rupert. 'It sounds like a game of cat and mouse.'

'That's exactly what it was,' said Frank. 'A game of cat and mouse. That's Carl's style. He was probing to see how much we knew.'

'And did you tell him?' blurted out Liz.

'Yes, I did. I had no option. I told him that we had discovered what appeared to be alien artefacts, probably from an advanced civilisation.'

'Thank God for that,' said a relieved Rupert. 'At least they know we found them too.'

'Yes, they do,' replied Frank. 'But, like us, they're unsure of the next step.'

'However,' interjected Viv, 'we did agree that the other teams should be informed. Carl's agreed to do that later today. I'm sure they'd have found them anyway.'

'Did he go into any detail about their findings?' asked Zak.

'A little,' replied Frank. 'I think he found it hard to contain his excitement. He wanted to share what they'd discovered but only told us the bare facts.'

'Have they found out more than we have?' queried Rupert tentatively, afraid he might be upstaged.

'It's hard to say. He only told us they'd discovered some unusual artefacts within the meteorite, probably of alien origin.'

'Have they detected any transmissions?' asked Liz.

'Yes, at about the same time that you did. They're trying to decipher them.'

As the discussion continued, both Liz and Rupert wished it had been them who'd informed the Americans rather than the other way round. They were disappointed, but it could have been much worse. The Americans hadn't gone public so at least they'd get a share of the glory.

'Carl has requested an immediate meeting between his team and ours before we inform our respective governments,' said Frank. 'They'll be at Jodrell Bank tomorrow.'

At first, the meeting was a cagey affair, like two boxers sparring, testing each other out. Probing to see what each other knew. Both sides were cautious about divulging what they'd found – they didn't want to divulge too much too soon. However, as the meeting progressed and it became evident that the Americans – Carl had brought two members of his team, Dr Simon Greer, a young, ambitious astrophysicist and Dr Lucy Fawcett, an even younger astrochemist – had found roughly the same things as them, both sides relaxed and opened up. The exchange of information and ensuing discussion was both lively and interesting, with each side trying to gain the upper hand, but nothing new emerged. One thing, however, became crystal clear: they had to inform the governments of Britain and America of their discovery. And they had to do it right away.

'I'll phone the Prime Minister,' said Viv.

'And I'll call the President,' said Carl, checking his watch. 'He should be up by now. I'm sure once we've told them they'll want a meeting as soon as possible.'

'Welcome to the White House,' said the President of the United States of America to the small gathering of scientists and top governments officials from Britain and America. 'As you all know, we're here to discuss the way forward regarding your, er, momentous discovery. The most significant discovery in the history of the human race. The Prime Minister and I have agreed to chair the meeting jointly. Isn't that right,' he said, glancing at the British Prime Minister.

'It is,' replied the Prime Minister. The President nodded for her to continue. 'Whatever is decided today, we have to act fast. News like this will leak out. Spread like wildfire. It's impossible to keep secret. As sure as night follows day, someone, somewhere will leak it. It's inevitable.'

'There are two things we need to address,' said the President. 'One. The scientific aspects. We need to learn as much as possible about the artefacts. Their structure, their source and the reason they were sent. Two. When and how do we make the discovery public? We don't want to be accused of withholding information yet we don't want to cause a mass panic either. It's a delicate balancing act.'

'You're right. We have to play this very carefully,' said the Prime Minister. 'The last thing we want is an outbreak of world-wide hysteria.'

'Absolutely,' said the President. 'We don't want a repeat of 1938.'

'1938,' said Liz. 'Why? What happened in 1938? Was it something to do with the start of World War II?'

'No. Nothing at all to do with World War II, unless…' said the President stroking his chin. 'Unless…Yes, in a way I suppose it was. It demonstrated the enormous power of radio to influence a mass audience, a fact that was well understood by the National Socialists in Germany. The Nazis, led by their astute propaganda chief Josef Goebbels, made radio their medium in a way that no one else, either before or since, has been able to replicate. But no, I wasn't referring to that but to the infamous radio broadcast by Orson Welles. It happened on the day before Halloween, October 30 1938, when millions of Americans tuned in to a popular radio programme that featured plays by, and often starring, Orson Welles. That evening, the performance was an adaptation of HG Well's science fiction novel, *The War of the Worlds*, about a Martian invasion of Earth. However, in adapting the book for radio, Welles made it sound like a news broadcast about an actual invasion from Mars, presumably to heighten the drama.

'As the play unfolded, dance music was interrupted a number of times by fake news bulletins reporting that a "huge flaming object" had dropped on a farm near Grovers Mill, New Jersey. As listeners sat on the edge of their seats, actors playing news announcers described the landing of an invasion force from Mars and the subsequent destruction of the United States. The broadcast did contain an explanation that it was a radio play, but if the listeners missed the brief explanation at the beginning, the next one didn't arrive until 40 minutes into the play. The broadcast was so realistic that a large proportion of the listeners thought they were hearing an actual news account of an invasion from Mars. And panicked. People packed the roads trying to flee the city, barricaded themselves into their homes, hid in cellars, loaded their guns, even wrapped wet towels around their heads as protection against Martian poison gas, in an attempt to defend themselves against the aliens. We don't want to precipitate anything like that,' concluded the President.

'That's really very interesting,' said Liz, enthralled by the story but amazed how gullible some people were.

As the meeting progressed, the scientists pushed for more time, a week, two weeks, to obtain more information. More information on the propulsion devices. More information on the sensing and transmitting devices. More information on trying to find the origin of the meteorites. And more information on the encrypted signals. More time to try and crack the code. The code that was proving so difficult to break.

Throughout the meeting, one question was at the back of everyone's minds. Nagging away. One question that kept coming back to haunt them. Why, if the aliens were trying to make contact, was the signal so difficult to decipher? Surely, they'd have made it as easy as possible to understand. Their language would be incomprehensible but the language of science wouldn't. It's universal: the same throughout the Universe. The only universal language. Surely, they'd have used that. The structure of the hydrogen atom, the simplest and most abundant element in the Universe and the fuel for all the stars. The structure of water, one of the simplest molecules and one essential for life. Mathematical equations. Drawings of galaxies. Drawings of themselves. But they couldn't find any of those, only extremely complicated algorithms. Why? Rather than being easy to decode, the signals were exactly the opposite, as if they weren't meant to be decoded. To be understood. It was both puzzling and worrying, as if they concealed some sinister, Machiavellian message.

In the end, a compromise was reached. The scientists would be allowed one week to conduct further tests. One week and one week only. Then, the discovery would be made public.

# 11

# LEAKS

Now their secret was out, at least to the governments of Britain and America, Viv and Carl took the decision to have the meteorites examined at specialist laboratories using their countries top experts. This was in no way a reflection on the efforts of either team – both had done really well – but rather to get results quickly. Time was of the essence. One week wasn't long at all to perform a thorough examination of a complex meteorite.

'Our first impressions,' said Professor Myles Lockhart to the small gathering of scientists sat in the meeting room of the Impacts and Astromaterials Research Centre (IARC) of Imperial College, London, 'is that your intact meteorite resembles a stony-iron mesosiderite and the pulverised one a stony chondrite, although both are harder and more dense than normal.'

'Come again,' said Viv, looking utterly confused. 'You've lost me. Completely.'

'And me,' said Liz.

'Me too,' said Rupert.

Frank's response was different but far more perceptive. He also hadn't the foggiest idea what a stony-iron mesosiderite was, or a stony chondrite, but he grasped the significance of what Myles had said. 'You mean the two pear-shaped meteorites from the Arctic belong to different classes?'

'The preliminary findings seem to suggest that, yes,' replied Myles. He paused, looked at the four scientists from Jodrell Bank, and smiled. 'I thought you might not be *au fait* with the intricacies of meteorite classification,' he said, 'so, before I go on, I think it's best if I give you a brief explanation of the types of meteorites and their structures.'

Viv had chosen the Department of Materials at the IARC to conduct the analyses but had insisted that a handful of other leading experts from around the UK (United Kingdom) be invited, experts in molecular engineering, propulsion, nuclear energy, chemistry and telecommunications, as well as himself, Frank, Rupert and Liz. He realised the risks. More people meant more chance of a leak, especially with news as hot as this, so he made it abundantly clear to everyone present that what he was about to tell them was of the utmost secrecy. Of the highest national security. Not a single word must leave the building. Satisfied that he'd rammed home the secrecy aspect, he then explained what they'd found and what they thought it might be. Now, he concluded, they needed some expert opinions as to whether they were right.

His counterpart in the US, Carl Ryan, had done the same thing, choosing the NASA/Johnson Space Center at Houston as the base for their analyses.

Professor Myles Lockhart surveyed his audience, the four scientists from Jodrell Bank and the five experts from around the UK, before continuing. 'I'll assume you know nothing, or very little, about meteorites,' he said, deliberately looking at Viv, Frank, Rupert and Liz, 'and start at the beginning.'

'A good assumption,' thought Liz, 'at least in my case.'

'You can tell the difference between a meteor and a meteorite as they travel through the Earth's atmosphere. Meteorites are generally much brighter than meteors, and look bigger. For these reasons, they are often referred to as fireballs.'

Liz's face lit up. 'That explains why the meteorite that hit my house looked so big, because it was a fireball,' she said excitedly.

Myles looked at her and nodded. 'That's right,' he said, then added, 'it must have been a frightening experience.'

'It was,' said Liz. 'Frightening yet… exhilarating too.'

'It's from these fireballs that most meteorites of measurable size originate,' continued Myles.

'Excuse my ignorance,' said Rupert, 'but what kind of sizes are we talking about.'

'The size of meteorites varies from microscopic to very large,' replied Myles. 'Most recovered meteorites measure between two inches and two feet in diameter, but the largest one is still in the ground in South Africa because it was too large to move.'

'When does a… No, it doesn't matter,' said Frank. 'Please continue.' He was going to ask at what size a meteorite became an asteroid, but decided there wouldn't be a definitive answer.

'Recovered meteorites fall into two classes, fall and find. A fall is when a meteorite is actually observed as it falls to Earth, for example when it lands on the roof of a house or in the backyard. A find is when someone stumbles across a strange looking rock but didn't see it fall to Earth.'

'So the one that hit my house was a fall,' interjected Liz, 'and the ones we found in the Arctic were finds.'

'That's correct,' said Myles. Continuing, he said, 'Meteorites consist of varying amounts of nickel-iron alloys, silicates, sulphides and several other minor phases. They are classified into three main groups based on their mineral compositions.

'Iron meteorites can contain as much as 90 per cent iron, together with some nickel, combined with non-metallic phases and sulphide ores. They are characterised by the presence of two nickel-iron alloys: kanacite and taenite. They are very dense and non-porous, being 3.5 times heavier than most comparably sized Earth rocks.

'Iron meteorites have a dark brown surface, the fusion crust, but silvery-coloured interiors. Their surface is fluted or scalloped, like thumbprints pressed into wet clay, an effect produced by ablation – severe frictional heating of the surface, but not the interior – of the meteorite as it plunged through the Earth's atmosphere.'

'But the one in my garden had a black, cinder-like surface,' said Liz, looking puzzled.

'That's because it had only just fallen from the sky,' replied Myles. 'Recently fallen meteorites usually have a black "ash-like" crust on their surface, evidence of their flaming passage through the Earth's atmosphere. After several years of exposure on the Earth's surface, it weathers to a rusty brown and then disappears altogether.'

'I see,' said Liz. 'Thanks.'

'These meteorites are well-known because the iron metal often crystallises in criss-crossing plates, known as a Widmanstatten pattern after the name of an Austrian count who was one of the first to describe them. However, this pattern is not really evident unless the meteorites have been chemically etched in the laboratory.

'Often, people mistake terrestrial magnetite for iron meteorites because it is heavy compared to most other terrestrial rocks and has a black to purplish-brown surface similar to the fusion crust of an iron meteorite. However, samples of terrestrial magnetite also have black to purplish interiors, in contrast to the silver-coloured interiors of iron meteorites,' concluded Myles.

'But none of our two pear-shaped meteorites are iron meteorites, are they?' said Frank.

'No, they're not,' replied Myles. 'But I included them for the sake of completeness. And because it was an iron meteorite that hit Liz's house.

'The second class of meteorites,' continued Myles, 'are the stony-irons. These consist of approximately equal amounts of nickel-iron alloy and silicate minerals. It's best to visualise them as small pieces of stone fixed in a body of iron.

'Stony-irons are divided into two sub-groups, the pallasites and mesosiderites. The pallasite group is characterised by olivine – magnesium orthosilicate – crystals surrounded by a nickel-iron structure which forms a continuous enclosing network around the silicate portion.

'The mesosiderites consist mainly of pagioclase and pyroxene silicates in the form of heterogeneous aggregates intermixed with the metal alloy. Unlike the pallasites, no distinct separation is apparent between the metal and silicate phases. As I mentioned at the beginning, we think your intact meteorite is a stony-iron mesosiderite.'

'I don't know about you,' chimed in Viv, finding it all a bit heavy going, 'but I'm starving. I think now's a good time to break for lunch. It gives us time to, er, pardon the pun, digest what you've said.'

'Aren't you surprised the two meteorites containing the alien artefacts belong to different classes?' Viv said to Frank, forking another chunk of sausage and mash into his mouth.

'I am,' replied Frank, swallowing a mouthful of tea, 'but I'm even more surprised by the change in the relationship between Liz and Rupert. They've gone from arch enemies to bosom buddies in the space of a week! I just don't understand it.'

'I was going to mention that,' said Viv. 'Everyone's talking about it. And have you noticed he calls her Liz too, not Beth,' he said, glancing across the canteen towards the two young people sat in the corner. Two young people in earnest conversation. Two young people who, until a week ago, fought like cat and dog. Two young people who apparently hated each other. The transformation in their relationship was simply amazing.

'Do you… do you think they're in love?' asked Viv. 'You know, like opposites attract. A rich, well-educated "posh" boy and a working-class girl made good sort of thing. It happens, you know.'

Frank almost choked on his mouthful of gammon and egg. 'I wouldn't go that far,' he said, 'but something's triggered a dramatic change in their relationship. I think it's the excitement of discovering the alien artefacts that's brought them together. Anyway, Liz already has a boyfriend, hasn't she?'

'Yes she has,' said Viv, his voice betraying his disappointment, 'but they don't seem to see each other very much. It would be nice if they were in love,' he said wistfully.

'Come on, you old romantic,' said Frank, gulping down the last dregs of his tea. 'Let's get back to the meeting room.'

At 55 years of age, Frank had seen it all. Been there. Done that. Got the T-shirt. He'd known Viv for over 20 years, first as a colleague and later as a friend, a very good friend. Friends who felt comfortable in each other's company. Friends who respected and trusted each other. Friends who could be frank and honest with each other. Frank's level, calm, approachable, easy-going, some would say laid back, manner made him the magnet of the group. The uncle who listened to everyone's problems. The practical, down-to-earth uncle who kept everyone's feet on the ground. The glue who held them all together.

Myles waited for the audience to settle down before continuing. 'The third and final class of meteorites are the stony meteorites. They're not as obvious as the iron meteorites because they resemble Earth rocks, especially basalt, in their appearance and composition, although their density is slightly higher, 1.5 times higher to be precise. They are the most abundant of the three groups.'

'How do you know if a rock is basalt or a stony meteorite?' asked Rupert.

'By the nickel content,' replied Myles. 'Earth rocks such as basalt have either very small or very large amounts of nickel, but in stony meteorites, the nickel content falls within a very specific range.'

'Thanks,' said Rupert.

'Stony meteorites are composed mainly of silicates with small amounts of a nickel-iron alloy,' continued Myles, 'which appear as small fragments within the surrounding rocky material and which are readily seen when a chip is broken off. They have the greatest variety in composition, colour and structure. One particular structural feature, called chondrules, divides the group into two sub-groups, the chondrites – those with chondrules – and the achondrites – those without chondrules.'

'Excuse me again,' said Rupert, 'but what exactly is a chondrule?'

'A chondrule,' answered Myles, 'is a small, spherical drop of solidified silicate ranging in size from fractions of a millimetre to several millimetres. Many scientists believe they represent the most primitive material in the solar system.'

'And you think the pulverised meteorite is a stony chondrite, right?' gushed Liz.

'As I said at the start, that's what our preliminary findings suggest, although it's much harder and more dense than all the other stony chondrites we've examined.'

'What puzzles me,' said Viv, scratching his head, 'is why the two meteorites belong to different classes? Why go to the trouble of sending two different types? Surely it would have been easier to send two of the same type.'

'It could be to confuse us. To make us more likely to think they're natural meteorites,' said Rupert.

'Either that or there's a technical reason,' said Frank. 'Perhaps one type is better for propulsion and the other for transmitting.'

'We'll bear that in mind,' said Myles, 'as we carry out the analyses.'

'I'm still fascinated by their shape,' said Liz. 'Why pear-shaped? None of the natural meteorites we found were pear-shaped.'

'Meteorites come in a great variety of shapes,' said Myles. 'They're seldom round, but angular fragments that are very irregular in appearance. During their flight through the atmosphere, some are tapered to a conical shape but I don't know of any that are pear-shaped. Most are split into fragments. In carbonaceous meteorites, the intense heat and pressure can transform the meteoritic graphite into minute diamonds!'

'Wow! I wouldn't mind finding a few of those in my garden,' exclaimed Liz.

'I think we'd all like to find one of those,' said Myles with a smile. 'Unfortunately, they're pretty rare.'

'But why pear-shaped?' repeated Liz.

'Perhaps that's the best shape to house the propulsion system and the transmission device,' said Viv, speaking aloud the first thoughts that came into his head.

'Or it's the best compromise for travelling through interstellar space and the Earth's atmosphere,' added Frank.

The meeting continued a while longer but no new information emerged. 'I think we should call it a day,' said Myles, scanning the tired faces of the people in the room, 'and sleep on what we've discussed. Perhaps after a night's rest we may have some new insights.'

The following morning Rupert dashed, indeed almost ran, into the canteen. 'Have you seen this!' he shouted, brandishing a newspaper in front of them. 'Have you bloody well seen this!!!'

Liz, Viv and Frank looked up at the young man interrupting their breakfast, and at the newspaper he was thrusting towards them. Their mouths fell open in disbelief. ALIEN PROBES DISCOVERED IN ARCTIC: PRELUDE TO ALIEN INVASION? screamed the headline. A headline that was no doubt splashed across every newspaper in the country.

'I knew it,' said Viv resignedly. 'I just knew someone would spill the beans. How can the biggest story ever be kept secret? The papers will have paid someone a small fortune to get a scoop like this. It just had to happen. It was just a matter of when.'

'Maybe,' said Frank, jabbing the headline with his finger, 'but this is just irresponsible scare-mongering by a tabloid newspaper, not responsible reporting.'

'And when have tabloids ever reported anything responsibly?' said Viv. 'They're all for sensationalism to boost their circulation.'

'Even if it causes a mass panic?'

'Even if it causes a mass panic,' replied Viv. 'All they care about is selling as many newspapers as possible.'

The sound of approaching footsteps made them pause and turn around. It was Myles. A broadsheet was cradled in his arm. 'I see you already know,' he said, noticing the paper in Rupert's hands. 'At least the broadsheets have been more accurate,' he continued, displaying the headline, SCIENTISTS DISCOVER STRANGE METEORITES IN ARCTIC: POSSIBLY FROM AN ADVANCED ALIEN CIVILISATION.

'Who do you think has leaked the information?' asked Liz.

'I've no idea,' replied Viv, 'and we'll never know. It could be anybody. A scientist, a government official, one of Carl's team, even one of us. Whoever it was will be extremely rich.'

'Surely there's a way to find out,' said Rupert, infuriated by the leak.

'Possibly,' said Viv, 'but now the news is out, we've more important things to consider, like finding out more about the meteorites and calming the situation. The Prime Minister will be furious.'

Viv's mobile phone rang. He glanced at the display. 'It's the Prime Minister.'

# 12

# GOING PUBLIC

The Prime Minister was indeed furious. 'Have you seen the papers?' she yelled. 'Have you seen the fucking papers?' What the fucking hell's going on?' she ranted.

'I'm as surprised as you are, Prime Minister,' replied Viv calmly. 'I've only just seen them myself.'

'It's bloody mayhem here. Pandemonium. My phone's red hot. It's never stopped bloody ringing. I've had the President of the United States, the German Chancellor, the French Prime Minister, everyone on at me. Every fucking leader in the world wants to know what the hell's going on!'

Viv said nothing, just listened to the tirade from Britain's most senior politician.

'Who the hell's leaked the information?' continued the Prime Minister in a calmer but still irritated voice.

'Is it one of your people?' she asked in an accusatory tone.

Viv repeated what he'd just told his colleagues. 'I really have no idea, Prime Minister. It could be anyone. But I'm not surprised. News like this was bound to leak out sooner or later. It was just a matter of time.'

'It's a pity it's sooner rather than later,' barked the Prime

Minister, still angry at the leak. 'Not only is it headline news in every national newspaper, it's also the lead story on every TV station around the world. People are beginning to panic. We need to do something fast.'

'I understand your concerns, Prime Minister,' said Viv. 'I'll discuss the situation with my colleagues and get back to you.'

'You do that! You fucking well do that!' spat the Prime Minister. 'You have one hour. In precisely one hour's time I want you and Frank in my office at Number 10. Do you understand?'

'Perfectly,' replied Viv. 'We'll be there.'

'Oh, and bring that bloody meteorite with you,' she said, slamming down the phone.

Viv looked at his colleagues. 'The Prime Minister's given us an hour to decide what to do,' he said. 'We need to tell the others immediately and formulate our response.'

In Downing Street, the Prime Minister was chairing an emergency meeting of the COBRA team on the very same topic.

As they were meeting, TV stations around the world were broadcasting news of the discovery. It was the top news story at every station. Just like the newspapers, some stations were factual and responsible whilst others went for sensationalism, either because they didn't have the true facts or because they were simply following the tabloids in order to boost their viewing figures. Audiences were confused. They didn't know what to believe. Had an alien probe really been discovered or was it one big hoax? If the probe did exist, were the aliens trying to make contact in a friendly, peaceful way, or was it the harbinger for a hostile invasion? People just didn't know and wanted answers. Answers from the government.

'Ah, come and join us,' the Prime Minister said to Viv and Frank, ushering them into the Cabinet Office Briefing Area (from where the acronym COBRA gets its name) to meet the rest of the COBRA team; the heads of MI5 and MI6, the Chief of the

Defence Staff, the professional head of the British armed forces, the Metropolitan Commissioner of Police, the Chief Scientific Advisor to the government and the Home Secretary. After the introductions were over, she addressed the meeting. 'Like you, we have been discussing our next move. People are confused by the conflicting news reports and are becoming scared. It won't be long before they start to panic. They need a clear, unequivocal statement of the facts, and reassurance. And they need them quickly. Are these your conclusions too?'

'Broadly, yes,' said Viv.

The Prime Minister continued. 'We need to go public, call a press conference to refute the wild speculations about an alien invasion, and present the true situation to allay public fear. Do you agree?'

Viv looked at Frank before responding. 'Yes, but we think the information should be presented in a cautious manner, saying that unusual meteorites have been discovered around the world which COULD be from an advanced alien civilisation, and that scientists are working round the clock to obtain a definitive answer. It's pretty close to the truth and should help calm the public anxiety. Finally, we think you should conclude by saying there'll be regular updates on their progress.'

'And how long will that definitive answer take?' asked the Prime Minister.

'How long is a piece of string?' replied Viv but, sensing the Prime Minister's annoyance at his glib answer, added quickly, 'one, possibly two, weeks.'

'I understood you were pretty certain that the meteorites were of alien origin,' said the Chief Scientific Advisor, 'but needed more time to analyse them in detail.'

Viv looked at Frank. 'That's correct,' said Frank, 'but I think we should break the news gently, as suggested. We don't want to cause a mass panic.'

'I agree,' said the Prime Minister. 'I'll call a press conference for 12 noon to disseminate what we've discussed, but I'll need one of you two present to answer any scientific questions,' she said, looking at Viv and Frank. 'Oh, and bring the meteorite along. I'm sure everyone's dying to see it.'

Back in the lab the experts were well into their analyses. The larger geodesic domes were arranged in an expanding helical pattern at the wide end of the pear-shaped meteorite. 'It's like a coiled spring,' remarked Dr Michio Ohta, a nuclear fusion expert who used to work for Hitachi, a world leader in the design and construction of nuclear power plants. 'A coiled spring that tapers from approximately six inches in diameter down to a single point.'

'A conical shape like that is very good for producing maximum thrust in jet engines and space rockets,' said Professor Gerald Numan, an expert in propulsion technology from Oxford University.

'I'm not absolutely sure,' continued Michio, 'but I think the basic materials of the geodesic dome are a unique combination of transition metals. An interlocked arrangement of selected transition metals enclosing atomic hydrogen, similar to a nano-sized football filled with hydrogen atoms.'

'But wouldn't the hydrogen atoms react to form hydrogen molecules?' said Gerald. 'Atomic hydrogen is very reactive.'

'That's true,' replied Dr Gregg Rutter, a bright young chemist from Manchester University and Liz's boyfriend, 'but transition metals like platinum and palladium are catalysts which facilitate chemical reactions. For example, by converting molecular hydrogen into atomic hydrogen. And,' he continued, 'maybe the aliens have found a way for them to facilitate nuclear fusion reactions too.'

Michio's face lit up. Gregg's last comment had sparked a Eureka moment. 'Transition metals like iron are not only catalytic, they're paramagnetic too, so perhaps the aliens have found a way to generate an intense magnetic field to contain the nuclear fusion reaction, or a matter/antimatter reaction, within the geodesic domes. Such nuclear fusion or matter/antimatter reaction chambers would generate an enormous amount of power for propulsion. Whatever it is,' he continued, in a less excited voice than his Eureka moment, 'it's way beyond our capabilities. But the geodesic domes are definitely of alien origin from a technologically advanced civilisation.'

'That's it!' exclaimed Liz excitedly. 'That's how the meteorite penetrated through 75 feet of ice to reach the ice cave without making a massive impact crater.'

Everyone turned to look at her, at the excited young woman who too had just had a Eureka moment. And waited for her to continue.

'Nuclear fusion not only generates enormous amounts of power, it also generates enormous quantities of heat too, right?' said Liz, looking at Michio.

'It does,' replied Michio.

'Then the meteorite would have been extremely hot and melted its way through the ice,' she said triumphantly. 'It didn't need to have been travelling at great speed. It explains everything.'

'Not quite everything,' chimed in Rupert. 'It doesn't explain why the second meteorite only penetrated 12 inches into the ice.'

In her excitement, Liz had forgotten about that. It was Frank who came to her rescue. 'That could be the reason why the two meteorites are different,' he said. 'Perhaps one was designed to penetrate deeply into the ice and the other to remain at or near the surface. Perhaps one got far hotter than the other.'

'It sounds good to me,' said Viv, having just returned from doing the press conference with the Prime Minister. 'Well done, Liz. And you too, Frank,' he added hastily.

Analysis of the smaller geodesic domes confirmed Liz and Rupert's first impressions, that they were arranged in clusters near the centre of the meteorite, probably for protection from damaging cosmic rays as it travelled through interstellar space and particularly from the intense heat as the meteorite entered the Earth's atmosphere. And from the impact as it hit the ice.

'They seem to be some kind of silicon-based semiconductor,' said Janet Blake, a telecommunications expert from Cambridge University and advisor to British Telecom, 'but of a type unknown to us.'

'The molecular engineering is incredible,' said Professor Stephen Gould, a leading expert on the subject from Strathclyde University. 'It's far more advanced than anything we have.'

'And the power of the signal is phenomenal for such a small device,' said Janet. 'Do you think they're powered by the nuclear fusion system?' she asked, looking at Michio.

'It's possible,' he replied, 'but if they are, I don't know how.'

'The clusters look a bit like chondrules to me,' said Liz, pleased with herself for remembering part of Myles's explanation of meteorite types. Her comment elicited smiles from the other scientists.

'Very good, Liz,' said Myles. 'At least someone's remembered something I said.'

'Because of their composition, location and arrangement, there's absolutely no doubt they're some kind of transmitting device,' said Janet.

'Do you think the transmissions happen of their own accord,' asked Rupert, 'or are they triggered by the, er, aliens?'

'That's a good question,' said Frank. 'For the aliens to be activating the signals, they'd have to be fairly close. In an astronomical sense,' he added. 'And if they are relatively close and sending signals, we should have detected them. But we haven't. Therefore, I think the meteorites, or should I say probes, are programmed to send back signals at predetermined intervals. If they originate from outside the galaxy, the signals would take tens of millions, even billions, of light years to reach their destination. However, if they originate from within our own Milky Way galaxy, which I think they do, they could take anything from a few light years to a hundred thousand light years. My guess is they're hundreds, or thousands, of light years away.'

'Why so far?' queried Janet. 'I thought the nearest star was only a few light years away?'

'That's correct,' replied Frank. 'The nearest sun-like star, Alpha Centauri, is indeed only four light years away, but it has no planets and, as far as I'm aware, neither have any of the other nearby stars. So, presuming the aliens live on a planet, which I'm sure they do, they must be many hundreds, probably thousands, of light years away.'

'Not necessarily,' said Rupert. 'Not if they've developed some sort of interstellar space travel. If they're in some kind of starship, they could be anywhere.'

'Good God' thought Liz. 'He's beginning to sound like me!'

'That's true,' said Frank, responding to Rupert's statement, 'but as I said earlier, we haven't detected any incoming signals.'

'No, but they could still be receiving the signals from the meteorites,' said Rupert.

Before Frank could reply, Liz changed the topic.

'Can we glean any clues as to their origin,' she asked. 'From their compositions, I mean,' she continued, looking at Myles.

'Yes, we can,' replied Myles, 'up to a point. By studying the chemical composition of a meteorite, it's possible to determine from which part of the solar system it came, how long its been in space and its age since formation. However, with meteorites from beyond our solar system, it becomes much more difficult, because we have no reference points to compare them to.'

'So you're saying we can't tell where these meteorites came from?' said Rupert.

'Well, we won't be able to pinpoint a precise location, no,' continued Myles, 'but it might be possible to place them from a particular region of the galaxy. But we'll have to wait and see what the analyses throw up.

'What I can say with absolute certainty,' he continued, 'is that they aren't from our solar system.'

'Are we any further forward in decoding the signals,' asked Liz, hoping for a positive response.

Janet's answer was short and sweet. 'No, we're not.'

'Bloody great,' thought Liz. 'We don't know why they were sent, where they're from or who sent them. What the hell do we know.'

In the USA, Carl Ryan's team faced the same dilemma. If the meteorites originated from a remote corner of the Milky Way, it would take tens of thousands of light years for them to reach Earth. That meant any interactive communication was out of the question. It would take tens of thousands of years for them to receive a reply and a further tens of thousands of years for us to receive their response. If, however, they originated from a star system much closer to home, or a starship, why hadn't they detected any signals? It was a conundrum. The meteorites definitely came from somewhere. BUT WHERE?

# 13

# RELIGION REFUTED

The analyses and discussions continued apace. There was much debate about the origin of the meteorites – were they from a remote corner of the galaxy tens of thousands of light years away, or from somewhere closer? – and about the information contained in the signals. The possibility that the aliens might even have discovered a way to transcend the speed of light, for example, by discovering wormholes to dramatically shorten the time to send and receive signals across the galaxy, was discussed and dismissed. Such a feat would not only require vast amounts of energy and unimaginable technology, it would also cause such a massive distortion of spacetime that they couldn't have failed to detect it. The most likely scenario, they concluded, was more mundane. The meteorites probably originated from somewhere much closer, either from an obscure star cluster a few light years away, or from a starship. Despite intensive efforts from both the UK and the USA, no such star cluster or alien spaceship was found. Also, as to their origin, analysis of the meteorites suggested they came from the far reaches of the galaxy many tens of thousands of light years away. As to which region, well, they were still working on that. It was baffling.

The press conference by the Prime Minister and Viv calmed the general populace, but only temporarily. As promised, the Prime Minister provided regular updates on the work of the scientists, including the fact that the meteorites were indeed from a technically advanced, alien civilisation. This pronouncement caused, if not outright panic, then great anxiety amongst most of the population. However, for some, it generated great excitement. The promise of a better life. An end to starvation. Cures for every disease. Unlimited supplies of green energy. And an end to all wars. But not everyone was either anxious or excited. Some were devastated, their lifelong beliefs shattered. The discovery of intelligent, alien life elsewhere in the Universe threw the world's religions into total chaos.

The discovery threatened to destroy their fundamental beliefs; to undermine them; to cast doubt on the two sacred tenets, that man was created in the image of God and that the whole Universe was created for the sole benefit of mankind. Neither could be the case if other intelligent beings existed. And, if one form of intelligent, alien life had been discovered, it was almost certain that others existed. Countless others in the vastness of the Cosmos, the 100 billion galaxies each with 200 billion stars. Approximately 20 billion trillion ($2 \times 10^{22}$) stars in the observable Universe. Even a chance as low as one in a trillion (1 in $10^{12}$) would mean there are 20 billion possible sites for life to have evolved.

Christians, Muslims, Hindus and Jews were in despair. Ordinary people were questioning the fundamental foundations of Christianity, Islam, Hinduism and Judaism and found them wanting. If two of their staunchest pillars had been demolished, what did that say about the rest?

As the weeks passed and the religious turmoil intensified, Liz and Rupert discussed the topic too. Although neither was religious, the boundaries of science and religion intrigued them. 'I know you're not religious,' said Liz, 'but don't you feel sorry for the billions of people who believed and have had their beliefs shattered?'

Rupert paused before answering, composing his response. 'Yes and no. I feel genuinely sorry for those people with little or no education who found great comfort in religion,' he replied, 'but not for those educated people who refuse to even consider the alternatives. The scientific facts. The beauty of the Big Bang theory of the creation of the Universe and the stunning simplicity and sheer elegance of the theory of evolution by natural selection. They're far more wondrous and awe inspiring than some supernatural being who's been around forever and who created everything in seven days.'

'Six,' interrupted Liz. 'God rested on the seventh day.'

Rupert ignored her interruption and carried on. 'The formation of the first atoms from the plasma of the Big Bang 13.7 billion years ago; the formation of the first stars as gravity crushed the hydrogen atoms together; the resulting nuclear fusion to produce light and heat, and the forging of the lighter elements, such as carbon, nitrogen and oxygen, in these nuclear furnaces; and spectacular supernovae to create the heavier elements such as silver and gold. And finally, for gravity to form all this stardust into planets, planets on which life evolved. Everything, Liz, absolutely everything, is made from stardust. Including you and me.'

'That's all perfectly true,' said Liz, about to play devil's advocate, 'but I don't see how what you've said undermines religious beliefs. After all, the Christian Church accepts the Big Bang theory of creation and even the Hindus don't dismiss it, do they?'

'You're right on both counts,' replied Rupert, 'and no, what I've just said doesn't undermine religion. But what I'm about to say does.'

'Go on,' said Liz.

'Well, both you and I believe that life, like the Universe, evolved naturally.'

'We do,' said Liz.

'That it arose spontaneously when molecules "learned" to replicate themselves. To make copies of themselves. These replicators, the RNA and DNA molecules, progressed to single-celled organisms and then, over approximately two billion years, to multi-celled organisms.'

'I know all of this,' said Liz. 'What's your point?'

'My point is that these multi-celled organisms eventually evolved into complex life forms, such as the dinosaurs, which ruled the Earth for hundreds of millions of years. Until their extinction 65 million years ago, they were the pinnacle of creation. So, if dinosaurs had religion, God would have made them in his image and God would have been a dinosaur.

'Following the extinction of the dinosaurs and other large land-based animals, a little mouse-like mammal flourished, a mouse-like mammal that led, eventually, to the hominids, the forerunners of homo sapiens. Of us. So, at that point in time, about two million years ago, the hominids were the pinnacle of creation, so God would have been a hominid.'

'I see where you're going with this,' said Liz, 'that at any point in time the dominant species regards itself as the pinnacle of creation.'

'That's right,' said Rupert. 'Currently, that pinnacle of creation happens to be us. But in one, ten or a hundred million years, our descendants will be totally different to us. And, if religion still exists, which I very much doubt, they too will believe they are created in the image of God. So you see, Liz, it's a transient thing. The image of God changes with time. The assertion that man was created in the image of God is a falsehood. The problem,' he concluded, 'is that evolutionary change is so slow and so subtle that no one notices.'

'Fascinating,' said Liz, clearly impressed with Rupert's explanation, 'but surely religion only applies to intelligent life, not to dinosaurs, mouse-like mammals and hominids?'

'I was making a point,' replied Rupert, 'and anyway, how do you define intelligence? Chimpanzees, whales and dolphins are intelligent. They all can't be made in the image of God.'

'I was thinking more of a highly advanced technological civilisation capable of communicating and travelling across interstellar space and interested in finding other intelligence's,' said Liz.

'You mean intelligent life like us,' said Rupert.

'I suppose I do,' replied Liz. 'Like us but much more technologically advanced.'

'Mm,' mused Rupert. 'Do I detect a lack of imagination here?'

Liz changed the subject. 'Don't you believe in anything… supernatural?' she asked.

'What do you mean, Liz?' queried Rupert. 'Ghosts?'

'No, not ghosts. Things like a… like a "Superintelligence" watching over the Universe. Guiding its progress.'

'Like a God?'

'No, not a God, like a… It's difficult to explain.'

'Well,' said Rupert, 'over the 13.7 billion year history of the Universe, I believe that life has arisen countless times. Most of it will have been primitive life but some will have evolved into intelligent life, of which some will have developed into extremely advanced life forms, advanced enough to discard their physical bodies and exist as pure energy. Pure thought. Whole civilisations existing as an amorphous mass of pure thought. Billions of minds coalesced into one. After all, Einstein showed that matter and energy are just two forms of the same thing with his famous equation, $E = mc^2$, where E is energy and m is matter.'

'Mm, a bit like a super soul,' said Liz thoughtfully, copying Rupert.

'You could look at it that way,' replied Rupert, 'but one that's evolved naturally. A Superintelligence.'

'And you think these could be, er, floating around the Universe, making sure it behaves itself?'

'Possibly,' said Rupert. 'It's more plausible than a God.'

A cough interrupted their conversation. A polite cough. It was Frank. He was standing at the door. 'I couldn't help overhearing the last part of your, er, metaphysical discussion,' he said. 'It's an interesting idea. The reason I'm here,' he continued, 'is because Viv wants us in the meeting room. I think he has some news.'

'Thanks for coming at such short notice,' said Viv to the scientists gathered in the meeting room. 'I've brought you here to report some good news.' An outbreak of expectant conversation filled the room. 'Some progress has been made on decoding the signals. By linking up to the world's most powerful computers, our scientists have managed to decode some of the algorithms, but not all of them. They appear to contain information on the local environment around where the meteorites landed. Information on the composition of the atmosphere, the land, the ice, the temperature and the microbial life. However,' concluded Viv, 'there's no sign whatsoever of any "contact message".'

# 14

# A LULL

The following weeks saw frenetic activity in observatories around the world. Every astronomer, every astronomical team, wanted to be the one to discover the source of the alien probes. To be immortalised. For eternity.

In the USA, NASA pulled out all the stops, deploying all its sophisticated resources, led by Carl Ryan's NEO team and the SETI team. Charged with the early detection of space objects that posed a potential threat to Earth, in 2008 the NEO team detected 11,327 objects of all sizes. But their main aim was to detect at least 90 per cent of all potentially dangerous objects that were one kilometre wide or more. Thankfully, they hadn't detected any of those.

The European Space Agency (ESA), particularly Viv's UK team, which relied on the radio telescopes at Jodrell Bank plus the Faulkes optical telescope, and Professor Alan Harris's NEO Shield team, part of Germany's Institute for Planetary Research, a multinational group of scientists based in Berlin, were modest by comparison, but still successful. All the teams tracked potentially hazardous objects by taking photographs of their positions on successive nights and then 'joined the dots' to see if they were on a collision course with Earth.

Employing this technique, the teams had discovered an asteroid about the size of three football pitches that will make the closest flyby of Earth in recorded history for an object that size. At about 10.00 p.m. London time on Friday, 13 April 2029, a most apt date, asteroid 2004 MN4, or Apophis as its been named, after the Egyptian god of destruction, will pass between the Earth and the moon, coming closer to the Earth than many of the telecommunications satellites in geostationary orbits. It is calculated to miss the Earth by a whisker, a mere 22,600 miles, less than a tenth of the distance to the moon. In fact, it will come so close it will be visible to the naked eye, appearing in the sky as a dim, fast-moving star, the first asteroid in modern times to be clearly visible from Earth without the aid of a telescope or binoculars. Residing in the asteroid belt between Mars and Jupiter, Apophis is unusual because so much is known about its orbit before it makes its closest approach to Earth – most asteroids are only detected on close approach. If Apophis did collide with Earth, an asteroid that size wouldn't create wide-scale damage, just major damage at the impact site, damage equivalent to about 20 hydrogen bombs.

The weeks of searching the heavens turned into months but, despite everyone's best efforts, no viable star cluster or starship was found. No one had earned the right to immortality.

The meteor showers stopped as abruptly as they'd started and, as first the weeks and then the months went by with no further activity, both the public interest and the media interest began to wane. The initial mass anxiety and excitement subsided. People put it to the back of their minds. Gradually, as nothing new happened, it disappeared as a topic in both the press and TV. Eventually, it was forgotten altogether. Only the scientific community remained interested and committed to finding out more.

There was a lull on the astronomical front.

'That's fine,' said Liz, 'we'll be here. See you soon.'

As she was putting down the receiver Gregg sidled up behind her and placed his hands on her breasts. 'Shall we go to bed?' he whispered in Liz's ear, 'and make each other happy.'

'We can't,' said Liz, removing his hands. 'That was Baby Blu. She's coming round with Rob. They've got something to tell us.'

'But we've still got time,' he continued earnestly, placing his arm around her waist. 'It'll only take ten minutes,' he implored.

'Look Gregg,' she said firmly, removing his hands for the second time, 'my little sister is coming round with her boyfriend with some important news. I've got to get ready. And I don't want a quickie. If we're going to make love, I want to do it properly.'

'Hi, Blu,' said Liz, flinging her arms around her little sister and kissing her on both cheeks, 'come in, come in. It's so good to see you. And you too, Rob,' she said, pecking him on his cheek. 'You know Gregg,' she continued as they entered the lounge.

Gregg stepped forward, kissing Blu on her cheek and shaking Rob's hand. 'Good to see you both,' he said. 'It's been a long time.'

'Would you like something to drink?' asked Liz. 'Tea, coffee, something stronger?'

'Coffee's fine,' said Blu.

'Rob?'

'Coffee for me too,' said Rob.

'Gregg, would you like one?'

'I certainly would,' he thought, but it wasn't a coffee that he had in mind.

'May as well,' he said. 'I'll have a coffee too.'

As Liz retreated into the kitchen to prepare the drinks, Gregg made small talk with Blu and Rob. Talk about the weather, about how they were doing and about their jobs.

'Coffee's ready,' said Liz, walking into the lounge carrying a tray with four mugs of steaming hot coffee and a plate full of chocolate biscuits. 'Help yourself to sugar and milk.' As Baby Blu and Rob added milk and sugar to their coffee, Gregg grabbed himself a Mars bar, one of his favourite snacks.

When they'd all got a drink and a biscuit, Blu looked at Rob and said, 'We've got a little gift for you.'

Liz looked surprised. 'Why, have you been away?'

'Er, yeah,' said Rob. 'Just a couple of days in Llandudno for a break. Nothing special. Just a couple of days away to recharge the batteries.'

As Blu handed her and Gregg the small, neatly wrapped packages, Liz was puzzled. Why had Blu been away without telling them? She'd never done that before. Her brain was whirling around as she tore the wrapping paper to reveal the gift beneath. It was a mug. A mug with a message. CONGRATULATIONS, AUNTY TO BE. Liz jumped up from her chair, dashed to her little sister and hugged her tightly. 'Oh Blu. Congratulations! I'm so pleased for you. And you too, Rob,' she said, hugging him too.

'Yes, congratulations to you both,' beamed Gregg, holding his CONGRATULATIONS, UNCLE TO BE mug.

'I know you're not an uncle yet,' said Blu, 'but it was the best we could do.'

'When's it due?' asked Liz excitedly.

'September 26th,' said Blu. 'I'm 12 weeks pregnant.'

'And that's not all, is it Rob?' giggled Blu.

'No, it's not,' said Rob, holding Blu's hand. 'It's not.'

'Don't keep us in suspense,' said Liz, half anticipating what was coming next. 'Come on, out with it.'

'Well,' said Blu, putting her arm around Rob, 'we're going to get married.'

Liz shrieked with joy, jumped up for the second time and embraced her little sister. 'That's great news. Absolutely great. Congratulations again.'

'Yeah. Congratulations from me too,' said Gregg, standing up and shaking both Blu and Rob's hands.

'When's the happy day?' asked Liz.

'Fourteenth of May,' said Blu. 'Before I get too big.'

'That's tremendous news, Blu. Really tremendous,' gushed Liz. 'We can't wait, can we,' she said, hugging Gregg.

'No, we can't. It's brilliant news. On both fronts.'

Although Blu would have preferred a more modest wedding, Rob's parents wanted their only son and his beautiful bride-to-be to have a very special day. A day to remember. The wedding was held at All Saints Parish Church in Thornton Hough, a charming, beautifully English village on the Wirral, with the reception at the nearby Thornton Manor, a place where the Queen Mother stayed when watching the horse racing at Aintree. Some brides arrived by helicopter. Or boat. They didn't go that far – it was too ostentatious – but Blu still arrived in style in a Hansom cab pulled by the loveliest horse that Liz had ever seen. It just reminded her of a giant yellow Labrador, a beautiful, gentle, graceful creature.

Both the wedding and the reception went off without a hitch. The falconry display sandwiched between the wedding ceremony and the Wedding Breakfast, staged by staff from the nearby Birds of Prey Centre at Blakemere, was a huge hit. In fact, the whole day was a complete success, helped in no small measure by the glorious weather.

A few months later, Blu gave birth to a beautiful baby girl – girls seemed to run in their family – a girl they named Charlotte, Charlotte Louise Manning, a lovely name and one without an embarrassing acronym.

For the next two years everything was quiet. The furore about the alien probes was all but forgotten and the world had returned to normal. Suddenly, that illusion was shattered. Viv received a call from Carl. His team had detected a huge rogue asteroid. A huge rogue asteroid on a collision course with Earth.

Part 3
· · ·
# COLLISION COURSE

Why should we subsidise
intellectual curiosity?

Ronald Reagan
Campaign Speech 1980

# 15

# ASTEROID

As she'd done many times before, Lucy Fawcett checked the image from the telescope before pressing the button. Checked that it was the correct region of the night time sky before committing it to film. Satisfied that it was, she pressed the button, let out a huge sigh and stretched her arms above her head. It had been a long, lonely night at NASA's NEO observatory in Houston, Texas. It was time for a coffee. Time to relax, read the morning papers and await the arrival of Carl and Simon. After the hectic activity of the past few years, it was good to get back to a normal routine, even if it was mundane.

As she sipped the hot, black liquid, Lucy reflected on another night of photographing the positions of unusual objects in the night sky. Objects that might, at some point in the future, pose a direct threat to Earth. But the night was like every other. Routine. Nothing unusual. Nothing out of the ordinary. Just the motion of the heavenly bodies on their celestial journey. Occasionally, very occasionally, the detection of a large object would cause a stir, generate a burst of excitement, but, without exception, it was always temporary: the large object never came anywhere remotely close to Earth. Smaller objects were commonplace but unexciting because, even if they did collide with Earth, they were too small to inflict much damage.

She smiled at the irony of the job she loved. On the one hand, a boring, routine night with no nasty surprises was ideal, what everyone wanted. It meant that planet Earth was safe. But on the other hand, well, she secretly longed for a nasty surprise, a large rogue asteroid heading straight for Earth, something to relieve the tedium. To generate some excitement. To test their mettle. Then again… they'd just witnessed the catastrophic outcome should that ever happen.

Ever since her birth in Portland, Oregon, Lucy Fawcett had been steeped in science. Both her parents were scientists who worked for Hewlett Packard's ink jet printing division in Corvallis, formulating inks for their range of ink jet printers. Yellow, magenta and cyan inks. She'd been amazed when her parents told her that these three coloured inks could produce a staggering 16.7 million different colours, just by mixing them in the correct proportions. At first, she refused to believe them, thinking they were pulling her leg. But it was true. The three subtractive primary colours of yellow, magenta and cyan, the famous YMC trichromat used to print every coloured publication on the planet, can indeed produce 16.7 million colours.

Like her parents, Lucy had an active, enquiring mind and a thirst for knowledge. As a child holidaying in Florida, she preferred the Kennedy Space Center to Disneyworld.

For most children the attractions of Disneyworld are irresistible. The Magic Kingdom, with its famous residents and rides. Exhilarating rides like *Thunder Mountain Railway*, or tranquil rides like *It's a Small World*. There's something for everyone. And, of course, there's Epcot, the more educational theme park. Although tempting, the Kennedy Space Center was still Lucy's favourite.

The size of the Saturn V rocket that carried the first astronauts to the moon took her breath away. She couldn't believe how something so big and so heavy ever got off the ground, never mind travelled to the moon and back. She stared at the plaque in disbelief.

SATURN V ROCKET

| | |
|---|---|
| Height: | 363 feet (60 feet taller than the Statue of Liberty) |
| Weight: | 6.2 million pounds (2,768 tons), equivalent to about 650 elephants, of which 2,067 tons is fuel |
| Power: | 160 million horse power producing a speed of 6,165 miles per hour (40 times faster than a Boeing 747) |
| Miles per gallon: | 5 inches |

It was the spark that fired her imagination. Her imagination for space. For the Cosmos. For the Universe. From the moment she first set eyes on that rocket, Lucy Fawcett was determined to become a space scientist. And she did, graduating as an astrophysicist and landing a job at NASA. Now aged 28, she was a clear-thinking, resourceful, likeable young woman who always sought the truth, even when it put her at odds with her colleagues. In a way, she was an American Liz Conway.

The team were disappointed, really disappointed, that they hadn't discovered the source of the alien probes. NASA had pulled out all the stops, focusing every possible resource in an attempt to locate their source, but to no avail. Despite working round the clock, day and night, for weeks on end, they found nothing. Zilch. It would have been devastating if another team had discovered the source, but they hadn't. No one had. For that they were thankful. But they'd keep on trying. The probes had to come from somewhere.

Her coffee break over, Lucy returned to the observatory and checked her watch. 5-50 a.m. Simon and Carl would be here in ten minutes. 'A good job too,' she thought, trying to stifle a huge yawn. The previous few years had played havoc with her sleeping patterns. She was ready to go home and catch up on some much needed sleep. Just two tasks remained: one, to check the image from an hour ago and two, to take a photograph of the next one at 6-00 a.m. She walked over to the telescope, collected the film, placed it on the glass-topped table and switched on the light. She scanned the illuminated film, making sure it was in focus, and was about to switch off the light when something caught her eye. A tiny, fuzzy, speck of grey. A faint, almost imperceptible, dot at the edge of a cluster of stars. She wasn't sure if it was real or a fault with the film. An imperfection. She rushed back to the telescope, pressed the button and waited, impatiently, for the image to appear on film. Eagerly, she grabbed the image, ran back to the illuminated table, and placed the new image next to the previous one. The dot was still there! Excitedly, she grabbed a magnifying glass to enlarge the image. It was definitely a dot, albeit a fuzzy, indistinct, grey-black dot, not an imperfection in the film. But where had it come from? It wasn't on the image she'd taken at 4-00 a.m., just two hours ago. Of that she was certain. It couldn't have appeared out of nowhere. She was bemused. A knock on the door startled her. 'Hi, Lucy.' It was Simon. 'Managed to stay awake then?' he said, flashing her a smile.

'Simon, come and look at this!' she shouted, her eyes glued to the dot on the illuminated image.

'Look at what, Lucy?' said Simon.

'At this... this dot,' she said, handing him the magnifying glass. 'There,' she pointed. 'There, at the edge of that star cluster.'

'Where,' he said, straining his eyes. 'At the edge of which star... I can see it!' he exclaimed. 'I can see it now,' he said excitedly. Then, almost as an afterthought, he said, 'What is it?'

'I don't know,' replied Lucy. 'I've only just seen it myself.'

'What's all this excitement,' said Carl, striding into the room. 'Have you discovered something exciting?'

'We don't know,' said Lucy, glancing at Simon. 'An object has just appeared out of nowhere.'

Carl shot her a sceptical look. 'Out of nowhere?' he said. '*Ex nihilo*. Come on, you can do better than that. There might be an object but it can't have materialised out of nowhere. Here, let me have a look.'

Lucy pointed to the faint, very faint, fuzzy dot and Simon handed him the magnifying glass.

Carl studied the image for several minutes before speaking. Studied it intently. 'You're right,' he said, 'there's definitely something there. But why do you say it appeared from nowhere?'

'Because,' said Lucy, passing him a sheet of film, 'it wasn't there two hours ago.'

Carl took the film but didn't examine it. 'I see,' he mused. 'That's interesting. Very interesting.' Suddenly, without any warning, his tone and demeanour changed, as if his whole body had been energised. 'Right,' he snapped, 'let's get to work.'

They tracked the mysterious object non-stop for the next 48 hours, eating, sleeping, living at the observatory, not daring to leave. Tracking its trajectory. Determining its orbit was the first step in identifying what it was: a planet, a moon, a star or an asteroid. A planet or a moon would have a small – in astronomical terms – well-defined, elliptical orbit. A star or an asteroid most likely wouldn't.

'What do you think, Carl?' asked Lucy, scrutinising the detailed plot on the computer screen, the line of dots displaying the object's trajectory. 'Do you think it's elliptical?'

'It's hard to tell,' replied Carl. 'We need more data points. Another couple of days of measurements should be enough.'

'I don't think it is elliptical,' said Simon, 'but, like Carl said, we'll know for sure in a couple of days.'

Dr Simon Greer shared many of the traits of his boss, Professor Carl Ryan. Both were products of the elite Ivy League university system, both were astrophysicists, both were full of their own importance and both would do anything to get to the top, including trampling over anyone who stood in their way. Simon had one other trait too. He always agreed with Carl, even when he knew he was wrong, because one day, he wanted his job.

'Do you think anyone else will have discovered the object?' asked Lucy.

'I doubt it,' said Carl. 'At the moment we've got sole access to the Hubble Telescope, the most powerful telescope in the world, so no, I very much doubt that anyone else has detected it. But they will. I reckon we've got 24, possibly 48 hours, before other teams detect the object. By then, we need to know what it is, how big it is and where it's heading. I want us to be the first to report it.'

'Shouldn't we tell the other teams now?' said Lucy, 'so they can be part of the discovery too.'

'NO!' barked Carl. 'Absolutely not. Not until we've worked out what it is and where it's heading.'

'And whether it poses a threat to Earth,' added Simon.

'But it seems so unfair,' continued Lucy, 'not to inform them. I'm sure they'd have…'

'That's my final decision, Lucy,' interrupted Carl. 'And anyway, I'm not sure they would have informed us if they'd discovered it first. They didn't with the meteorites.'

Lucy let it rest. He wasn't going to change his mind.

Twenty-four hours later, it was obvious the object wasn't a planet or a moon. It was either a star or an asteroid. They deliberated for hours before reaching a decision. One thing they all agreed on was that if it was a star, it had to be very far away. And that created a problem. 'If it is a star,' said Simon, 'which is very far away, then it must be moving at an incredibility high velocity to have travelled this distance in just 72 hours,' he said, jabbing the path travelled by the object with his finger, 'almost the speed of light, which is highly improbable. It must be an asteroid.'

'I agree,' said Lucy. 'It must be an asteroid which is much closer and moving much slower.'

'You're right,' chipped in Carl, 'it must be an asteroid. Have we any idea of its size or position?'

'We're working on it,' said Simon looking at Lucy. 'At this point, we can't be precise but I'd say it's pretty large, somewhere between 50 to 750 miles across, probably closer to 250 to 550.'

'Jesus Christ!' exclaimed Carl. 'That's one huge sonofabitch.'

'And the distance?'

'Depends on its velocity,' said Lucy. 'It's difficult to determine accurately because the object, er, asteroid, is fuzzy and indistinct. But if I were to hazard a guess, I'd say it was travelling extremely fast for an asteroid, about 215,000 miles per hour.'

'Bloody hell,' said Carl. 'That is fast. Are you sure?'

'No, I'm not. As I said, it's just a best guess.'

'Well, keep on it. We need to go public in a couple of hours. I'll start making preparations for the announcement. Focus most of your efforts on its trajectory and whether it poses a direct threat to Earth. That's what people will want to know. Okay? I'll see you in a couple of hours.' With that, he departed to prepare the framework for his announcement and to put on his best suit for the media interviews.

Lucy and Simon toiled tirelessly for the next two hours, Lucy calculating and recalculating the likely trajectory of the asteroid and Simon its size and distance from Earth. Ideally, they'd have liked more data points, but that wasn't going to happen before Carl gave his announcement. 'Why?' thought Lucy, 'can't he wait another 48 hours. Just another 48 hours to enable them to calculate, with absolute certainty, the path of the asteroid. But no, that wasn't his style. He wanted to hog the limelight again. To be the centre of attention. To be the person who discovered the asteroid. They might not have discovered the source of the meteorites, but he wanted the world to know that he was the one who discovered the asteroid.'

While Simon focused on determining the size and velocity of the asteroid, Lucy concentrated on calculating its path through space. Its trajectory. As the results of the final calculations appeared on the screen, Lucy couldn't believe her eyes. 'Fucking hell,' she uttered, surprising herself by her choice language, 'it's on a collision course with Earth!'

'What!' exclaimed Simon, turning away from his screen to look at Lucy's. 'What did you say? Are you sure?'

'The calculations predict that the asteroid will pass within 50,000 miles of Earth,' said Lucy. 'With a mean deviation of plus or minus 75,000 miles, it could miss the Earth by 125,000 miles or…'

'Or it could smash straight into it,' said Simon, finishing the sentence for her.

'Can't you be more precise?' said Simon. 'A mean deviation of 75,000 is pretty big.'

'With the data I've got, no. If I had a few more days of data, yes, I could be more precise. But I haven't, so that's the best I can do.'

'How about you? Have you got a better handle on its size and speed?'

'Well, like you, I can't be totally sure but the calculations show that it's approximately 400 miles in diameter and travelling at about 199,000 miles per hour. I reckon it'll reach the Earth in about two years time.'

'Fucking hell,' exclaimed Lucy, surprising herself for the second time, 'a 400 mile wide lump of rock on a collision course with Earth in just two years. We'd better tell Carl.'

Lucy urged Carl to present the full facts, that the asteroid would probably miss the Earth, that the probability of an impact was low, but he was having none of it.

'Godammit it, Lucy,' he shouted, 'I want this to be the headline news for weeks. If we say there's only a slight chance of an impact, it won't be. No, I'll say there's a 50:50 chance of a collision. It's not too far from the truth.'

'It fucking well is,' thought Lucy, surprising herself for a third time. 'It's a fucking long way from the truth.'

'I agree with Carl,' said Simon. 'Let's go for sensationalism and get the attention.'

'And the kudos,' added Carl. 'After all, we're not saying that it will definitely hit the Earth, just that there's a 50 per cent chance that it will.'

'I'm not happy with…'

'For fuck's sake, Lucy,' bellowed Carl, 'I'm the team leader and it's my call. That's the end of it. Okay?'

Lucy said nothing, just turned on her heels and stormed out of the room. He was doing it again. Had he learned nothing? It was *deja vu* all over again.

Carl picked up the phone. 'Hi, Viv. I've got some exciting news for you.'

# 16

# COLLISION COURSE

Carl's announcement did indeed make headline news around the world. Every TV station, every radio programme, every newspaper, ran it as their top story. Every day. His prediction that there was a 50 per cent chance the Earth would be destroyed by a huge asteroid in two years time caused mass panic. People were terrified. The impending end of the world, their world, scared them to death. The United Nations held emergency meeting after emergency meeting trying desperately to formulate contingency plans. Everyone looked to the world's most powerful and technically advanced nations for leadership. Looked to America, Russia, Europe and China for a plan. A plan to avoid Armageddon. The episode with the meteorites was forgotten. Compared to what was happening now, it was an inconsequential triviality.

The scientific community adopted a more rational approach. In every observatory around the world, telescopes, both optical and radio, were trained on the approaching asteroid. They wanted more information, more data points, to calculate precisely the path of the asteroid. To calculate it without any error. With absolute certainty. To know, beyond any shadow of doubt, whether it would hit the Earth.

Viv's team were one of the first on the scene. They trained all their radio telescopes, plus the Faulkes optical telescope, on the approaching asteroid hurtling towards them. And spotted a problem. Carl had been over optimistic in thinking they'd need only two days to calculate its precise path. They'd need at least several weeks, even months, because not only was the asteroid fuzzy and indistinct, it also had a 'wobble'. A wobble which meant that its path wasn't a 'straight line', but an extremely shallow sine curve. The asteroid alternated between deviating, ever so slightly, first to the left and then to the right, making it very difficult to predict with any degree of certainty whether or not it would collide with the Earth.

The uncertainty introduced by the wobble meant that teams around the world came up with different answers. Fierce disagreements broke out. Some teams predicted the asteroid would miss the Earth by 125,000 miles, others predicted a direct hit, whilst some predicted a glancing blow. One team even predicted a collision with the moon, an event that would be every bit as catastrophic as a full-blown collision with Earth. Such a collision would cause both the asteroid and a large part of the moon to shatter into countless massive fragments, fragments which would drench the Earth. Drench it with thousands of huge lumps of rock. Thousands of large asteroids raining down on Earth. It would be disastrous.

Conflict also flared between Carl's team and Viv's team, opening up old wounds. Carl's team, led by Lucy and Simon, calculated that the asteroid would miss the earth by 50,000 miles, a mere whisker in astronomical terms. Viv's team, led by Frank and Rupert, calculated it would hit the Earth a glancing blow, not a full-blown collision. Each team, not just Carl or Viv's, believed their calculations were correct, but only one could be correct. The question was, which one?

As the months rolled by and the disagreements raged on, countries, governments and families started making their own contingency plans. Plans for different outcomes. Plans for what everyone hoped and prayed would be a near miss or, at worst, a glancing blow. No one wanted a full-blown collision. But even a near miss, a close encounter at 50,000 miles, would still cause extensive damage. Damage from the massive tidal surges caused by the asteroid's gravitational pull. Tidal surges bigger than any seen before. Bigger than any tsunami. The damage to coastal and low-lying areas would be enormous. Countries like Holland would be obliterated, submerged under a mass of water, and areas prone to tidal bores, such as the Severn Estuary, would suffer a devastation far worse than the Great Flood of 1607, the worst in recorded history.

'What would you do, Rupert?' said Liz, 'if the worst came to the worst. If you knew that, say, in six months time, the asteroid would crash into the Earth. That it was an absolute certainty and there was nothing we could do. What would you do? Would you carry on as normal, doing the same things you'd always done, or would you abandon your current lifestyle – work, commuting, going to the pub, going to watch rugby union – and spend all your remaining time with your loved ones? Your family. Your girlfriend. Or would you embark on a bucket list, cramming everything you'd always planned to do in your lifetime into those final few months? Exotic holidays, sky diving, climbing the Himalayas, bungee jumping, flying a plane… Or even a wild hedonistic fling, gorging yourself on fine food and wine, and having sex with as many beautiful women as possible? What would you do, Rupert?'

'All of them, Liz,' smiled Rupert. 'All of those – if I had the time.'

'Come on, be serious,' said Liz. 'You must have thought about it.'

For a while, Rupert said nothing. Then, what he did say shocked Liz to the core. 'I'd like to spend all my time with you.'

Liz was speechless. Her shocked expression amused Rupert, bringing a smile to his face. 'I said be serious,' she uttered, regaining a little of her composure.

'I am being serious, Liz. I'm being deadly serious. I'd like to spend my last months on Earth with you.'

Liz had pondered the same question herself. And come up with a definitive answer. She'd spend most of her time with her little sister, Baby Blu, and her niece, Charlotte – both her parents were dead – and her long time boyfriend, Gregg. Steady, safe Gregg who loved football and sex – in that order. Gregg, who was rarely passionate or exciting, but reliable and caring. Gregg, who wanted a career but didn't know if he wanted children. She'd spend some time with him but she'd spend most of her time with Baby Blu and Charlotte. But this bombshell had come out of the blue. Blindsided her. A man she'd hated, no, not hated, loathed, for years and years had just professed his dying wish was to spend his remaining time on Earth with her. With Liz Conway. It had certainly thrown a spanner in the works.

With Rupert it had been hate at first sight. During the five years she'd known him they'd never got on, but the discovery of the alien meteorites changed all that. It brought out a new person. A person she never thought existed. An emotional, enthusiastic, passionate person who respected her. A person she really liked. A person she could, maybe, fall in love with.

After the initial shock and furore regarding the asteroid had quietened down, the recriminations began. The politicians were furious. Furious with the scientific community. With all the billions spent on the latest sophisticated detection equipment, why hadn't such a huge asteroid been detected earlier? They stopped short of accusing them of incompetence, but secretly, that's what many of them thought.

It was a question the scientists had asked themselves. How could an asteroid 400 miles wide get to within 3.5 billion miles of Earth before being detected? Get past Pluto before being spotted? It shouldn't have happened, not with all the equipment at their disposal. But it had. The question was how?

One reason it had been difficult to detect the asteroid was its shape. Somehow, its surface scattered electromagnetic radiation in a similar way that a Stealth bomber scatters radar, making it almost invisible. As a result, it only became 'visible' when it got fairly close to Earth. Also, it was right at the edge of a large star cluster, another factor that made detection difficult. But the bigger question was how it had appeared so suddenly, apparently out of nowhere. On this point there was much speculation. Every possibility was examined, from the plausible to the metaphysical.

'Could it have appeared out of hyperspace?' said Liz mischievously.

'And what exactly is hyperspace, Liz?' asked Frank.

'You know, the space that Starship Enterprise enters when it goes into warp drive.'

'I won't dignify that with an answer,' said Frank. 'Star Trek is science fiction.'

'What about a wormhole?' asked Rupert. 'I know we've discussed that before but what if there are natural wormholes where the distortion of spacetime isn't so obvious?'

'It's a possibility, but it's highly unlikely,' replied Frank.

'Could it have been travelling close to the speed of light,' said Liz. '186,000 miles per second, and then suddenly decelerated? That would explain its sudden appearance out of nowhere. And,' she added, 'objects travelling close to the speed of light shrink in size, making them more difficult to detect.'

'It's a nice idea, Liz,' said Frank, 'but again, highly unlikely. To accelerate an object the size of an asteroid close to the speed of light would take an enormous amount of energy. It's very unlikely, but not impossible.'

Although far from ideal, the best solution they came up with as to why the asteroid hadn't been detected earlier was a combination of its unique, reflective surface and its proximity to the large star cluster.

As the months went by and more data became available, the calculations on the asteroid's trajectory began to converge, to come closer together. To begin to show signs of agreement. And the results were terrifying. It was headed straight for a full-blown collision with Earth!

# 17

# BLACK DEFLECTION

The results were conclusive. Definite. Absolute. Scientists around the world came up with the same answer. In just eight months time, the asteroid would crash directly into the Earth.

The plan had been to inform the governments first and then for the governments to inform the people. But it didn't happen like that. News of such monumental importance was impossible to contain; the public received the news at the same time as the governments. Not surprisingly, it caused a global panic. Governments around the world did their best to try and calm the situation, but to little effect. In the public's mind, the end of the world was nigh and they were all going to die a horrible death.

A world summit was convened comprising top politicians and scientists from the world's leading countries. The world's best brains gathered together with a single aim: to formulate a plan to deflect the asteroid. To knock it off its collision course with Earth. It wouldn't take much deflecting. A deflection of just a fraction of a degree would be sufficient to ensure it missed the Earth. But deflecting a 400 mile wide asteroid travelling at 199,000 miles per hour was easier said than done.

The world was in turmoil. The mass panic caused by the impending destruction of Earth brought the world to a standstill. People stopped going to work. Students stopped going to university. Children stopped going to school. What was the point if they were all going to die in eight months time? Public transport came to a grinding halt. No buses, no trains, no ships, no planes. Private transport followed quickly as the petrol stations ran dry. Shops and supermarkets were stripped bare as people scrambled to stock up on food and drink. Looting was rife. The social infrastructure had all but broken down. Law and order was hanging by a thread. As the shortages became acute, the killing started. Ordinary people killing fellow citizens just to provide food for their loved ones.

The government did its best, drafting in what remained of the armed forces to try and restore some semblance of law and order, and making frequent appeals for calm and restraint, saying that scientists were close to finding a way to deflect the asteroid, deflect it sufficiently to miss the Earth. It worked, up to a point. The lootings stopped, mainly because there was nothing of value left to loot, and the killings abated, partly because of the army's shoot to kill policy of anyone breaking the curfews and partly because of the government's reassurance that the asteroid would be deflected. In the total scheme of events, they were minuscule improvements, but at least they slowed the slide into outright anarchy.

Scientists around the world worked feverishly trying to decide the best course of action to deflect the asteroid. The NEO teams had trained for such an event for years. Trained using simulations. This time, however, it was for real.

It had been agreed at the summit that it was best if the NEO teams worked independently at the beginning, and than liaised to thrash out the final solution. But they didn't have much time. The closer the asteroid got to Earth, the more they'd have to deflect it. It was a race against time. A race they couldn't afford to lose.

A number of options were discussed. For the best chance of success, they all had one thing in common. Early detection. The early detection of an approaching asteroid offered the best chance of deflecting it because the further it was from Earth, the smaller the deviation needed to deflect it. According to NASA, it would take a couple of years to build a rocket powerful enough to deflect an asteroid and allow enough time for the deflection's effect to alter its trajectory sufficiently for it to miss the Earth. But early detection was a luxury they didn't have. The asteroid was less than eight months away. They'd have to find another way.

Methods for deflecting an asteroid fall into two categories; nuclear and non-nuclear. Although the nuclear option is the most common method some, like in the 1998 film *Armageddon*, where Bruce Willis lands on an asteroid and blows it up with a nuclear bomb, are pure science fiction. Even if such a feat could be accomplished and the bomb blasted the asteroid to smithereens, most of the fragments would still hit the Earth, causing untold damage and destruction. Even a fragment of rock one mile wide would produce catastrophic global events, including wiping out 25 per cent of the human race. Hundreds would wipe out the entire planet. Blowing up the asteroid was a non-starter.

'The best of the nuclear options,' said Frank, 'is Black Deflection. Professor Alan Harris's NEO Shield team in Berlin have done extensive research into asteroid deflection and concluded that detonating a powerful nuclear bomb close to one side of an asteroid is the best way to deflect it. The neutron radiation, or neutron wind if you like, from the nuclear explosion, would cause a slight deviation to its trajectory, enough, hopefully, for it to miss the Earth.'

'Wouldn't it have to explode very close to the asteroid to be effective?' asked Viv.

'That's a very good question,' replied Frank. 'Yes, it would have to be close to maximise the effect of the explosion, but not so close that it fragments the asteroid.'

'So what's the optimum distance?' asked Rupert.

'Ah, that's a matter of some debate,' said Frank. 'A stand off distance of approximately 20 yards is often mentioned to achieve maximum deflection, but no one knows for certain.'

'Surely you'd need more than one hydrogen bomb to deflect an asteroid 400 miles wide,' said Liz. 'You'd need dozens, probably hundreds.'

'At least,' said Frank, 'and then it's by no means certain they'd deflect it sufficiently to miss the Earth, especially as it's so close.'

'Have we got so many rockets capable of carrying powerful nuclear warheads into space?' asked Liz. 'Didn't the Russians and Americans destroy a lot of them after the Cold War ended?'

'They were supposed to,' said Viv, 'but those rockets weren't any good anyway. They were only designed to travel a few thousand miles, from one continent to another. That's why they were called intercontinental ballistic missiles or ICBMs. They aren't powerful enough to travel to outer space. For that, we need rockets even more powerful than the Saturn V rocket.'

'And do those exist?' asked Rupert.

'I don't know,' said Viv, 'but I suspect the Americans and Russians will have one or two stashed away.'

'But it'll take more than one or two nuclear bombs to deflect a 400 mile wide asteroid,' reiterated Liz.

'Yes, it will,' replied Viv, 'but we can only use what we've got.'

'But shouldn't such rockets be capable of carrying a multiple payload?' asked Frank. 'Five, maybe even ten, nuclear bombs. So, if the Americans and Russians can muster, say, five such rockets, that means 50 nuclear bombs could be exploded near the asteroid. It's still not ideal but it gives us a fighting chance.'

'Possibly,' said Viv, 'but aren't we jumping the gun here. There's the non-nuclear options too.'

'You can rule out solar sails,' said Frank. 'It's far too late for them.'

'What about gravitational tractors?' asked Rupert.

'Or a direct impact?' asked Liz.

'A direct impact could work,' said Frank, 'if we had a massive spaceship to crash into the asteroid. But we haven't. The rockets we've got would only work on asteroids up to 100 yards wide. So that's a non-starter.'

'By a gravitational tractor, do you mean where a spaceship, a rocket, lands on the surface of the asteroid, is tethered to it with a towline and then uses its engines to "push" on the asteroid, deflecting its path or slowing it down?' queried Frank.

'I do,' replied Rupert.

'Well, the thrust from conventional chemical rockets is far too weak, but it's achievable using a 20 ton nuclear-electric rocket proposed by NASA. The problem is, no such rocket exists.'

'I remember reading a study by researchers at the University of Glasgow that the best way to deflect an asteroid is the "Mirror Bees" method,' said Liz.

'Mirror Bees? What the hell's that?' said Rupert.

'It entails sending a group of small satellites equipped with mirrors 30 to 100 feet wide into space to "swarm" round the asteroid and trail it. The mirrors would tilt to reflect sunlight on to the asteroid, vaporising one spot and releasing a stream of gases that slowly move it off course.'

'I've read that paper too,' said Frank, 'and the operative word is slowly. It's a plausible idea if the asteroid is far away but it's too late for that now. And anyway, we don't have the satellites.'

'Couldn't we combine the two?' said Rupert. 'The nuclear and non-nuclear options. For example, explode nuclear bombs to cause the main deflection and then use a gravitational tractor or direct impact to cause a further deflection?'

'In theory, yes, in practice, no. The asteroid's too close for that now.'

Liz voiced what they were all thinking. 'Then our only option is Black Deflection. To explode as many nuclear bombs as possible, simultaneously, close to one side of the asteroid.'

'I'm afraid so,' said Frank. 'Even then, I'm not sure it'll work.'

In the end, every team in the world came to the same conclusion. Black Deflection was their only option. Their only hope.

Between them, America and Russia managed to muster five rockets. Five rockets each armed with ten of the world's most powerful nuclear bombs. Scientists worked tirelessly programming the coordinates and synchronising the times. It was imperative that all five rockets reached the asteroid at precisely the same time, and that all the bombs detonated in unison. Six months before the asteroid would hit the Earth, the rockets were launched.

Two months later, 300 million miles from Earth in the asteroid belt between Mars and Jupiter, four of the five rockets – one had malfunctioned and drifted off into deep space – reached their target and detonated their deadly payloads. Forty of the world's most powerful nuclear bombs exploded close to the asteroid. But not simultaneously and not 20 yards from the asteroid. For that to have happened after a 300 million mile voyage would have been a miracle, and miracles simply don't happen. The explosions occurred over a period of a few minutes, the nearest 400 yards from the asteroid, the furthest one mile away. It wasn't perfect, but it wasn't too bad of an outcome. Anyway, it was the best they could do. Had it done the trick, or was it too little too late?

The world held its breath.

# 18

# ILLICIT LOVE

While the scientists in America and Russia worked frantically against the tightest deadline they'd ever known to prepare the rockets for launch, NEO teams around the world tracked the asteroid, tracked its trajectory to the nearest inch to provide the most accurate data possible for them to feed into the rockets' guidance systems. There was no room for error. All five rockets had to reach the asteroid at precisely the same time, otherwise the plan would fail.

During the same period, governments began implementing their contingency plans, moving people away from the coast, away from estuaries and away from low-lying areas. Once thriving coastal resorts became ghost towns as people moved inland to higher ground. Entire areas such as East Anglia were emptied of people. If the asteroid smashed directly into the Earth, it would all be a pointless waste of time but if, as everyone hoped, it was a near miss, countless lives would be saved. Either way, it kept people occupied. Helped take their minds off the approaching asteroid. Helped lessen the feeling of hopelessness.

Billions of people the world over had a decision to make: who to spend their final few months with? Seven billion people had to make that decision. For Liz, it was a no-brainer. She would spend her remaining time with the people she loved most. Her little sister, Baby Blu, and her three-year-old niece, Charlotte. And, of course, she'd spend some time with her boyfriend, Gregg.

As she watched her niece running around giggling and laughing with her mummy, she thought about the rank unfairness of it all, the cruel blow dealt by the hand of fate. Millions of innocent babies and children, children just like her little niece, would be wiped from the face of the Earth. Obliterated before their lives had barely begun. Where was God now? It was bad enough for everyone, but at least the elderly and people like herself had had a taste of life.

As the reality of the situation hit home, people began to accept their fate. Resign themselves to the fact that their world was coming to an end. A solemn determination replaced the hysteria. A determination to enjoy what little time was left with the people they loved. Their spouses, their children, their families, their friends. If they were going to die, they were determined to die happy. It was a sad yet uplifting time. A time which demonstrated the strength and dignity of the human spirit. It felt good to be a human being.

It had been a long night at the Jodrell Bank Observatory. Rupert and Liz were exhausted. The frenetic activity of the past few months was taking its toll. The constant stress had made people tired and edgy, ready to explode at any moment. Nerves were frayed. As they joined the dots on the screen predicting the asteroid's path, it was Liz who broke the uneasy silence. 'Rupert. Can you predict where the asteroid will strike the Earth?' she asked, adding quickly, 'if we fail to deflect it.'

'Pretty much,' replied Rupert. 'It's heading for England. London actually.'

'Well,' said Liz after a brief pause, 'at least we won't suffer. Death will be instantaneous.'

Rupert said nothing, just continued plotting the asteroid's path.

'Rupert?'

'Yeah.'

'Do you really think the nuclear explosions will knock the asteroid off course? Deflect it sufficiently to miss the Earth?'

'Do you want my honest opinion, Liz?'

'Of course I do,' she retorted. 'I wouldn't have asked otherwise.'

'Then no, I don't think they will. I think they'll deflect it a little, but not enough to miss the Earth. I think the best we can hope for is a glancing blow.'

Noticing the consternation on Liz's face, he added, 'But look on the bright side. It's depleted the world's stockpile of nuclear weapons, making…' He was about to say, 'making the world a safer place,' but stopped when he realised the irony of his intended pronouncement.

As Liz took over plotting the asteroid's path, Rupert watched her in silent admiration. Watched the young woman he'd come to like. Like a lot. Sat at the computer screen, she looked so lovely, so beautiful, so desirable. At that moment, in the peace and tranquillity of the observatory's control room, he wanted her more than anything. Wanted her with every atom of his body. Wanted to kiss her and make love to her. Before he knew it, he'd grabbed her shoulders, spun her round and was kissing her passionately.

Liz was startled. Taken aback. She resisted, struggling to free herself from his strong grip, eventually managing to push him away. She slapped his face. Hard.

'What the hell do you think you're doing?' she spat.

'I… I couldn't stop myself,' said Rupert, rubbing his red, smarting cheek ruefully. 'I don't know what came over me. You looked so lovely. So desirable. I just had to. It's what I've wanted to do for a long time.'

He felt ashamed at what he'd done but he'd had to do it. It was now or never. At the very least, he had to kiss the woman he loved before the world came to an end.

Liz felt ashamed too. Ashamed that she'd slapped his face. Slapped it hard. But ashamed because she'd enjoyed it. Enjoyed his spontaneous moment of passion. Secretly, it was something she'd longed for too. Deep down, she wanted more than a kiss. She wanted mad, passionate sex.

'I'm sorry for slapping you,' she said apologetically. 'It's just that you... startled me. Took me by surprise.'

'I'm sorry too,' said Rupert. 'I shouldn't have done it.'

At that instant, Liz surprised herself. She flung her arms around him, kissing him passionately on the mouth. Really passionately. A surprised Rupert responded in kind, returning the passionate kiss and hugging her tightly.

'Oh, Rupert,' she said. 'I've wanted to do that for ages.'

'So have I, Liz,' said Rupert, unable to stop the throbbing erection developing in his groin. 'So have I.'

What she did next both surprised and delighted him. She slid her hand down his torso and placed it on the growing bulge in his trousers. 'I want more than a kiss, Rupert,' she whispered hoarsely in his ear. 'I want to make love to you,' she said, unzipping his flies. Moments later, she was straddling him on the floor and making the movements of love. Forceful, rhythmic, deep movements. Rupert groaned with delight, his hands digging into her buttocks. It felt so good. Although she was betraying Gregg, at that moment she didn't care. She was consumed by passion. The guilt could wait.

As they were getting dressed, the guilt arrived. Swept over her. What had she done? For a few moments of instant sexual gratification, she'd jeopardised her five year relationship with Gregg. Put at risk everything they'd built together. All for a few moments of passionate sex with a man who, until a few months ago, she'd loathed. But it was done now. Done and dusted. She'd acted on impulse. On an urge to satisfy a deep longing. But it hadn't worked. Rather than resolve the situation, it had made it worse. But it presented her with an opportunity to ask a question that had been gnawing at her. 'Rupert, why have you behaved so horribly towards me?'

'I could ask you the same question,' thought Rupert, but he didn't say it. He didn't want to spoil the moment.

'Resentment really,' he replied. 'I've always liked you, liked you a lot, but I felt I couldn't have you. That you were out of reach. You already had a boyfriend so I teased you, tried to upset you. To hurt you. I'm sorry.'

Although they didn't make love again, the feeling of guilt persisted. The atmosphere between her and Rupert became awkward. Uncomfortable. He'd started it by his unexpected kiss but she'd undoubtedly finished it by fucking him. No, not fucking him, by making love to him. She'd done it with feeling. With love.

As the asteroid got closer – it was now less than four months away – Liz was torn between Gregg and Rupert. She agonised over what to do. The nuclear bombs had exploded near the asteroid several weeks ago and they were tracking its trajectory carefully to see if it had been deflected. Deflected enough for it to miss the Earth. In a few days time they'd know the answer. Know for sure. She had to make a decision. To choose who to spend her last few months with. Should it be steady, reliable Gregg, her long time boyfriend, or unpredictable Rupert? And which was the real Rupert anyway? Was it the arrogant, condescending, superior Rupert she'd loathed for so long, or the emotional, passionate Rupert she'd come to love? She didn't know, but she had to decide. They could all be dead in a few months.

# 19

# A SURPRISE

It would miss! The asteroid would miss the Earth! The nuclear explosions had done the trick. Deflected it sufficiently to knock it off its collision course with Earth. Scientists the world over hugged and congratulated themselves on a job well done. Politicians were relieved. People rejoiced, singing and dancing in the streets. A common threat had been averted. The world celebrated. Some semblance of normality returned as people gradually resumed their daily lives.

The NEO teams celebrated too. Carl, Simon and Lucy in America and Viv, Liz and Zak, together with Rupert and Frank, in England. Everyone was relieved. And delighted. Delighted their lives wouldn't be cut short. Some had questioned the wisdom of spending millions on such nefarious ventures, but not now. The NEO teams worldwide had played a major role in ensuring a positive outcome. Their existence had been vindicated. Fully.

The positive outcome gave Liz more breathing space. More time to make her crucial decision. Would it be Gregg? Or would it be Rupert? Gregg knew nothing about her one night stand with Rupert. No one did, except Rupert, and he wouldn't tell. But was it a one night stand or was it something far more serious? On that point, she was still undecided.

Those of a religious disposition flocked to their places of worship to thank their Gods for sparing the world. For sparing them. For giving them a second chance. But it wasn't over yet. A flyby of a 400 mile wide asteroid at 55,000 miles would still cause extensive flooding and devastation, but the evacuation of vulnerable areas should ensure that any loss of life would be minimal.

As the asteroid approached, people watched in fascination as its size grew bigger and bigger in the night sky. Initially, it seemed like a dim 'star', a dim fast moving 'star' that grew bigger every night until finally, on its closest approach to Earth, it was bigger than a full moon.

The floods were as bad as they'd feared. Giant tidal surges wreaked havoc. Coastal resorts were razed to the ground, flattened by massive tidal waves, whilst low-lying areas were submerged beneath a wall of water. The damage was extensive but, thanks to the evacuation, there was little loss of life, at least in the developed countries.

Despite the devastation caused by the tidal surges, people throughout the world rejoiced, grateful for a new beginning. Street parties, carnivals, parades, even mardi gras, were the order of the day.

Suddenly, everything changed. Instead of careening off into space, the asteroid changed trajectory to take up orbit around the Earth.

Part 4
. . .
# DARK DAYS

To a primitive society, any
form of advanced technology
seems like magic

Arthur C Clark

# 20

# EARTH ORBIT

The scientists were puzzled. The public were puzzled. The whole world was puzzled. And afraid. Very afraid. They thought they'd seen the last of the asteroid. Seen the back of it. But they were wrong. For it to swing into orbit around the Earth was the last thing that anyone expected.

'What the hell's going on?' asked Rupert, staring in disbelief at the asteroid's dramatic change of direction on the computer screen. 'How on earth has that happened?'

'I don't know,' replied Frank, looking as bemused as the rest of them. 'I just don't know.'

Neither did scientists at observatories around the world. Everyone was baffled and bewildered. It shouldn't have happened. It was very strange and very frightening.

Scientists scratched their heads. Could such an occurrence be natural? A 400 mile wide asteroid taking up orbit around the Earth. They knew that objects travelling through space could be attracted by the gravity of a massive object, such as planet or especially a star. Captured by their gravitational pull and then held in orbit. But was the Earth's gravitational pull strong enough to capture a 400 mile wide asteroid and hold it in orbit?

'I don't think it is,' said Frank. 'It's strong enough to have an effect, that's for sure, to alter it's trajectory ever so slightly into a large elliptical orbit which could bring it back to the vicinity of Earth in tens of years, a bit like what will happen with Apophis, but it's not strong enough to pull it into a direct orbit around the Earth. I've never seen such a dramatic change in trajectory.'

'Could it be caused by an unusual alignment of the inner planets?' asked Liz. 'Are Mercury, Venus and Earth all in alignment, creating a uniquely strong gravitational field?'

'I don't think so,' said Frank.

'No, they're not,' said Rupert, turning around from punching keys on the computer. 'That's not the explanation.'

As the discussion continued, the ideas became more bizarre, more extreme.

'What about a black hole?' said Rupert. 'Could there be a small black hole lurking nearby? The gravitational pull would be enormous.'

'I certainly hope not!' exclaimed Frank. 'And anyway, wouldn't we have detected its effects?'

'I suppose so,' said Rupert dejectedly. 'But a small black hole is most certainly one object which could have produced such a dramatic change in the asteroid's trajectory.'

'And on the Earth's and the moon's too, if it existed,' said Frank. 'No, that's not the answer either.'

Could there be any natural explanation? They racked their brains searching for one, but nothing emerged. Try as they might, they couldn't think of any natural explanation for the asteroid's bizarre behaviour. And neither could anyone else.

'Well,' said Liz, 'if it's not natural, then it has to be... unnatural. Alien. An alien asteroid. An alien starship in disguise.'

'It must be,' said Frank. 'Strange as it may seem, it must be some sort of alien spacecraft. I can't think of any other explanation.'

'Neither can I,' said Viv. 'It must be a starship under alien control.'

Rupert and Zak were of the same opinion.

'Do you think the asteroid, er, starship, actually has a crew of aliens onboard, or is it uninhabited and controlled remotely?' asked Liz.

'If I had to make a guess,' replied Frank, 'I'd say it's controlled by aliens actually on the asteroid. Why would they send such a massive object if it wasn't inhabited? No, I think it's a large object because there are thousands, possibly even millions, of aliens on that asteroid. It's like a mini world.'

Frank had voiced what most of them were thinking, that a mini world of technically advanced, intelligent, alien beings was circling the Earth. Circling their prey. Waiting for the right moment to strike. It scared the living daylights out of them.

The asteroid settled into a steady orbit about 100,000 miles from Earth. Not just any random orbit, but an orbit which positioned it precisely between the sun and the Earth, an orbit designed to block out some of the sunlight, like a partial eclipse of the sun when the moon's orbit crosses between the sun and the Earth.

During the next few weeks, nothing changed. The asteroid remained in the same geostationary position, blocking out some of the sun's life-giving heat and light. Some, but not enough to cause alarm. The initial public consternation had subsided, replaced by a curious fascination. It was like the Earth had two moons, one of which was in a constant state of partial eclipse.

The extra moon proved a source of fascination. The romantics loved it. Two moons adorning the night sky. It was like a scene from a science fiction movie, as if they'd been beamed to another world. But it wasn't a movie, it was happening right here. Right here on Earth.

Around the world discussions raged as to what the asteroid really was. Where was it from? What was its purpose? Was it connected to the meteorites? Was it controlled by aliens? Was it inhabited by aliens? So many questions and so few answers.

'I've no idea where it's from,' said Liz, 'but I think it's definitely connected to the meteorites. I think the meteorites were probes to gather information about the Earth and relay it back to the asteroid. And,' she continued, 'I think they found the data to their liking and have come to, er, investigate further.'

'You mean come to invade and conquer us if the planet meets their requirements,' said Rupert.

'Quite possibly,' replied Liz.

'This is all pure conjecture,' said Viv, getting a little irritated with all the speculation about doom and gloom. 'I agree the asteroid is probably controlled by intelligent, alien life, but we don't know what they want. It might be nothing more than a fact-finding mission. A tour of the galaxy to find and map other planets with intelligent life.'

'Maybe,' said Frank, 'but the way they've acted so far doesn't exactly fill me with confidence. But it does explain a few things. For example, the surface of the asteroid, er, starship, is obviously an advanced form of camouflage to make detection difficult.'

'Like the cloaking device of the Klingon starships in Star Trek?' said Liz lightheartedly. Frank shot her a withering look before carrying on. The time for frivolity had long since passed.

'It could also explain the asteroid's wobble. It's obviously deliberate, either to keep us guessing whether or not it would hit the Earth or, more likely, because it's related to the asteroid's method of propulsion, like alternating bursts of energy from two very powerful engines.'

'And it could account for its sudden appearance out of nowhere,' said Viv. 'If the aliens really are a technically advanced civilisation, then maybe it did appear from some kind of wormhole, or hyperspace,' he said, winking at Liz who was still a little upset at Frank's response to her playful query. 'Or it could even have been travelling close to the speed of light. Such ideas are not so fanciful now.'

'But still highly improbable,' said Liz, returning to the fray.

'To us, yes. But remember Arthur C Clark's famous quotation: *To a primitive society, any form of advanced technology looks like magic.* To our early ancestors, today's technology would seem like magic beyond their wildest dreams. So, if we're a primitive civilisation compared to the aliens, it's no surprise that their technology seems highly improbable to us. And,' continued Viv, 'now we know why the asteroid didn't smash into the Earth. It wasn't the nuclear bombs – they had some effect, yes, but it was too little, too late – it was the aliens who steered it away from Earth.'

'And it was probably the aliens who engineered the collision between the asteroid and the comet,' said Frank, 'to provide cover for their meteorite probes. Although such an event isn't impossible, it's very, very rare.'

'I think you're right,' said Viv. 'It's all beginning to come together now.'

Similar discussions took place around the world, but nobody came up with any convincing answers regarding the origin and purpose of the asteroid. Or the aliens. However, fear was growing that their coming wasn't in peace. The concealment of the meteorites, the type of information sent back, and the disguise and behaviour of the asteroid, weren't acts associated with a peaceful encounter. Far from it. They were acts associated with war.

As the weeks went by, rather than view it as a benign, friendly, second moon, people began to view the asteroid as a giant version of the Death Star from the Star Wars films. A giant Death Star about to inflict untold devastation and misery on the human race. On planet Earth.

In top level meetings around the globe, politicians, scientists and military leaders debated what to do. It was agreed, although not unanimously, that the first course of action should be communication. To try and make contact with the aliens. To find out why they were here. What they wanted. Had they come in peace? How had yet to be decided.

If that failed, they should wait. Wait for a while and see what developed. As usual, the military pushed for using force to try and destroy the asteroid but, as was pointed out by the scientists, they'd already exploded 40 of the world's most powerful nuclear weapons close to the asteroid, and that hadn't destroyed it. Furthermore, it had used up most of the world's stockpile of nuclear weapons. Also, if rockets armed with nuclear warheads, or even poisonous chemical weapons, were launched against the aliens, they almost certainly possessed the technology to intercept and destroy them before they reached their target. And, if they wished, to retaliate. Retaliate with weapons of unimaginable power and destruction.

As the debates continued, astronomers noticed a subtle change in the asteroid. A slight ridge had appeared around its circumference. Around its belly. A ridge that was growing bigger each day.

# 21
# NUCLEAR WINTER

At first, the change was barely perceptible. Just a minute ridge straddling the 'equator' of the asteroid. Even viewed through the most powerful telescopes, it was difficult to make out what it was. However, as the days passed and its size increased, it became patently obvious what it was: it was a concentric, fan-like array of interlocked solar panels. A thin fan-like sheet of solar panels spreading out evenly from the asteroid. As the array grew in size, it reminded Liz of the rings around Saturn. An ever expanding halo around the belly of the asteroid.

'There,' said Viv, studying the image on the telescope. 'It's like I said. They're harnessing the power of the sun to recharge their batteries. To "refuel" the asteroid before moving on.'

'You still think it's just a fact-finding mission?' exclaimed Frank incredulously. 'That they'll leave when they've gathered sufficient data and recharged their batteries?'

'It's a possibility,' replied Viv, feeling less sure after his colleague's questioning remarks.

'And how long will this fact-finding mission take?' asked Frank. 'How long will it take them to gather all the information they need?'

'How long is a piece... I don't know,' replied Viv, remembering the Prime Minister's acerbic response to his glib answer. 'A week, two weeks, a month. I've no idea.'

'That's bullshit!' exclaimed Rupert, releasing his pent-up frustration. 'No fucking way is it a peaceful fact-finding mission. It's something far more serious than a bloody fact-finding mission. Something... sinister.'

'Like what?' said Viv, visibly taken aback by Rupert's blunt outburst.

'Like they've come here to destroy us. Destroy us and take over the planet. Colonise it for themselves.'

As the days turned into weeks, the size of the fan-like array kept on increasing, blocking out more and more of the sunlight. The Earth was getting darker. Not dark enough to worry about, at least not yet – it was just like a cloudy summer's day – but if the array continued expanding, it would, eventually, block out all the sunlight, creating a total eclipse of the sun. A permanent total eclipse. A state of total darkness. A nuclear winter similar to that which caused the extinction of the dinosaurs.

The possibility of that scenario, and its dire consequences, spurred them into action. Had them calculating the time when the array would block out all the sun's light. But it wasn't straightforward. The rate of increase of the array wasn't uniform, but inversely proportional to its size. In other words, the rate of growth became slower as the array grew bigger. To the scientists, this made perfect sense. As the array expanded, its surface area increased exponentially relative to its distance from the asteroid, meaning that the same surface area covered less distance the further it was from the asteroid. Assuming the exponential growth would continue, the calculations predicted they had about six months before the asteroid and its array blocked out all the sun's light. And heat.

The world was thrown into a cauldron of activity. Astronomers, physicists, chemists, biologists, scientists of every description worked around the clock deciding on the best way to communicate with the aliens. Politicians and governments formulated contingency plans and did their best to try and placate the public, a public that was getting increasingly restless and worried. Very worried. The military were busy devising plans to attack the asteroid, particularly its more vulnerable array. Everyone was busy doing something or other.

Along with hundreds of other scientists worldwide, the teams at Jodrell Bank were wrestling with the communication issue. What was the best way to try and make contact with the aliens?

'Just because we communicate using radio and TV,' said Frank, 'doesn't mean the aliens do. They could use other methods, other regions of the electromagnetic spectrum.'

'Frank's right,' said Rupert. 'Radio and TV waves only represent a tiny part of the electromagnetic spectrum, the long wavelength, low energy end. What if they communicate using other parts, such as microwaves, infrared or ultraviolet?'

'Or even the very high frequency end of the spectrum, the X-rays and gamma rays,' said Liz.

'And don't forget the visible region,' said Rupert. 'That's arguably the most important region of all, the region in the middle of the electromagnetic spectrum where the sun's output is greatest.'

'And the reason why eyes have developed to sense precisely that region,' said Viv.

'Absolutely,' replied Rupert.

'Do you think aliens have eyes?' asked Zak, digressing from the main task. 'I mean eyes similar to ours?'

'Almost certainly,' said Liz, drawing on her biological knowledge. 'Eyes have developed independently on Earth many times, biological devices to capture the sun's peak output of energy to aid the survival of the organism. And not just any old eyes, but camera eyes like ours. Did you know that an octopus, a creature that looks remarkably alien, has a camera eye just like ours?'

'No, I didn't,' said Zak.

'Well, it does. And since the energy profiles of stars are similar, at least those that last long enough for life to have developed, I'd be amazed if intelligent life on other planets didn't have eyes very similar to ours.'

'That's all very interesting,' said Viv, 'but let's focus on the task in hand. What are we saying about trying to contact them. What are you saying we should do?'

'Despite what's been said, radio and TV are still the most likely method of communication,' said Frank. 'Therefore, first and foremost we should bombard them with every possible radio and TV frequency containing information and pictograms about Earth and ourselves.'

'I agree,' said Viv, 'but we should focus on certain regions, like the natural frequency of hydrogen at 1421 MHz (MegaHertz), and the "Water Hole" between 1420 and 1640 MHz, the gap where space is relatively radio quiet.'

'We should transmit in the microwave too, even the infrared and visible,' said Rupert. 'The microwave region from 1,000 to 10,000 MHz has low cosmic background noise, and there are no natural infrared or visible lasers.'

'So,' said Liz slowly, 'if ever we detected red, green or infrared laser light emanating from deep space, it must be of alien origin?'

'Absolutely,' replied Rupert. 'That's why SETI teams have started searching for laser light in the Universe.'

'I didn't know that,' said Liz. 'You learn something new every day.'

It was Zak who asked the obvious question. 'What part of the electromagnetic spectrum do the transmissions from the meteorites use?'

'Good question,' said Frank. 'They use different frequencies for each transmission. Short pulses of energy in the radio, TV, "Water Hole" and the microwave regions, but different frequencies each time.'

'But not the visible or infrared?' asked Rupert.

'No. And nothing in the ultraviolet, X-ray or gamma ray regions either,' said Frank.

'Why pulsed transmissions?' queried Liz.

'Because a short, intense burst of radiation is the best way to transmit and encode data,' replied Frank.

'And,' added Viv, 'a narrow band width of less than 300 Hz distinguishes them from natural cosmic radiation which, apart from the radiation from hydrogen and the hydroxyl group (OH) in water, is broad.'

'But shouldn't we just focus on the frequencies they're using?' said Zak. 'Surely that makes the most sense.'

'That's what everyone's been doing,' answered Frank. 'On those and others in the same regions – the radio, TV and microwave regions. But so far without any response.'

'What if,' said Liz, gathering her thoughts, 'what if the aliens were "cruising" the galaxy and just happened to pick up the first radio transmissions from Earth. After all, we've been broadcasting ourselves unintentionally to the rest of galaxy for nearly 100 years, ever since the first radio broadcasts in the 1920s, followed by the first TV broadcasts in the 1940s.'

'Good point,' said Frank. 'That means the Earth's radiosphere, the area covered by the broadcasts, is about 200 light years. They could have picked them up and decided to investigate.'

'You mean they'd have picked up the BBC Overseas Service, The Archers and Desert Island Discs,' said Liz smiling.

'They would,' said Viv, 'and the broadcasts from World War II. I'm surprised it didn't put them off.'

'I'll bet they had a good laugh over Popeye, Mickey Mouse and The Munsters,' chimed in Rupert.

'And God knows what they'd have made of Coronation Street and Eastenders,' said Viv.

'And if they've seen the X-Factor, Big Brother and I'm a Celebrity, Get Me Out of Here,' said Frank, drawing curious looks from the rest, 'they must think we're bonkers.'

His comments brought chuckles from the others. Did a respected fifty-odd-year-old Professor really watch such inane TV programmes? They doubted it.

Liz spoke again. 'Do you think the aliens come from within a 100 light years of Earth?' she asked.

It was Frank who answered. 'It's unlikely. One hundred light years is tiny compared to the 100,000 light year diameter of the Milky Way galaxy, a drop in the ocean. I'd say they're from much farther away but picked up the signals when the asteroid, er, starship, entered the Earth's radiosphere.'

Liz's eyes lit up again. Her thought processes were in overdrive. 'I've just had another thought,' she gushed, the words tumbling out of her mouth like bullets from a machine gun. 'The Earth's radio noise increased rapidly as radio and TV became more and more popular, reaching a peak in the late 1960s. However, since then it has declined due to the spread of cable TV and fibre optics. And…'

'And directed communications, beaming and digital broadcasting,' interjected Frank, finishing the sentence for her. 'Compared to what it was, the Earth is now relatively radio quiet. Is that what you were getting at, Liz, that the aliens are so technically advanced that their planet, wherever it is, is radio silent?'

'Yes, it was,' said Liz, a little irritated by Frank's premature interjection. 'And,' she continued, 'I think that's why they sent the meteorite probes to gather information, so they wouldn't betray their presence on the asteroid.'

'Good thinking, Liz,' said Viv, pleased it was his protégé who'd come up with the idea. 'But why do you think they're maintaining radio silence now?'

It was a good question and one to which she didn't have a satisfactory answer.

'This is all very interesting,' said Viv, repeating his earlier comment, 'but we still haven't decided how to communicate with them? What are our recommendations? What frequencies should we use and what information should we send?'

'Well,' said Rupert, 'there's no need to send data about Earth or ourselves, they can see all that firsthand from their orbit around the Earth. They're only 100,000 miles away.'

'I disagree,' said Viv, remembering Rupert's blunt comments about his suggestion. 'It's not so simple. The Earth's atmosphere and the cloud cover make direct viewing difficult. I think we should include some pictograms of ourselves, our culture, our science, even our music. But the main message has to be: WHY ARE YOU HERE? They should have grasped our language by now and be capable of responding – if they want to. Indeed, they may even have picked up some of this information already if they encountered the Pioneer and Voyager spacecraft.'

'Possibly,' said Rupert, sensing that Viv was exacting some sort of revenge for his earlier outburst, 'but I still think...'

'I don't see any reason not to send it,' said Viv, cutting him off in mid-sentence. 'It can't do any harm.'

'No, it can't,' said Frank, sensing the tension between the two of them. 'Let's include it.'

'To summarise,' said Viv, 'we should focus on the frequencies used by the aliens with their meteorite transmissions, but saturate the rest of the radio, TV and microwave regions too. Also, we should try infrared and visible lasers. Do you all agree?'

'Yes,' said Rupert, 'but we'll have to tread carefully with the lasers. They might think we're attacking them.'

'Not if the lasers are used at low power,' replied Frank, doing his best to avoid another confrontation.

'We'll include that in our recommendations,' said Viv.

'If we're using light,' said Rupert, 'we may as well try sound.'

'Sound? What do you mean?' queried Viv.

'Send a range of musical notes, like in the film *Close Encounters of the Third Kind*. We've got nothing to lose.'

Eventually, after further discussions, they agreed their recommendations would be to send pictograms of humans, some science – the structures of DNA, hydrogen and water – some mathematics, like the Arecibo message which used the product of two prime numbers 23 x 73 = 1679 to generate a pictogram, and a musical message. But without a doubt, the two main messages should be: WHY ARE YOU HERE? and WE MEAN YOU NO HARM.

The final message triggered another thought in Liz's head. A horrible thought. 'You don't think they viewed the act of exploding 40 nuclear bombs right next to the asteroid as an act of aggression, do you?'

'That's an interesting point, Liz,' said Frank. 'I'd never thought of it like that.' None of them had.

'But why should they interpret trying to deflect an asteroid on course to destroy us as an act of aggression?' said Viv. 'After all, we didn't know it was a starship.'

'No, we didn't,' said Liz, 'but maybe all their starships look like asteroids. And we never tried to make contact, did we?'

'Why on earth would we try and make contact with an asteroid?' said Rupert, getting irritated at the way the discussion was going.

'Because it wasn't an asteroid, was it?' retorted Liz. 'It was a starship.'

Their old animosity was beginning to surface again.

'Okay, okay,' said Viv, calming the situation. 'Maybe we should have sent some signals, but everyone thought it was an asteroid, not a starship, including you, Liz,' he said, shooting her an icy glance. 'Let's leave it at that.'

'So are we all agreed?' continued Viv, bringing the discussion to a close, 'that we should send information about ourselves, our culture, science and mathematics on every possible radio, TV and microwave frequency and see what happens?'

'Don't forget the infrared and visible lasers,' said Rupert, 'and the music.'

'Ah, yes. They're all included,' said Viv, checking his notes, 'I just forgot to mention them.'

'Isn't music a sign of a civilised society?' asked Liz.

'Some people think so,' said Frank.

'Are these everyone's views?' asked Viv one final time, looking at Frank, Rupert, Liz and Zak. He wanted to be absolutely sure he'd got it right. The fate of the world hung in the balance. Four heads nodded their assent. 'Okay, I'll relay our findings to Carl. He's coordinating the work.'

A few days later, the transmissions were sent. And resent. Time and time again. From transmitting stations around the world. Transmissions not just in the radio region of the electromagnetic spectrum, but also in the microwave, infrared and visible. Over and over again. But there was no response. Just silence. A total, deafening silence.

Failure to communicate with the aliens prompted a flurry of activity. The world's leaders engaged in new discussions. Urgent, frantic discussions. Discussions addressing the key issues. Had the aliens come in peace? Were they simply taking their time to contact us? Were the solar panels really to provide energy or was there a more sinister motive? Were the aliens deliberately intending to block out all the sunlight, all the sun's life-giving rays, plunging the Earth into total darkness and making it a cold, dark, lifeless planet. Because that's what would happen. Without the sun's heat and light, all life would be extinguished. First, all the green plants. Green plants which depend on sunlight to survive, using the green pigment chlorophyll to photosynthesise glucose and oxygen from water and carbon dioxide. They'd be the first to go. All the grasses, all the trees, all the flowers. And all the food crops too. Wheat, corn, barley, potatoes, carrots, cabbages, cauliflowers… everything would perish.

And it wasn't just the land-based plants that would die. All the green phytoplankton in the world's oceans, the trillions of tiny organisms at the bottom of the marine food chain, would die too. The organisms that provide most of the world's oxygen. Oxygen essential for animal life. The lungs of the world. Extinguished.

As the plants died, the herbivores would follow quickly. Deprived of their food source, they would starve. The wild herbivores first. Elephants, rhinos, hippos, buffalo, wildebeest, zebra, giraffe, antelope, gazelle, deer… All would perish. Domestic herbivores would survive longer, sustained by stockpiles of hay and grain, but as these ran out, they too would die. Cattle, horses, sheep, pigs, chickens, turkeys. All would die.

Plants could still be grown indoors using artificial heat and light. Grown in giant greenhouses with fluorescent lighting. But only for a while. Only while the energy supplies lasted.

With the herbivores gone, the carnivores wouldn't last long. Deprived of their prey, predators such as lions, tigers, leopards, jaguars and cheetahs would starve. And, although we might survive a little longer, humans would perish too.

The last remaining life on Earth would be microbial. The tiny microscopic microbes invisible to the naked eye. The bacteria and viruses. In time, however, they too would die, leaving the Earth a cold, dark, lifeless void.

## 22

# ALIEN LIFE

The lull in proceedings as the world's leaders debated what to do presented Liz and her colleagues with a rare moment of quiet. A chance to relax and unwind from the stresses and strains of the past months. To sit and chat over a cup of coffee, just like they did in the old days, putting the world to rights. As she leaned back in the sumptuous leather armchair in the 'snug corner' of the canteen, Liz studied the man sat opposite, the man she liked so much, the man who'd recruited her at Jodrell Bank. The kind, caring, compassionate, thoughtful, intelligent man who reminded her so much of her late father.

'Liz,' said Viv, placing his mug of hot tea on the table between them, 'what do you think the aliens look like? Do you think they'll look humanoid, like the extraterrestrials depicted in the movies? You know, like the greys with their large heads and big eyes, or bipedal reptilians like the Romulans in Star Trek. Or even like ET (Extra Terrestrial) himself. Or will they be more like the monsters in the Alien and Predator films?'

Liz sipped her coffee and smiled before answering. Her colleagues knew she'd written a dissertation on alien life as part of her PhD. 'That's how most people visualise aliens,' she said, 'but that's got more to do with the power and influence of the movie makers rather than science. However, it might not be too far from the truth.'

'You mean they might look like that?' gasped Viv. 'Like humanoids I mean.'

'They might,' said Liz. 'Extraterrestrial life has always fascinated me. Intrigued me. That's why I did my doctorate in astrobiology. It's something I've thought about a lot. And read about too.

'A good starting point,' continued Liz, 'as to what extraterrestrials might look like, is to study the evolution of life on Earth.'

'Why's that?' said Viv, leaning forward in his chair. 'Tell me more.'

'Well,' continued Liz, 'one of the nice things about biology, and evolution for that matter, is that from really rather different starting points, in the tree of life, again and again, the same sort of solution arises. We call these universal characteristics, properties that are similar in species which are not closely related. For example, things like limbs – arms, legs and tentacles – eyes, flight and photosynthesis.

'There are parochial characteristics too, properties unique to one species, like an elephant's trunk or a panda's thumb, properties not found in any other species. But let's focus on the universal characteristics.

'Universal characteristics are so useful they've evolved many times in many forms. Eyes are a prime example. The ability to sense light is probably the most useful feature of any organism, so it's hardly surprising that eyes are common in many Earth species, often in radically different forms. Did you know that 96 per cent of animal species have eyes?'

'No, I didn't,' said Viv.

'Well, they do. The simplest eyes, like those of primitive worms, consist of just a few photoreceptors, nothing like enough to form an image but sufficient for the worm to distinguish light from dark. Then there's the compound eyes of insects, the parietal eyes of reptiles and the most advanced eyes of all, the camera eyes of mammals, including ourselves.'

Continuing, she said, 'At the molecular level, every eye in the world works the same way. Every one has a molecule that detects light – rhodopsin. As soon as light hits the rhodopsin molecule, it changes shape, causing its colour to change from pink to yellow. This change in structure triggers an electrical signal which ultimately goes all the way to the brain, where the signal is transformed into an image. It's this chemical reaction that's responsible for all vision on the planet. Molecules closely related to rhodopsin lie at the heart of every animal eye, which tells us that it must be a very ancient mechanism. Although we've been separated in evolutionary terms for over one billion years from a green algae called Volvox, we share one surprising similarity – the Volvox have light sensitive cells that control their movement and the active ingredient is a form of rhodopsin so similar to ours that we must share a common ancestor. That common ancestor is thought to be cyanobacteria, one of the first forms of life on Earth.'

'I'm amazed that the first photosensitive cells appeared so early, and even more amazed that they were used for movement rather than sight,' said Viv, enthralled by Liz's detailed knowledge.

'It's surprising, I know,' replied Liz, 'but eyes are complex structures that took tens of millions of years to evolve.

'Without eyes,' she continued, 'most organisms would die quickly. For instance, how long would a blind human last in the wild? Unable to see his surroundings, to find food or water, to sense danger, to see and evade predators, he would quickly perish. So would other blind animals. It's sad, but nature is cruel. Cruel to be kind. It has to be to ensure that only the fittest survive.'

Liz paused to take a sip of coffee. Viv did likewise, taking a huge gulp of tea. 'Please continue,' he said, still leaning forward in his comfy leather chair. 'I think I'm beginning to see where this is leading.'

'The driving force behind universal characteristics is convergent evolution,' said Liz. 'Convergent evolution describes how similar traits are acquired by totally unrelated lineages. I've already mentioned eyes as a prime example of convergent evolution but wings are another good example. The wings of bats – a mammal – and birds – theropods, descendants of dinosaurs – are just extensions of limbs, of arms, having extended fingers or claws covered by membranes or feathers. The shape of wings is determined by physics: they have to be a certain shape in order to fly, so evolution converges on those shapes. If it didn't, the wings wouldn't function and the creatures wouldn't fly. It's the same for eyes – there are only so many ways to sense light. Convergent evolution always progresses towards an optimal solution to fit the prevailing environment. In a way, it's a sort of determinism.'

'But there's another force at work too, isn't there, Liz?' said Viv. 'Contingency.'

'Yes, there is,' said Liz, surprised by Viv's knowledge of evolution. 'Contingency, or radical diversity, is the impact of random, unpredictable events on evolution. Events that dramatically change the course of evolution. In a way, it's the opposite of convergent evolution. But it isn't a case of one or the other. Both convergent evolution and radical diversity operate together.

'Perhaps the best example of radical diversity,' continued Liz, 'is the impact of the massive asteroid 65 million years ago which wiped out the dinosaurs, the dominant life form on the planet at that time.' She paused, looked at Viv, and said, 'Have you ever thought what would have happened if that asteroid hadn't hit the Earth?'

'It's crossed my mind,' said Viv, 'but no, I can't say I've thought deeply about it.'

'If that asteroid had missed the Earth,' said Liz, 'then most likely we wouldn't be here. Dinosaurs would be the dominant life on Earth and mammals would still be small fur balls living between the cracks of an ecosystem dominated by dinosaurs. Most likely they'd have developed intelligence and the world would be run by intelligent dinosaurs. Dinoman would rule the Earth.'

'It's a sobering thought that such random, unpredictable events have such a profound effect on the course of evolution,' said Viv. 'It's scary.'

'It is,' said Liz, 'and we see the same thing in the Cambrian explosion.'

'I know a bit about that,' said Viv, pleased by his smattering of knowledge on evolution. 'It's the explosion of life that occurred around 600 million years ago, isn't it?'

'It is,' said Liz, 'and it heralded the first appearance of an animal with a backbone. The first chordate. There must have been many early chordates but only one survived, the pikaia chordate, the ancestor of all creatures with backbones, including the dinosaurs and ourselves. Why? Why did pikaia chordates survive and not the others? Why did these fail and pikaia and its ancestors become us? We don't know. That's what's meant by radical diversity – there are no guarantees.'

Continuing, she said, 'The genus homo has only been around for approximately two million years and the reason we're in a mammal dominated world, not a dinosaur dominated world, is mainly because of the random, unpredictable event of an asteroid colliding with Earth. Determinism may dictate the shape and structure of eyes and limbs but that determinism can be changed in an instant by contingency, by radical diversity. Convergent evolution and radical diversity are in competition all the time and the direction evolution takes depends on which has the upper hand. The dinosaurs were optimally adapted for the conditions that existed 65 million years ago, but mammals, like us, are optimally adapted to the current conditions. It's all a bit of a lottery really.'

'So,' said Viv thoughtfully, 'if I've understood it correctly, convergent evolution produces universal characteristics, such as eyes, limbs and wings, that are extremely valuable to the organism, but such evolutionary pathways can be derailed, altered completely, by radical diversity.'

'Spot on,' said Liz. 'You've grasped it well.'

'And you think alien life will have developed along similar lines?' said Viv.

'The laws of physics, chemistry and biology are the same throughout the universe, so yes, I do. I expect to see similar trends in extraterrestrials. I expect them to have light sensing organs – eyes – skeletons to counteract gravity and stand upright instead of being a blob of matter, and I expect them to have limbs – arms, legs, tentacles and wings. In short, I expect them to have evolved physically optimal structures for sensing the environment, counteracting gravity and moving around. They'll probably have parochial characteristics too, suited to their own particular environment. Despite the randomness of evolution, they have to obey the same physical laws, so we'll probably recognise them quite easily when we see them. In fact, the humanoid and bipedal reptilian aliens depicted in the movies isn't too crazy after all.'

'What about intelligence? Is that a universal characteristic?' asked Viv.

'Intelligence is probably the most important characteristic of all to ensure the survival of an organism,' said Liz. 'Look at us, at homo sapiens. We currently dominate the planet because we're the most intelligent species. But intelligence requires a large brain. Not only have large brains evolved independently in totally unrelated species, for example in apes, dolphins, octopuses, even crows, but in each case their cognitive world – what they sense and see – is surprisingly similar to ours, which supports the view that thinking, or intelligence, will be the same throughout the Universe.

'What most people don't realise,' continued Liz, 'is that large brains developed in tandem with sight in order to process all that data. As I mentioned earlier, an octopus has a sophisticated camera eye like ours and, like us, it also has a large brain. In fact, an octopus is the most intelligent non-vertebrate.'

'I didn't know that,' said Viv.

Liz continued. 'The last common ancestor between ourselves and an octopus existed 600 million years ago, suggesting a tantalising link between sensory processing and the evolution of intelligence.

'But for one species, the desire to gather more and more sensory information has become overwhelming. That species is us. The increasing amount of data gathered by our senses drove the evolution of our brains and those increasingly sophisticated brains became curious and demanded more and more data. And so we built telescopes to extend our senses beyond the visible horizon and discovered a universe that was billions of years old and contained trillions of stars and galaxies. Our insatiable thirst for information has been the making of us.'

'That's fascinating,' said Viv, obviously impressed by Liz's knowledge and deductions, 'but will alien life be based on carbon, like Earth life is, or are there other possibilities?'

'Good question. Non carbon-based life is a favourite theme with science fiction writers,' said Liz, 'but carbon is unique. It's the most important of the four light elements essential for life, the famous CHON quartet – carbon, hydrogen, oxygen and nitrogen. It's the sixth element in the Periodic Table.* Its electron configuration gives it remarkable properties. Carbon can form single, double and triple bonds, combine with itself in a myriad of

---

\* Hydrogen is the first, nitrogen the seventh and oxygen the eighth

ways to form complex chains and rings, and with other elements, especially hydrogen, oxygen and nitrogen, to form countless millions, even billions, of molecules. No other element in the Periodic Table comes close to matching these properties.

'The molecules based on carbon, hydrogen and oxygen are the carbohydrates, the sugars and fats. Proteins and DNA use the same three elements plus nitrogen. Along with the two heavier elements, phosphorus and sulphur, these are the chemicals of life.'

'But what about silicon-based life, isn't that feasible?' asked Viv.

'Silicon is in the same Group as carbon in the Periodic Table,' replied Liz, 'so, like carbon, silicon also has four valence electrons in its outer shell, but its properties are quite different to those of carbon. Unlike carbon-carbon bonds, silicon-silicon bonds are weak, about half the strength of carbon-carbon bonds, so silicon can't form long complex chains or rings. Also, its bonds with other elements, such as hydrogen and oxygen, are also weak, meaning it can't form silicon analogues of carbohydrates, proteins or DNA. But there is one silicon compound which is very stable and very abundant. Silicon dioxide. Sand. Silicates are the most common minerals in the Earth's crust, but they are inorganic, not organic, molecules and are useless for life. So no, silicon-based life is extremely unlikely.'

'So we're stuck with good, old-fashioned carbon-based life then,' said Viv, draining the last dregs of tea from his mug.

'I'd say so,' replied Liz. 'I can't think of any other feasible alternatives.'

'That's been most enlightening, Liz. Thanks. But I've got one final question. Do you think the aliens will be peaceful?'

Liz hesitated before answering. 'No, I don't think they will,' she replied, trying desperately to remember a quote she'd once heard, a quote that disturbed her. Suddenly, it flashed into her head. 'Chances are,' she said, 'that when we meet intelligent life forms from outer space, they're going to be descended from predators.'

'What was that!' exclaimed Viv. 'What did you say?'

'It's a quote from Michio Kaku, an American physicist. And you know what, I think he's right.'

As they were getting up to leave, Viv suddenly remembered where the alien meteorites had landed. 'Liz, can life exist in extremely cold conditions?'

'I'm glad you asked me that,' replied Liz. 'A large part of my thesis was on life at the edge, about organisms that can survive, even thrive, under extreme conditions. These so-called extremophiles can survive in really harsh environments, including extremes of hot and cold, and...'

Liz's answer was cut short by Rupert entering the canteen. 'Frank wants us all to assemble in the meeting room. I think the world's leaders have reached a decision.'

# 23

# PLANS

Manhattan in the dark should have been a beautiful sight. The most iconic skyline in the world ablaze with a kaleidoscope of coloured lights. Wall Street skyscrapers, the Empire State building, the equally impressive Chrysler building and the Rockefeller Center, all shining like beacons in the night. But not tonight. The buildings were still there, they hadn't changed, but the lights had gone. Apart from a few dim specks emanating from the windows of inhabited apartment blocks, they stood in the gloom, forgotten relics silhouetted against a sombre, dark sky, like candles in the dark.

It was against this depressing backdrop that the world's leaders, top scientists and military experts gathered together for one last face-to-face meeting. One last chance to meet in person before international travel became impossible. One last chance to try and resolve the deepening crisis engulfing the planet. Here, at the UN (United Nations) headquarters on the east side of Manhattan, New York. In future, any such meetings would have to be held using videoconferencing.

The meeting began with the General Assembly, giving all the nations of the world a chance to participate, to express their views. Their concerns. But it didn't work. There were too many conflicting views, too many dissenting voices but, most of all, too much parochialism, with each country looking after its own interests. The main problem, however, was that 90 per cent of the countries represented had little to offer in the way of a solution. Few resources and even fewer, or no, technical capabilities. The world had done its duty by involving each nation but, after that first day, the remainder of the meaningful discussions were conducted by the UN Security Council, the small, powerful group of nations having the most advanced technology. Countries like the USA, Russia, Britain, France, Germany and China. These were the countries with the technological clout.

The meeting started off with good intentions but the gravity of the situation, coupled with the stresses and strains of the past few years, quickly got the better of some of the delegates. Tempers flared. Nerves were frayed. Heated exchanges took place. Accusations flew. Finger-pointing was rife. Why do countries find it so difficult to cooperate, to work together, even in times of impending doom?

'Is that the fucking best you can come up with?' spat the German Chancellor in her heavy Teutonic accent, glaring at the British delegation and thumping the table with her fist. She'd put up with obstructions and veto's from Britain on various EU (European Union) proposals for years, and now the anger and frustration came pouring out. Pouring out like a torrent. In a way, it was payback time.

The British Prime Minister met fire with fire. If the German Chancellor wanted to rant and rave, then so would she. 'At least we discovered the fucking things!' she shouted with venom. 'It's more than your lot did.'

'Please, ladies and gentlemen,' interrupted the President of the United States, 'this behaviour is getting us nowhere. Let's stop the accusations and finger-pointing and concentrate on the task in hand – to save our planet from destruction.'

His intervention had the desired effect, calming them down.

'We need to address the key questions,' he continued. 'Why are they here and what do they want? We've already tried, and failed, to communicate with them, so the question is: what do we do next?'

On that point there were splits and divisions, not only between the scientists and the military, but also between the hawks and the doves. The hawks wanted immediate military action, the doves a more measured, peaceful approach. Once again, heated, sometimes acrimonious, exchanges took place. Old animosities resurfaced. Even the clear and present threat of a common enemy couldn't unite the nations of Earth. At the end of the day, no matter how much they huffed and puffed, their options were limited.

Forty of the world's most powerful nuclear bombs exploded close to the asteroid had failed to destroy it, so attacking the asteroid itself was a *non sequitur*. The best option, they decided, was to send a single rocket, either manned or robotic, to the asteroid to try and instigate some direct, physical communication. The problem was, no robots existed that could take the place of a human being.

'Couldn't we send an unmanned rocket crammed with information about ourselves and our culture, and land it on the asteroid?' asked the French President. 'At least, if they shoot it down there's no loss of life.'

Everyone agreed the single rocket option was the least threatening to the aliens. If 40 rockets had had little effect, a single rocket posed no threat whatsoever. The majority of those present agreed.

'If that fails,' said the Russian President, 'we have no option but to send a manned rocket, a single rocket containing one or two brave cosmonauts.'

'Only if they don't destroy the first rocket. There's no point sending two astronauts to a certain death,' said the President of the United States, deliberately emphasising the word 'astronauts', the term used by Americans to describe people sent into space.

Once again, most of the delegates concurred.

They had to act fast. To find two brave humans to undertake what would be a one way mission. And to prepare the rocket. Their mission would be to land on the asteroid, gather whatever information they could, and try to communicate with the aliens. There'd be no return journey, unless the aliens possessed the technology, and the desire, to send them back. Under normal circumstances, volunteers for such a Kamikaze mission would be few and far between but, given the present circumstances... well, it offered a chance to die a meaningful death, an honourable death, doing something positive.

There were risks associated with such a strategy, of course there were. They knew that. The risk that the astronauts would be captured and interrogated by the aliens and subjected to extensive physical scrutiny, possibly even dissection and death. An intensive examination to discover everything they could about human physiology. But it was a risk worth taking. There were no other options anyway.

To placate both the Americans and the Russians, it was decided that one astronaut and one cosmonaut should be sent. These two countries had dominated the space race: no other countries came close to matching their experience in space exploration so it was only fitting that the volunteers should come from these two countries.

While preparations were made to get the manned rocket ready, the unmanned rocket was launched from the Kennedy Space Center in Florida. To everyone's relief, the launch was successful and the rocket wasn't destroyed. Eighteen hours later, it reached its destination, landing safely on the surface of the asteroid. They waited anxiously to see what would happen. Waited for a response. A response to the information, and questions, they'd sent, but none came. One day passed, two days, a whole week and still no response. The rocket remained precisely where it had landed. The aliens made no attempt to investigate it or to check its contents. It was time to send the manned rocket.

The ensuing days saw a frantic rush to get both the rocket and the two space travellers ready. To select the best examples of our culture, our science, our mathematics, even our music, and decide on the best way to convey that information. In the end, it was decided to display the data in digital form on laptops, but to take hard copies as back-up. The astronaut and cosmonaut underwent intensive training on how to conduct themselves, what to say and how to say it. And to explain to the aliens the damage they were inflicting on the planet and its people. Most of all, they needed to find out why they were here. What they were doing? What was their purpose? And to make it clear that the exploding of 40 nuclear bombs close to their starship wasn't an act of aggression, just an attempt to deflect a giant asteroid off its collision course with Earth. They needed to do all of that and relay the answers back to Earth.

Even at this late hour arguments raged. Trivial arguments such as which language to use. The Americans and most other nations favoured English, not because it was their own language, but because it was the language used in the early radio broadcasts, the language the aliens would have encountered as they entered the Earth's radiosphere.

'Why not Mandarin?' said the Chinese President indignantly. 'It's the most widely spoken language in the world.'

'Only because there are 1.3 billion Chinese,' retorted the American President, irritated by these trivial arguments. 'English is the universal language, the language spoken in most countries, not Mandarin.' And he was right. The Russians felt their language should be used too seeing they were sending a cosmonaut, but in the end, common sense prevailed and English was the language chosen.

Twelve days after the launch of the unmanned rocket, the rocket carrying the astronaut and the cosmonaut lifted off the launch pad for its 18 hour voyage. The world held its breath.

'Oh my God,' said Bubba Watkins to his Russian colleague, 'look at that. Just look at that. It's like a giant golf ball.'

As the rocket approached the asteroid, it did indeed look like a giant golf ball. A dark, grey-black golf ball. From a distance, its smooth but dimpled surface reminded Bubba of a grey-black version of the 'golf ball' at Epcot, only infinitely bigger and infinitely more sinister.

'You're right,' said Nikolov Spasky, 'it's gigantic, like a small moon.'

As the rocket got closer, they could see that the surface was composed of interlocking hexagonal panels, very large hexagonal panels. Strangely, there were no lights and no sign of any activity. Away in the distance, the unmanned rocket stood exactly where it had landed.

'What are those?' said Nikolov, straining his eyes trying to make out the dim shapes.

Bubba followed his gaze. 'They look like... dishes. Radio dishes. And those... spikes look like antennae,' he said, pointing to the profusion of spike-like protrusions emanating from one of the panels.

Bubba and Nikolov looked at each other. Both were thinking the same thought but it was Nikolov who spoke it. 'If they have radio dishes and antenna, why the hell haven't they responded to our signals?'

'I don't know,' said Bubba. 'I just don't know. But I don't like it.'

Houston was listening to their conversation. 'Is everything okay up there?' asked the senior controller.

'Yes, everything's fine,' replied Bubba. 'We're about to make preparations to land.'

'Is there still no sign of life? No lights? No activity?' asked the controller.

'Negative,' replied Nikolov.

'What about the fan-like array? Is it composed of solar panels?'

'We'd say yes, definitely,' replied Bubba, looking at Nikolov who was nodding his head in agreement. 'Giant solar panels. The engineering is fantastic, out-of-this-world. It's incredible.'

As they began manoeuvring the rocket into a position for landing, Nikolov noticed a small aperture in the centre of one of the panels. An aperture that was growing bigger.

'Houston, we have activity,' he said. 'An opening is appearing in one of the panels, and it's getting bigger.'

'Roger that,' replied Houston. 'Keep us informed Carpathia One.'

The aperture continued to grow in size, revealing an enormous, dark tunnel. A gaping black void. 'Do the aliens live in total darkness?' thought Nikolov. 'Surely not.' Suddenly, he felt something invisible tug on the rocket. Take control. He tried his damnedest to wrest control back, increasing the rocket's thrust to full power, but it was hopeless. Whatever force had taken hold, it was far stronger than the rocket's chemical engines.

'Houston, we have a problem,' he said, a message reminiscent of that sent by the astronauts on board the ill-fated Apollo 13 moon mission in 1970. 'We appear to have lost control of the rocket. We're in the grip of a powerful force, a sort of tractor beam. It's pulling us towards the opening.'

'Roger that,' said Houston. 'Is there nothing you can do?'

'Come in, Carpathia One,' said Houston. 'Come in.'

'Houston, we can't escape the...'

The signal ended abruptly as the dark tunnel engulfed the tiny rocket, like an elephant swallowing a gnat, and the aperture began to close.

Despite repeated attempts by Houston, there was no further contact with Carpathia One.

'I knew it. I just fucking knew that would happen,' said the spokesman for the military faction. 'We told you we should have attacked them.'

'Look,' said the President of the United States, 'we've tried a peaceful approach and it appears to have failed. So now, you have your chance.'

The military had discussed the options for days – there weren't many – and formulated a plan of action. It would be futile to attack the asteroid itself – it had already withstood the force of 40 nuclear bombs – so they'd focus on the more vulnerable fan-like array of solar panels. If they could destroy some of that – it was now too big to destroy completely – it might affect their power supply, a power supply that must surely be depleted after years travelling through interstellar space. The asteroid may be powered by nuclear fusion, or matter/antimatter, but internally, it would almost certainly be powered by electricity. And that would need replenishing. Recharging. They couldn't damage the asteroid itself, but they could disrupt its energy supply. The Earthlings could still bite.

They decided against sending dozens of rockets armed with nuclear warheads. They'd be intercepted and destroyed, and the resulting nuclear fall-out would contaminate the Earth. No, to increase their chance of success, messages should first be sent saying they were sending two more rockets in a final, peaceful attempt at communication. That way, there was less chance of them being destroyed. After all, they'd already allowed two rockets to reach the asteroid. One rocket would be loaded with the latest chemical weapons – a lethal poisonous gas and neurotoxins – and sent to the point where Carpathia One was swallowed up. The other, armed with a nuclear warhead, would be directed at the fan-like array. At the same time as the rockets unleashed their deadly payloads –

timing was crucial – lasers, both ground-based and satellite-based, the Star Wars technology initiated by Ronald Reagan, would be fired at the fan-like array. Hopefully, the rockets would distract the aliens, diverting their attention away from the lasers. In the best case scenario, both the rockets and the lasers would do their job. In the worst case scenario, well, they didn't want to think about that. Either way, the two brave astronauts were deemed expendable.

On the day of the launch, everyone was tense. The two rockets sat on their launch pads ready to go. One armed with chemical and biological weapons and one with a nuclear warhead. The lasers were powered up and ready to fire. All that was needed was the go-ahead from the Security Council. It came at 12 noon.

'Five, four, three, two, one, we have lift off,' said the controller. The engines burst into life and began to lift the two rockets off their launch pads. Slowly at first, then faster and faster as they disappeared into the dark sky, like two tracer bullets leaving a wispy, white vapour trail in their wake. A nervous 18 hours lay ahead.

As the two rockets approached the asteroid and prepared to unleash their deadly cargos, the lasers opened up. What happened next took everyone by surprise. The aliens' response was both immediate and deadly. Almost the instant the lasers switched on, they were destroyed. Destroyed by powerful bursts of radiation from the asteroid. The two rockets met the same fate, destroyed before they could unleash their deadly payloads. It was as if the aliens had anticipated what they were doing.

It had been a feasible plan, a well thought out plan, but it had backfired. Big time. They'd played their trump card, and failed. All they could do now was wait. Wait and see what the aliens would do. But time was running out. The Earth was getting colder and darker every day.

# 24

# LIFE AT THE EDGE

Silence. Complete and utter silence filled the room. Permeated the air like some invisible presence. They stared at the screen in disbelief. Moments earlier, two rockets were about to unleash their deadly payloads. Now they were gone. Blown to smithereens. Just a pile of debris floating in space. For an instant, they'd seen the lasers hit the array, but only for an instant, because they too had been destroyed. Extinguished. And with them the last realistic chance of averting the catastrophe looming over planet Earth.

They just stood there. All five of them. Liz, Rupert, Viv, Frank and Zak. Stood there in stunned, shocked silence. Stood there in the underground bunker that was the Simulation Chamber. Stood there harbouring their own, private thoughts. And a common feeling of complete hopelessness.

Gregg was in the Simulation Chamber too, but in a different room with the other chemists and biologists, no doubt experiencing the same emotions of shock and despair.

It was Viv who broke the silence. 'Well, that's the last throw of the dice. There's nothing more we can do now except wait. Wait and see what develops.'

'There must be something we can do,' said Rupert, angry at the failure of the mission. 'We can't just sit around twiddling our thumbs waiting to freeze to death.'

'No, we can't,' said Frank. 'It's not fair on the billions of people out there who are depending on us.'

Frank's last remark brought images of Baby Blu and Charlotte flooding into Liz's head. She tried her best to suppress her emotions, to stem the tears rolling down her cheeks, but to no avail.

'Are you okay?' asked Rupert, noticing her tears.

'I'm fine,' replied Liz, wiping away the tears with her hand. 'I was thinking of Baby Blu and Charlotte.'

'Don't worry,' said Rupert, putting his arm around her. 'It'll be alright. We'll think of something.'

Her mother had used the very same phrase when telling her of her father's illness. It wasn't alright then and it wouldn't be alright now.

'Do you think the aliens intend to block out all the sunlight,' said Rupert. 'Block out all the light and heat, plunging the Earth into total darkness and extreme cold, or will they let a little through, just enough to attain and then maintain their preferred temperature? Whatever that might be,' he added quickly.

'That's a good question,' said Frank, pondering what Rupert had just said. 'I suppose it depends on their intentions. If they want to extinguish all life on Earth, to sterilise it as a prelude to colonising it for themselves, then yes, they could very well block out all the sunlight for months, even years. That way, they'd be certain that all life on Earth would be dead. Exterminated. Then they would retract the array to allow just enough sunlight through to warm it back up to the temperature they prefer. Or,' he continued, 'they may decide to skip the total darkness stage and halt the expansion of the fan-like array when the Earth has reached their preferred temperature. That would save them a considerable amount of time but it wouldn't necessarily have killed off all life on Earth.'

'Can life exist in total darkness and extreme cold?' asked Viv, remembering his interrupted conversation with Liz.

All eyes focused on Liz. On the woman who was the expert, the specialist, on life in extreme conditions, at least in this group of people. She was the centre of attention. She'd always been intrigued by life at the edge, both on Earth and alien life. It was her favourite topic, the reason she did her PhD in astrobiology. She'd have to be careful not to go overboard, not to get carried away, to confine herself to answering the questions on the current situation. Not to digress. But it wouldn't be easy.

'The answer to your question is yes and yes. Life is very tenacious and very adaptable,' said Liz. 'There are organisms, called extremophiles, that have adapted to living, even thriving, in extreme environments, environments which include total darkness and extreme cold.

'Chemoautotrophs are creatures that live in total darkness. They're found in deep caves and in the depths of the ocean. Unlike green plants, which utilise sunlight and photosynthesis to provide food and energy, chemoautotrophs oxidise hydrogen sulphide and methane to provide their food and energy, a process known as chemosynthesis.

'Most creatures that live in the dark,' continued Liz, 'don't have eyes – they don't need them – and are generally white or pale-coloured. There's no point wasting precious reserves developing eyes or pigmentation if there's no light to see or to sense colour. Instead, they sense their surroundings by touch, developing extra long, extra sensitive limbs or hairs.'

'So, are you saying the aliens won't have eyes, that they'll be blind?' asked Zak.

'No, I'm not,' replied Liz. 'I think it would be very difficult for blind creatures to develop advanced technology. And anyway,

I don't think they live in total darkness. I think they're blocking out the sun's light and heat to make the Earth cold. The darkness is just a by-product.

'To answer the second part of your question,' she continued, looking at Viv, 'life can and does exist at very low temperatures. Cold temperatures are bad for most organisms. Freezing temperatures damage cells, both by superosmosis, which desiccates them, robs them of their water, and by the formation of ice crystals, which rupture them. Cold also increases viscosity, limiting the availability of both nutrients and waste products, which causes a build-up of waste that poisons the organism. Finally, cold temperatures cause cell proteins and enzymes to stiffen, inhibiting their function.'

'The exact opposite of what happens with men, then,' said Rupert, laughing, and winking at Viv, Frank and Zak. As the penny dropped, they all laughed, including Liz. Even in the darkest days, humans could still raise a smile. It was uplifting.

'Cold loving organisms are called psychrophiles,' continued Liz. 'They have adapted to life at low temperature by natural selection over multiple generations, developing flexible enzymes and proteins that act like antifreeze. They're found in glaciers, Arctic ice, snow and soil, and deep oceans.'

'Wasn't the meteorite you found in the ice cave near to some bacterial growth?' asked Viv. 'Was that a psychrophile?'

'Yes, it was,' replied Liz, 'and yes, the meteorite was found lying near to the bacterial growth.'

'Do you think the aliens landed it there deliberately?' continued Viv. 'Near to the bacterial growth, to study Earth life at low temperatures? Or do you think it was just fortuitous?'

'The latter,' said Liz. 'I think they wanted to find out about the conditions 75 feet below the surface – things like the temperature, the atmosphere and the light level – and to see if life existed under those conditions. I don't think they deliberately targeted that life.'

'Liz,' said Frank thoughtfully, 'were extremophiles the first form of life on Earth? The conditions on the primeval Earth were pretty harsh and extremophiles are the organisms that can survive in harsh conditions.'

'That's very perceptive, Frank,' replied Liz, 'and yes, many scientists believe that extremophiles were the first forms of life, but not psychrophiles. They believe that thermophiles, the heat loving extremophiles, could have been the first form of life on Earth. High temperatures are bad news for most organisms. They degrade the green pigment chlorophyll, stopping photosynthesis, an effect seen in the kitchen when cooking green vegetables – the green colour disappears. The vegetables are blanched. Heat denatures proteins, causing them to stop working, an effect seen when eggs are fried. The change in colour from clear to white is a clear sign of denaturing, the unwinding of the proteins. Heat also decreases the amount of carbon dioxide and oxygen in water, making them less bioavailable. Over billions of years, thermophiles have evolved proteins and enzymes that work at high temperatures by successive mutations and natural selection. Thermophiles can live at temperatures above the boiling point of water (100°C), the sort of temperatures found near deep hydrothermal vents at the bottom of the ocean, and it's here that life, protected from the harsh surface of the young Earth, is thought to have begun. The hydrothermal vents are thought by many to be the cradle of life.

'Until the 1970s,' continued Liz, 'it was thought that psychrophiles and thermophiles, indeed all the extremophiles, were prokaryotic bacteria, the simplest form of life. These mainly single-celled organisms lack both a nucleus and cell membrane, in contrast to the eukaryotes, organisms whose complex cells contain both a nucleus and a cell membrane, and on which nearly all present life is based. But DNA evidence showed that the extremophiles were not really bacteria at all, but a new class of life, which they called archaea. And it's the archaea which could well have been the earliest form of life on Earth. Indeed, DNA traces support that view, showing that prokaryotes tend to be more heat tolerant than eukaryotes. It's thought that as time passed and the conditions on Earth became more comfortable for life, some of the archaea evolved into eukaryotes.'

'I presume the organisms that live in hot springs and geysers are also archaea,' said Frank.

'Yes, they are,' said Liz.

'Are extremophiles a rarity? Are they just a niche form of life which only exist in a few exceptionally hot and exceptionally cold spots on Earth?' asked Rupert.

'That's what most people think,' said Liz, 'but they're wrong. Overall, extremophiles may constitute one third of the Earth's biomass.'

'Wow!' exclaimed Rupert. 'I thought there were just tiny pockets of such organisms. I'm amazed.'

Frank changed the topic. 'I know the 40 nuclear bombs exploded near the asteroid didn't do much physical damage, but what about all that radiation? It must have penetrated the asteroid. Surely that must have had some effect on the aliens?'

'If the aliens are carbon-based life forms, which I think they are, then quite possibly,' said Liz. 'Ionising radiation is hazardous to life. It changes DNA. If the change is minor, caused by a low dose of radiation, the DNA can repair itself, but a large dose of radiation, a lethal dose, results in death. Intermediate or non-lethal doses result in mutations.'

'What kind of doses are we talking about here?' asked Rupert.

'The radiation dose is the energy absorbed per kilogram of body mass,' said Liz. 'To give some examples, a medical X-ray is approximately 0.002 joules per kilogram, and the background radiation we're exposed to on the surface of the Earth is 0.0003 joules per kilogram per year, an extremely low figure. For humans, a dose of 10 joules per kilogram is lethal, but it takes six times that amount, 60 joules per kilogram, to kill an E Coli bacterium.'

'So a little bug is more resistant to radiation than we are? That really makes me feel good,' said Rupert sarcastically.

'And the radiation from the nuclear explosions…' continued Frank.

'That will have been very high for a very short period of time,' said Liz.

'But obviously not high enough to have killed them,' said Frank.

'Not yet, anyway,' said Liz. 'But it could have damaged their DNA, provided that's what they have, and caused longer term damage.'

'Like cancer,' said Rupert.

'Yeah, like cancer,' said Liz.

'But they could be resistant to radiation,' continued Liz. 'Some organisms have developed a very high resistance to radiation. For instance, some of these so-called radioresistant extremophiles can survive doses of 5,000 joules per kilogram, 500 times more than the lethal dose for humans. Some can even absorb up to 15,000 joules per kilogram with a 37 per cent viability. In other words, 37 out of 100 would survive such a dose.

'The reason that radioresistant extremophiles can survive such high doses of radiation,' she continued, 'is because they possess very efficient DNA repair mechanisms and because they carry four to ten copies of their genome, not just one like we do. So, if one, or two or even more copies are destroyed, they have several more back-up copies to replace them. They are such tough little beggars that they've been given the nickname Conan the Bacterium, after the tough character Conan the Barbarian played by Arnold Schwarzenegger in a film of that name. In fact, they're so resistant to radiation they could be used to transport life through space.'

'That's fascinating, Liz, absolutely fascinating,' said Rupert, intrigued by what she'd just said. 'Do you think the aliens are radioresistant?'

'I don't know, but if they've been inveterate space travellers, they could have developed such resistance.'

'Well, one thing's for sure,' said Viv. 'If we ever wipe ourselves off the face of the Earth with a nuclear war, there's no doubt who the survivors will be.'

'You're right,' said Liz, 'the radioresistant extremophiles and the endoliths.'

'The what!' exclaimed Rupert.

'The endoliths,' said Liz. 'Organisms that live inside rocks and between mineral grains. They've been found as deep as three kilometres below ground. Not surprisingly, most are chemoautotrophs that only reproduce about once a century.'

'And I thought my sex life was poor,' said Rupert smiling.

Liz smiled too and carried on. 'That's not the only surprising fact about endoliths. Even more surprising is that the total biomass of endoliths could exceed that of all surface life!'

'Are there any conditions on Earth where life can't survive?' asked Frank, amazed by the versatility and sheer tenacity of life to adapt to almost any environment.

'In theory yes, in practice no,' said Liz. 'The one requirement that life definitely needs is water. We don't know of any life that can exist without liquid water. One of the driest places on the planet is the Atacama desert in northern Chile. It's so dry that the Viking 1 and 2 expeditions to Mars practised in the Atacama desert in 2003. As expected, they didn't find any life in the top 10 cm of desert, but did find viable bacteria at a depth of 30 cm. So, even in the driest places, if there's just a microscopic amount of water, as there was 30 cm below the surface in the Atacama desert, life can gain a foothold.'

'Isn't that what the Earth's becoming now, a dry, barren planet?' said Rupert.

'Yes, it is,' replied Liz, 'another factor that will aid the extermination of life.'

All the talk about liquid water triggered a thought in Viv's head. 'Could the interior of the asteroid be full of water?' he asked. 'Like a giant goldfish bowl. Could the aliens be an aquatic species, an intelligent, advanced aquatic species that live in water? After all, a lot of the meteorites fell in the sea.'

'You mean like a super intelligent dolphin or octopus?' said Rupert.

'I was thinking more along the lines of an aquatic humanoid, but who knows,' replied Viv.

'I think a lot fell in the sea because 70 per cent of the planet is covered in water,' said Liz, 'not because the aliens directed them there, and it's possible they're an aquatic species, but it wouldn't be top of my list. However, we shouldn't rule it out. After all, life on Earth originated in the oceans, in the salty seas, and some scientists believe that life existed in the salty seas of the early Mars, and may exist in the salty seas of present-day Europa.

'To conclude,' said Liz, quite enjoying her time in the spotlight, 'extremophiles are also known that thrive in conditions of high salinity, like the Dead Sea and the Great Salt Lake in Utah, high acidity – even in conditions resembling battery acid – and high alkalinity. In fact, life can exist almost anywhere.'

'That's all very interesting,' said Viv, 'but will it help us defeat the aliens?'

'It might,' said Liz. 'It just might.'

# 25

# THE DARK FREEZE

If the creeping darkness wasn't enough to chill the bones, the freezing cold certainly was. The increasing lack of sunlight caused the temperature to plummet. People struggled just to keep warm. It wasn't just a cold snap, a short, sharp spell of exceptionally cold weather. Such events were commonplace. This was a cold snap without end. A cold snap that was getting colder by the day. Already the average temperature had plunged to minus 30°C, as cold as an Arctic winter, and it was continuing to drop. People wondered how much colder it would get. They didn't know. But the scientists did. Not precisely, because that depended on a number of factors, but approximately. Once all the sun's light had been blocked, the temperature would eventually drop to a mind-boggling minus 140°C, similar to the temperature on the dark side of the moon, another place untroubled by sunlight. To put that in perspective, the coldest temperature ever recorded on Earth was minus 89.2°C at Vostock, Antarctica on July 21 1983 and the coldest temperature in the Universe, the coldest temperature possible, is minus 273°C, absolute zero. It was a frightening prospect.

People panicked. They rushed to buy warm clothes. Clothes normally used for extreme weather were worn inside their homes to keep them warm. Within weeks, shops, stores and supermarkets were stripped bare, not only of warm clothing but of blankets and duvets too. Duvets with the highest TOG (derived from the Roman word toga for garment) ratings went first, followed quickly by every single item which could be used to help people keep warm. To stave off hypothermia. And death. Blankets, rugs, towels, even curtains. What they couldn't buy, they looted. Shops everywhere were emptied. Denuded of stock. People were desperate.

As the cold and darkness bit deeper, the government rationed vital supplies. Priorities were assigned. Top of the list was energy. Energy supplies were strictly controlled. The amount of electricity, gas, oil and coal which households were allowed was reduced dramatically and diverted to places such as power stations. It was absolutely essential that power stations continued to function. Continued churning out electricity, electricity vital for producing light and heat. Light and heat that we'd come to take for granted. Oil, gas and coal earmarked for other uses was also diverted to power stations. They were the top priority.

Critics of the 'Green Movement' had a field day. What use were windfarms and solar panels now? No sun, no solar power. No sun, no weather. No weather, no wind. They were as useful as a snowball in hell. Why hadn't successive governments invested more in nuclear power? Hadn't they foreseen a scenario such as this? Probably not. The 'Greens' could argue all they wanted about 'clean' energy and protecting the environment but, at the end of the day, they ignored the facts. Ignored an inconvenient truth. The entire Universe, everything, is powered by nuclear energy. By nuclear fusion. It's the process that powers every star in every galaxy. It is the ultimate energy source. Although we don't yet have the technology for nuclear fusion – except in destructive hydrogen bombs – nuclear fission isn't a bad second option.

As well as power stations, the government also prioritised hospitals – at least they didn't abandon the sick and infirm –

food production – people needed to eat – and water supplies – they needed to drink too. But it wasn't easy. The challenges were enormous. Reservoirs had frozen over, as had most of the mountain streams and rivers that supplied them with fresh water. The government did its best trying to run the country as near to normal as possible, at least at the beginning, but it was extremely difficult. They were fighting a losing battle.

As the power cuts became more severe, people reverted to the old-fashioned ways of keeping warm. They purchased paraffin heaters and wood burning stoves, even braziers, to provide their warmth. Barbecues were brought inside. Candles became a necessity to provide light, and a little heat, for when the power was off. Families huddled together in a single room to conserve precious energy supplies. To eke out what little energy was left. As the supplies of paraffin, coal and wood ran out, they resorted to cannibalising their homes and gardens.

Gardens were attacked first. Garden sheds, summerhouses, gazebos and pagodas were broken up, fences torn down, decking ripped up, and the wood used as fuel to provide vital heat and light. When this supply had been exhausted, they turned to their homes. Wooden chairs and tables were broken up and burned. Wooden banisters, wardrobes, kitchen units, all broken up and burned. Even treasured pieces of furniture, precious family heirlooms, were broken up and burned just to stay alive. Nothing was spared.

The burning of all these fossil fuels exacerbated another problem: it used up oxygen, oxygen that was no longer being replenished.* Without the photosynthesis of green plants, the world's supply of oxygen was diminishing, being consumed

---

\* It created carbon dioxide too, the greenhouse gas, but that didn't matter. Without sunlight, there was no greenhouse effect, an effect that would have been most welcome under the current circumstances.

by animals and the burning of fossil fuels, as well as by natural phenomenon such as volcanoes and forest fires. Due to the lack of light and rain, the dry, dead vegetation was like a tinder box, just waiting to catch fire.

Scientists monitoring the oxygen level in the atmosphere noticed a decrease, but a decrease so small that it would have no discernible effect in the short term. However, if it continued to decrease, then in the long term the oxygen level would reach a critical value. But that didn't matter. Long before that point was reached, all life on Earth would be dead.

As the dark freeze intensified, fuel rationing became more strict. More severe. More controlled. The frozen seas – the sea ice was over three feet thick – made shipping impossible. Oil tankers couldn't sail, couldn't deliver their precious supplies of oil. Inland, on the large land masses of Arabia and Russia, the temperature was so low that the oil in the pipelines froze. Restocking the declining oil reserves was impossible.

Ships were stranded in mid-ocean, locked in a sea of ice. Cargo ships and luxury liners which had failed to reach port before the oceans froze over. Some of the crew and passengers were rescued by helicopter, but not many. Fuel was getting too scarce to mount repeated rescue operations and the intense cold made flying hazardous. The temperature was so low that petrol, and especially diesel, were beginning to freeze. Most of those on board were left to die a slow, painful death marooned in a sea of ice.

Dwindling petrol and diesel reserves were controlled ruthlessly by the government. Armed soldiers with instructions to 'shoot to kill' guarded the oil refineries, plus those petrol stations that hadn't run dry. Priority was given to the armed forces and the emergency services; the police, ambulance and fire service. Public transport received a little fuel, but not much, just enough to maintain a restricted service. Private transport got none. Cars were banned, as was air travel, except for the Royal Air Force and medical helicopters. In effect, all travel ceased.

In a way it didn't matter. With a temperature of minus 30°C and dropping, fuel was beginning to freeze, or at least become mushy and unusable. Diesel-powered vehicles were affected first. Unfortunately, most commercial vehicles – trucks, vans, buses, even trains – run on diesel, a fuel which freezes between minus 6°C and minus 18°C, depending on its composition. However, diesel powered vehicles equipped with fuel heaters or diesel containing special additives to lower its freezing point can and do operate at low temperatures. Lorries in Alaska and other cold climates function at temperatures as low as minus 46°C using these techniques, and such vehicles were the only ones useable in the dark freeze. Petrol driven vehicles are useable down to minus 60°C, the temperature at which petrol begins to freeze, but were of little use – they were mainly cars and cars were banned – but it gave the government time to convert some of the commercial vehicles to petrol, to use when the diesel ran out.

The cessation of travel caused great heartache. Families were disrupted, split up, unable to spend whatever time was left together. Husbands stranded abroad on business trips. Relatives scattered around the country. Grandparents, many living alone, deprived of seeing their grandchildren one last time. Families everywhere unable to spend their final moments together.

The curfews imposed at the start of the crisis to prevent looting and killing were no longer necessary. The extreme cold meant that venturing outside was suicidal. Temperatures of minus 40°C froze the eyeballs in seconds. Even fully protected, staying outside for more than a few minutes invited death. People were prisoners in their own homes. The homes that would become their tombs.

As time passed, the food and water shortages became acute. The inability to farm crops and livestock due to the frozen fields and the absence of grass caused massive problems. Indoor food production was cranked up but provided just a fraction of the food that was needed. Over 99 per cent of the world's food is grown and reared in the great outdoors. Domestic animals kept alive in gigantic indoor farms supplied a trickle of meat to the fortunate few, but as the cattle, sheep, pigs and chickens were slaughtered, meat, both of the red and white variety, became a rarity.

It wasn't just meat that was scarce, food in general was scarce. Wheat, grain, vegetables and root crops were all running out. Even bread and butter was becoming a luxury. The food shortage was so bad the government advised people to have their pets put down. Put down to save precious food supplies. Some families ignored the advice but some went one step further. Starved of meat, not only did they kill their precious cats and dogs, cats and dogs they'd come to love, cats and dogs that were part of the family, they ate them too. Eating dog and cat meat was better than the alternative. Starvation and death.

If food is essential for life, water is absolutely vital. A person can survive for weeks, even months, without food, but without water, they die within days. Supplying water had become a problem. Like the fresh water lakes and the oceans, reservoirs had frozen. But not completely. Water displays its maximum density at 4°C, a fact which ensures that the water at the bottom of ponds and reservoirs never freezes, a fact essential for aquatic life. And a fact which meant that water could still be transported from the bottoms of reservoirs to the water treatment plants in underground pipes. But, as the temperature continued to drop, the water in the water treatment plants froze. Eventually, the only reliable source of fresh water was from underground wells and aquifers. It was better than nothing but certainly not enough to sustain the entire population. Mobile standpipes from specially heated lorries supplied a limited amount of water to desperate households, but even that ceased as the temperature became too cold for people to venture outside.

The extreme cold caused another problem: the sewage works froze, meaning that people could no longer use their toilets. In the past, before indoor toilets became the norm, people 'did their business' in a poe, a round, ceramic bowl with a handle, stored under the bed. It was emptied in the outside toilet the following morning. Hardly hygienic, but that's the way it was. Nowadays, poes are extinct so, with the toilets out of action, people did their business in buckets, or washing up bowls, even cooking pans, throwing the excrement and urine into the garden, where it froze instantly. At least the extreme cold had one benefit: it prevented diseases. And smells.

Ironically, the countries coping best with the dark freeze were those like Iceland, countries with an abundance of geothermal hot springs. Unlike other countries, which relied on coal, oil, gas or nuclear power, the hot springs supplied all of Iceland's heating and hot water.

The dark freeze changed the weather patterns completely. No sun to evaporate water from the oceans meant no water vapour in the atmosphere. No water vapour in the atmosphere meant no clouds. No clouds meant no rain. The last remaining water vapour in the atmosphere fell as snow and hail but once that was gone, nothing fell from the sky. No snow, no rain, no hailstones. Nothing. The Earth was a frozen, dry, barren wasteland. It was like the beginning of an ice age. A dark ice age.

The government provided whatever shelters they could for the poor and homeless to give them some respite from the freezing conditions. And small rations of food and drink. But the sick and weak died quickly. As the food ran out, the survivors faced a stark choice. Starve and die, or resort to cannibalism and live, at least for a little longer. It was a difficult choice. A personal choice. Some chose to starve and die. What was the point of eating a dead person if it only delayed the inevitable? But some did eat the dead. There was no right or wrong, just a decision on when to die.

Families too faced the same stark choice. Should they eat those who'd died? Their mothers? Their fathers? Their children? Their brothers or sisters? Their grandparents? Eat their loved ones in order to live a little longer? Or should they accept their fate and die with dignity? Eating a stranger was one thing but eating a loved one was completely different. Eating your own flesh and blood proved abhorrent to the majority of families: most chose to die with dignity.

Millions died. Of thirst. Of hunger. Of hypothermia. Of a combination of all three. But at least the cold prevented the bodies from decomposing and causing disease. It was as if they were stored in a deep freeze.

The government, both national and regional, moved into the underground bunkers designed specifically for such emergencies. Moved in with others deemed necessary for the survival of the human race. Scientists, engineers, doctors, surgeons, nurses, dentists, industry leaders… The teams at Jodrell Bank, Viv's team and Frank's team, moved to the relative safety of the Simulation Chamber, cocooned from the outside world in an underground tomb.

Liz was in turmoil. She'd vowed to spend her last days with Baby Blu and Charlotte. And with Gregg too. But what about Rupert? She still hadn't decided between them. But time was running out. Viv and Frank wanted her to stay with them. With the team. To work until the last moment to try and find a solution. A way to save planet Earth. Rupert wanted her to stay as well. Of course he did. But they didn't pressurise her. Didn't try to force her to stay. They knew how much she loved her little sister and young niece. They left the decision to her.

What should she do? If they were all going to die, she preferred to die with Baby Blu and Charlotte. Of that she was sure. But if there was the slightest chance of saving planet Earth – and with it Baby Blu and Charlotte – she wanted to be part of that too. But she couldn't do both. It was one or the other.

Liz agonised over her decision for days. What really annoyed her was that an elite few were deemed worthy of saving – at least for the time being – but the vast majority, including her little sister and niece, were deemed expendable. Unworthy of saving. Abandoned and left to die. She thought it grossly unfair. And unethical. Who had the right to play God? If there was a God, which she very much doubted, it should be him and him alone who made such decisions, not the government.

As they sat huddled together in Baby Blu's small apartment near Chester, Liz, Baby Blu and Rob clasped their hands around their hot mugs of coffee as they watched Charlotte play with her dolls. They didn't know which was best; to drink the coffee quickly and let the hot liquid warm their insides, or drink it slowly, letting the hot mug warm their hands. It was a trivial decision compared to the one she had to make; whether to spend her last days with the team at the Simulation Chamber or with her little sister and young niece.

Fuel was so scarce that this was the last time she'd be able to visit her family. Her final chance to make her decision. The army driver was outside, waiting in his specially heated jeep. She'd been allowed one hour, and half of that had gone.

Gregg had already made his decision: he was staying at the Simulation Chamber with the rest of the team. So were Viv, Frank, Rupert and Zak. For Rupert and Zak, the decision was easier to make. They were young, single men with no family ties. But for Viv and Frank, it must have been the most terrible, heart-breaking decision of their lives. Both had families. Wives and children. She didn't know how they'd arrived at their decision, but it must have been awful. Saying goodbye to those you love the most knowing that you'd probably never see them again must have been absolute torture. But it was a decision she was going to have to make in the next 30 minutes.

In a way, Gregg staying at the Simulation Chamber made her decision simpler. At least she didn't have to make her choice between Gregg and Rupert now. Both were at the Simulation Chamber. However, what she had to do was decide whether to stay here with her family in Chester, with Baby Blu and Charlotte, or go back to Gregg, Rupert and the rest of the team at the Simulation Chamber.

'Come and play, mummy,' shrieked Charlotte. 'Come and play dolls.'

'In a moment, darling. When mummy's finished her coffee.'

'Okay mummy,' said Charlotte, clearly disappointed that her mummy couldn't play right away. 'But please hurry up and drink your coffee. Pleeeease,' she pleaded, drawing out the word, 'please hurry up and play.'

Liz didn't know whether to laugh or cry. 'Oh to be young again,' she thought. 'Young and innocent with not a care in the world, shielded from the harsh realities of life. Completely oblivious to the impending disaster that was about to engulf them all.'

'She's so lovely,' said Liz, embracing her little sister as she watched her young niece cuddle her dolls. 'And cute. You should be so proud.'

'We are, aren't we Rob?' said Baby Blu, holding his hand. 'We both are.'

'Yes, we are,' he said, 'very proud.' Tears filled his eyes as he watched his three-year-old daughter cuddle her dolls, waiting impatiently for her mummy to finish her coffee.

Liz paused for a moment, trying to find some courage before speaking. 'Blu, I've been thinking...'

Blu put her hand over her elder sister's mouth, looked her in the eye, and said, firmly, 'Look Liz, we know how much you love us. We always have. And we love you. Very much. But staying here achieves nothing. We'd love you to stay, of course we would. You know that. But as long as there's the faintest chance of averting this disaster, it's better if you're at work helping your team. Helping Gregg and the others end this… this dark freeze. Please Liz, do it for us. For me and Charlotte. Please Liz.'

Tears streamed down the faces of both Liz and Baby Blu. They both knew what she'd said was true, that it was better if she was back at the underground bunker trying to find a way to end this nightmare. But how could she leave the people she loved the most to die a slow, painful death while she lived? It wasn't right. She was facing the most difficult decision of her life, of anyone's life, and time was running out. Her heart implored her to stay with her family, but her head told her to go back to the Simulation Chamber. When feeding the squirrels, her heart had won the day. This time, her head prevailed.

'You're right,' she said hoarsely, her voice choking with emotion. 'You're right,' she repeated. 'I should be at work helping my colleagues.' She hugged her sister so tightly Blu thought she was going to break her ribs, kissed her tenderly on both tear-stained cheeks, and said, 'I love you so much. And you too, my little princess,' she continued, bending down and hugging and kissing Charlotte.

She hugged and kissed Rob, turned on her heels and virtually ran to the door. Tears streamed down her face. 'I love you. I love you all,' she blubbered, disappearing through the door.

'Are you okay?' asked the army sergeant noticing Liz's distress.

'I'm fine, thanks,' replied Liz, wiping the tears from her face with a handkerchief. 'Just a little emotional, that's all.'

'Have you made your decision?' he asked in a quiet, understanding voice.

'Yes, I have,' said Liz. 'Take me back to the underground bunker please.'

# 26

# ACTIVITY

The failure of the mission cast a sombre mood over the entire world. Everyone was despondent. In the depths of despair. Even the most optimistic were melancholy.

The fan-like array had continued to expand for a further six days since the abortive attack, and then stopped. Stopped as abruptly as it had started. Stopped before it blocked out all the sun's light. And heat. The temperature had dropped to minus 60°C, much colder than an Arctic winter, leaving the Earth a dry, barren, frozen planet.

'Is this their ideal temperature?' asked Viv, 'or the temperature they think will have killed off all the life?'

'The former, I would think,' said Liz. 'They must know that life can exist below minus 60°C, especially if they come from a cold planet.'

'Do you think their planet has become uninhabitable and they're seeking a new home?' asked Frank.

'They could be,' said Liz. 'Who knows.'

'Hey, look at this!' shouted Rupert excitedly. 'Come and look at this!' Liz, Viv, Frank and Zak dashed over to the screen where Rupert was sat. 'There,' he said, jabbing the screen with his finger.

'There,' he repeated, 'right in the centre of that hexagonal panel. Can you see it?'

They could. Right at the centre, a pinprick, a tiny aperture had appeared. An aperture that was growing steadily bigger. After about 30 seconds, it stopped. They watched in hushed silence, their eyes glued to the hole on the screen. And waited. Waited for the next development. At first, nothing happened. No movement, no lights. Nothing. Then, suddenly, they saw it. Something was emerging from the hole. It looked like a… a pear-shaped object. A spacecraft similar in shape to the meteorites but more pointed at the narrow end. A pear-shaped spacecraft heading towards Earth.

## Part 5
· · ·
# END GAME

Chances are, when we meet
intelligent life forms in outer
space they're going to be
descended from predators

Michio Kaku

# 27

# SCOUTING MISSION

Around the world scientists huddled in groups, their eyes glued to the scout ships on the screens, watching in awed silence as they made their short journey to Earth. There were five in total, heading, they presumed, for the sites where the meteorites landed; the Arctic, Alaska, Siberia and the Himalayas in the northern hemisphere, and the Antarctic in the southern hemisphere. As the scout ships entered the Earth's atmosphere, tracking stations across the planet lost contact due to the intense static. The brief lull provided Viv with an opportunity to ring his counterpart in the US.

'Hi Carl, it's Viv. I've got a proposition for you.'

'Go on,' said Carl.

'If you agree, we'd like to focus our attention on the, er, scout ship in the Arctic, while you focus on the one in Alaska, but we need one of your reconnaissance satellites to provide detailed, close-up images. Is that okay?'

'That's fine,' replied Carl. 'I was thinking the same thing myself. Like you said, it's best if we each focus on just one ship; you on the one in the Arctic and ourselves on the one in Alaska. I think that's where two of them are headed.'

'Excellent,' said Viv. 'We'll keep you informed.'

'Likewise,' said Carl. 'Good luck.'

'You too,' said Viv, replacing the receiver.

Other teams followed the progress of the remaining three scout ships. The Russians followed the one that landed in Siberia, the Chinese and Japanese focused on that which landed in the Himalayas, and an international team tracked the one in the Antarctic.

As contact with the scout ship heading for the Arctic was re-established, the satellite tracked its descent to the region where Liz's team found the meteorite in the ice cave. They watched as the scout ship slowed down in readiness for landing, watched as it made its final descent.

'Whatever method of propulsion they're using,' said Frank, 'it's certainly not chemical. There's no sign whatsoever of any exhaust flames.'

As the ship neared the snow-covered ice, four short, stubby protuberances emerged from the rear of the ship. Landing legs. Landing legs with large disc-like attachments at the end, presumably to spread the weight of the ship. They watched as the ship descended the last few feet slowly and smoothly before settling effortlessly on the snow.

Everyone stared at the screen. And waited. Waited for a first glimpse of... Liz took a sharp intake of breath as the circular hatch at the bottom of the ship suddenly dropped down, catching them by surprise. 'That wasn't very subtle, was it?' said Liz. Almost immediately, a geodesic-shaped object about two feet in diameter, a robot of some kind Liz presumed, emerged from the open hatch and hovered in mid-air between the ship and the ground. Once again, no flames were apparent. Suddenly, without any warning, the geodesic-shaped 'hovercraft' zoomed off into the distance, skimming the ground at great speed before disappearing from view. At the same time, a second geodesic-shaped 'hovercraft' emerged before it too sped off. The process was repeated twice more, with each geodesic-shaped 'hovercraft' heading off in a different direction.

'Well,' said Viv, 'they certainly like their geodesic shapes.'

'It looks like they've gone north, south, east and west,' said Frank, 'probably to gather information and samples.'

'Do you think one will go down the ice cave and take samples of the bacterial life?' asked Liz.

'Quite probably,' said Frank. 'After all, that's where one of their meteorites, er probes, ended up.'

They strained their eyes to see if any aliens alighted from the scout ship, but none did. The absence of alien life prompted a debate. 'Are the aliens machines?' asked Rupert. 'Advanced, intelligent machines, not carbon-based life.'

'Why should machines need specific temperatures and light levels?' said Frank. 'Surely they can function over a wide range of conditions.'

'And why do they need to kill off all life first? It doesn't make any sense.'

'I agree,' said Viv. 'I think the machines are just an advanced scouting party gathering information and samples to take back to the asteroid. Detailed, firsthand information. The aliens will come later.'

'There's not much we can do except wait and see what develops,' said Frank. 'Let's have a brew.'

As they sipped their drinks waiting for the machines to return, they reflected on the unique happenings of the past few years. The unprecedented meteor showers, the sudden appearance of the asteroid, its position in geostationary orbit and especially the emergence of the huge fan-like array. They wondered what kind of technology was required to produce such a gigantic, fan-like array. A fan-like array that had expanded to a staggering 800 miles, making the overall diameter of the asteroid a whopping 2,000 miles, the same as that of the moon.

Viv did a quick calculation. 'I estimate its area to be about 302,000 square miles,' he said, 'almost a third of a million square miles.'

'Bloody hell!' gasped Rupert, 'how do they manage to keep something so big and so thin so rigid and stable?'

'And how do they store and transport something that huge around the galaxy?' asked Liz.

'I'm not sure,' said Frank. 'The nearest material we have on Earth is graphene, a monoatomic layer of interlocked hexagonal rings of carbon atoms, a bit like a single sheet of graphite but far stronger. Being only one atom thick, graphene is essentially two dimensional.'

'I've heard of graphene,' said Viv. 'It was discovered by scientists at Manchester University, wasn't it? Scientists who were awarded the Nobel Prize for its discovery.'

'It was and they were,' said Frank. Continuing, he said, 'Graphene is very tough, extremely strong – stronger than steel – flexible and conducts electricity. Also, being just one atom thick, it's extremely light. Their array could be made of something similar, but much more advanced.'

'That's very interesting,' said Rupert. 'I wasn't aware of graphene.'

'Neither was I,' said Liz. 'Thanks for that, Frank.'

About six hours later, the machines returned to the scout ship and entered the hatch. A few minutes later, the ship lifted effortlessly into the dark sky on its return journey to its mother ship, the asteroid. Exactly the same scenario was re-enacted at the four other locations.

There was nothing they could do except wait for the next scout ships to arrive, the scout ships with aliens.

## 28

# FIRST GLIMPSE

Two days later the scout ships returned. All five of them. To the same locations. Liz and her colleagues gathered round the screen showing real time images of the one in the Arctic, images beamed directly from one of America's orbiting spy satellites. Images that were crisp, clear and life-sized, even in the Arctic gloom. Were they about to get their first glimpse of the aliens? To see what they looked like. Or would there just be more machines to gather more information? They waited in eager anticipation, eyes fixed on the spacecraft in the centre of the screen.

For a while, nothing happened. Then they saw it. The hatch began to open. Not quickly like before, but slowly, just a small crack in the hull of the spacecraft, a small crack through which vapour of some kind, probably water vapour, escaped into the cold Arctic air.

'It's probably some sort of pressure hatch to equalise the pressure,' said Viv, his eyes fixed on the screen.

'Probably is,' said Frank, staring intently at the small opening that had appeared in the hull of the spacecraft.

As the hatch opened wider, light from the interior of the spacecraft spilled into the Arctic darkness, illuminating the patch of snow immediately below the hatch with an eerie bluish-grey glow.

'So they don't live in the dark,' said Liz.

'Doesn't look like it,' said Rupert.

'I didn't think they did,' said Frank. 'As Liz said earlier, the darkness is just a by-product in their attempt to attain the right temperature.'

'Look!' exclaimed Rupert, 'something's happening.'

With the hatch now fully open, steps began to descend to bridge the gap from the spacecraft to the ground, a gap of approximately ten feet. Everyone's eyes were glued to the screen, itching to get their first glimpse of the aliens. They didn't have to wait long. A foot appeared on the first step. Then another. Two feet and two legs clad in a dark grey spacesuit. As the alien descended the steps, a torso appeared followed by a spacesuited head. The movie makers and Liz had been right. The aliens were bipedal, upright humanoids with two arms and two legs.

'Is it me or do they look smaller than us?' asked Liz.

'You're right. They do look smaller. More the size of a chimpanzee,' replied Rupert.

'I think they're bigger than that,' said Frank. 'Somewhere between the size of a human and a chimpanzee. About five foot tall I'd say.'

As the alien alighted on the snow-covered ground, it removed an instrument from the belt on its spacesuit, took some readings and studied the results. Satisfied, it removed its helmet. Liz gasped. What met her eyes wasn't the face of a humanoid, but a face that was a cross between a chimpanzee and a seal pup. The nose was small and flat, like a chimpanzee's, as were the ears. Its mouth was also small, with thin lips, but the feature that really caught her attention was its eyes. They were large, round and dark, in complete contrast to the pallid colour of its face. Superficially, they reminded Liz of a seal pup, but only superficially. Whereas the eyes of a seal pup are endearing, charming and loveable, these were dark, sinister and foreboding. They made her shiver.

Short, thick, white hair surrounded the pale-coloured, pallid face, hair that reminded her of a polar bear.

Satisfied that everything seemed fine, the alien made a gesture with its hand. A few moments later, a second alien began descending the steps, an alien without a spacesuit. An alien shorn of all attire except what could best be described as a pair of dark grey shorts and a 'vest', a lighter grey garment that covered its upper torso. And, like its companion, it also had a belt around its waist.

Liz's fist impression was that the alien looked like a miniature Yeti, a miniature version of the abominable snowman. Its arms and legs were covered in thick, greyish-white hair and, she presumed, so was the rest of its body. As a child, she'd been fascinated by tales of the abominable snowman, a mysterious creature reputedly seen in the Himalayas. There was no way her parents would take her to the Himalayas, but every winter she implored them to take her to the snow-capped mountains of Snowdonia where she'd hoped to catch sight of a Yeti, but never did. Yet here she was looking at something remarkably similar. 'Could it be,' she wondered, 'that these very same aliens had visited Earth before, and been spotted? Spotted and dismissed by a sceptical public? Probably not, but then…'

'Look, they're moving,' said Viv. And they were. The two aliens were 'walking' away from the spacecraft with a gait that was a hybrid of a human and an ape. Every so often, they stopped to test the air and drive a rod-like probe into the snow-covered ground, recording the readings on the instruments on their belts.

'This should be interesting,' said Rupert, pointing to a dim shape in the distance. The keen nose of a polar bear must have picked up an unfamiliar scent and come to investigate. Liz could just make it out in the distant gloom. It stopped when it saw the aliens, stood on its hind legs to get a better view, and sniffed the air. It hadn't encountered scent like this before. The bear remained where it was, unsure what to do. However, curiosity got the better of it and it began to edge closer towards the aliens. Carefully, cautiously, inch by inch, like a predator stalking its prey. In a few moments time, the first ever encounter between alien life and Earth life would take place. What happened would reveal a lot about the aliens' intentions. Would they act peacefully or would they…

Suddenly, one of the aliens looked up, pointed to the polar bear and said something to its companion. Almost immediately, its companion withdrew a strange looking object from its belt, aimed it at the polar bear, and fired. What happened next both startled and horrified them. An intense white flash engulfed the polar bear and, as that disappeared, so did the polar bear. It had gone. Vanished. Vanished into thin air. Not a trace remained. Nothing to show that just a few seconds earlier, a polar bear had stood on that very same spot. It had vanished without a trace.

'Bloody hell!' gasped Rupert. 'Did you see that.'

'We did,' came the reply. 'We most certainly did.'

'What the f… hell was it?' said Liz, managing to restrain herself from using the eff expletive, an expletive she thought unladylike.

All eyes turned towards Viv and Frank. 'Either it's been atomised and destroyed,' said Frank, 'or it's been transported to another location.'

Liz couldn't help herself. 'You mean transported like in Star Trek? You know, like "beam me up, Scotty".'

'Yes, like that,' replied Frank, smiling in spite of himself. 'But if I had to choose, I'd say it was atomised.'

'What do you mean, atomised?' queried Rupert.

'Well, I think what they used was some sort of quantum ray, a weapon designed to destroy the quantum states of atoms. And if you destroy an atom's quantum states, you destroy the atom.'

'But you can't destroy an atom, can you?' said Liz. 'It contradicts the conservation of matter and energy law.'

'Perhaps destroy was the wrong word,' said Frank.

'What I meant was if you destroy the quantum states of an atom, the quantum energy levels of the electrons collapse and the electrons fall into the nucleus.'

'Where they'd combine with the protons to form neutrons, emitting lots of energy in the process,' interjected Rupert, 'explaining the intense flash of light which enveloped the bear.'

'That's right,' continued Frank, 'and since an atom is almost entirely empty space, the resulting pile of neutrons would be invisible to the naked eye. In a way, it's as if the polar bear collapsed to a nano-sized neutron star.'

The ensuing silence was broken by a concerned looking Viv. He seemed far away, as if deep in thought.

'Did you know that when different civilisations have met on Earth, it's usually been disastrous for one of them. The most technologically advanced civilisation invariably takes over, sometimes wiping out the other in the process. I hope the same thing doesn't happen to us.'

'But it might,' thought Liz. 'Perhaps Michio Kaku was right.' From their actions thus far, it looked very likely that these aliens were indeed descended from predators.

# 29

# ORIGINS

'Where the hell do you think they're from?' asked Rupert, disgusted and frightened by the aliens' destruction of the polar bear. 'Where the fucking hell are they from?'

'I don't know,' said Viv, 'but I certainly wouldn't fancy them as neighbours.'

'Let's consider it objectively,' said Frank, the group's expert on stars and planetary systems in the Milky Way galaxy. 'The nearest star is Proxima Centauri…'

'I thought the nearest star was Alpha Centauri,' interrupted Liz.

'It's the nearest sun-like star, a G-type star, yes, but the nearest star is Proxima Centauri, a red dwarf that's only a fraction the size and luminosity of the sun,' continued Frank. 'Most of the stars in the solar neighbourhood, within say 15 light years of the sun, a total of less than a 100 stars, are red dwarfs. Only a few per cent are like our sun. If we double the size to 30 light years, 75 per cent of the stars are still red dwarfs and only 7 per cent are like our sun. Even within a 100 light years, most of the stars are red dwarfs.'

'Do red dwarfs have planets?' asked Rupert, 'planets capable of supporting life.'

'They do,' replied Frank. 'Of the 600 or so exoplanets discovered thus far, some orbit red dwarf stars. As to whether they could support life, well, it's possible. Because red dwarf stars are much cooler and have a lower luminosity than G-type stars like our sun, the planets would have to be much nearer the star to receive sufficient light and heat for life to have evolved.'

'In other words,' said Rupert, 'the habitable zone, the so-called Goldilocks zone, would be much closer to a red dwarf star than for a G-type star.'

'Correct,' said Frank, 'but I don't think red dwarf stars are the best place for life to have evolved, especially intelligent life. I think the most likely place for life to have evolved in our own galaxy is on planets orbiting stars near its centre. A spiral galaxy like ours is a thin disc, barely 1,000 light years across, except at the centre where it bulges into a spheroid and it's here, in that galactic bulge, that the highest density of stars are found. Three per cubic light year compared to just four per ten cubic light years in the spiral arms of the galaxy. Not only that, but they are older stars – some are 10 billion years old – allowing plenty of time for life to have evolved. Intelligent life. You could say the bulge is the city of the galaxy and we're in the suburbs, some 26,000 light years away.'

'But if they're from the galactic bulge, how can they have travelled such a vast distance?' said Rupert. 'Even light, the fastest thing in the Universe, would take 26,000 years to reach us.'

'To have a chance of bridging interstellar distances, you need to accelerate a starship to near light speed,' said Viv, 'but even then it would take hundreds, even thousands, of years just to explore the solar neighbourhood, never mind the entire galaxy. Daedalus, a nuclear fusion starship proposed by scientists in the UK in the 1970s, travelling at 0.12c (12 per cent of the speed of light), would take 50 years to reach Barnard's star, just six light years away. As for intergalactic space travel, well, that seems totally out of the question.'

Liz was about to say 'remember Arthur C Clark,' but decided against it. Instead, she said, 'But we're decades away, even from that technology.' Doing a quick calculation in her head, she continued, 'For instance, it'll take Voyager 1, the fastest spacecraft ever built, 74,000 years just to reach the nearest star, Alpha, er, Proxima Centauri! Travelling at 38,000 miles per hour, it'll take 74 millennia to travel just 4.3 light years.'

'You're absolutely right,' said Frank. 'It certainly puts things in perspective doesn't it. In terms of space travel, we haven't even left our own backyard.'

'One of the biggest problems,' continued Frank, 'is the need to carry vast amounts of fuel. Acceleration requires fuel, which has mass. The more the total mass, the more energy required to accelerate it... The more energy required, the more fuel you need... It's a "Catch 22" situation, known as the "Rocket Equation" – faster acceleration requires exponentially more fuel.

'Our current technology,' continued Frank, 'employs chemical fuel. It's heavy and bulky and, in relative terms, it's power output is extremely low. Nuclear fission, and especially nuclear fusion, are infinitely superior, but the best fuel of all is matter-antimatter. However, such technologies are hundreds, possibly thousands, of years into the future.'

'But the aliens could have them, right?' said Liz.

'They could,' replied Frank. 'We already know they can travel much faster than 38,000 miles per hour.'

'Another way,' said Viv, 'is not to carry all the fuel but scoop it up along the way.'

'Ah, like the Bussard "Ramjet",' said Rupert, 'which scoops up interstellar hydrogen gas to feed the nuclear fusion engine as the starship travels through space.'

'Or more likely photon sails,' said Liz, 'like the ones they're using now to block out the sunlight.'

'Photon sails to collect starlight, solar energy, and convert it into power?' queried Rupert.

'Yes,' replied Liz. 'To use the energy that powers the Universe, an unlimited supply of free energy, to power your ship as it travels through space.'

'Like they're doing now,' said Rupert, 'using the stars as "petrol stations" to fill up their starships.'

'That's a good analogy,' said Liz.

'What you've all said is perfectly true,' said Frank, 'but I think the question of how the aliens arrived here boils down to one of two possibilities. One, they're travelling, cruising might be a better word, the galaxy at sub-light speed in a mini world, a mini planet, the asteroid, taking thousands of years; or two, they've found a way to transcend the speed of light.'

'And which is your preferred option?' asked Rupert.

'By the way the asteroid suddenly materialised out of nowhere, I'd have to say they've found a means to travel faster than light.'

'I don't think people realise just how vast and empty and lonely space is,' said Viv. 'For instance, if we shrunk the sun to the size of a golf ball, the nearest star, Proxima Centauri, would be at Istanbul, some 1,700 miles away. Space is empty. A vast nothingness, just like an atom. Empty space. In fact everything, you, me, our surroundings, the planets, the stars, the entire Universe, is essentially composed of empty space. Even things we consider heavy and solid, like a lump of lead, are really just empty space.'

'It's a sobering thought,' said Liz.

'What is?' asked Viv.

'That we and everything else are nothing more than just empty space.'

'Frank?' queried Rupert, changing the subject, 'are you saying that the meteorites came from the bulge of stars at the centre of the galaxy? It would have taken them millions of years to reach Earth.'

'No, I'm not saying that,' said Frank. 'I think the meteorites were sent from the asteroid, but I think the asteroid itself originates from a star system in the galactic bulge.'

'Couldn't we ask Myles to check that?' said Viv. 'It might not be possible to give a definitive answer, just an indication that the meteorites, and therefore the asteroid, originate from the bulge. It might give us something to work on.'

'We've got nothing to lose,' replied Frank. 'I'll ask him.'

# 30

# ASTEROID BELTS

'They can't be absolutely sure,' said Frank, 'but Myles and his team believe the meteorites could originate from the galactic bulge at the centre of the Milky Way.'

'In that case,' said Viv, 'it's almost certain that the asteroid originates from there too.'

'But it's 26,000 light years away!' said Rupert. 'That's one hell of a long way to travel.'

'Yes, it is,' said Frank, 'but since the presentation by Myles I've been reading up on asteroids and asteroid belts.'

'What for?' asked Rupert.

'Partly to answer a question I almost asked him,' replied Frank, 'but primarily to find out more about the alien asteroid.'

'I remember,' said Liz. 'You started to ask him something then said it didn't matter. What was it, Frank? What were you going to ask him?'

'I was going to ask him at what size a meteorite becomes an asteroid.'

'And have you found the answer?'

'Yes, I have,' replied Frank. 'Asteroids range in size from a few metres to hundreds of kilometres across. From boulders to mini planets. Anything less than that is a meteorite.'

'I see,' said Liz. 'Something else I didn't know.'

'But how did the aliens travel 26,000 light years in an asteroid,' said Rupert, bringing the discussion back to the central theme. 'It's a bloody long way.'

'I've thought about that,' said Frank, 'and I think I may have an answer. I said before that I thought the aliens had found a way to travel faster than light. Now, I'm not so sure. Having read about asteroids and asteroid belts, I think there's a more plausible explanation.'

'And what's that?' asked Rupert.

'Well,' said Frank, 'asteroids and asteroid belts are extremely common throughout the galaxy. They're everywhere. Most solar systems have them. The star, Epsilon Eridani, just ten light years away, has not one but two asteroid belts, and another star has an asteroid belt 25 times larger than our own. Asteroid belts are the fragments left over after planets have formed, so they tell us a lot about their solar systems. By studying asteroids, we are studying relics of the distant past.'

'Isn't an embryonic solar system just a mass of asteroids orbiting a star?' said Viv.

'It is,' replied Frank. 'All rocky planets are formed from the accretion of asteroids. As they orbit the star in the same direction, they collide with each other, slow collisions that result in accretion, a sticking together of the asteroids. It's a bit like two cars travelling in the same direction having a bump – they stick together. However, it would take billions of years for a planet to form just by accretion of asteroids, but we know that isn't the case. Planets are formed over millions, not billions, of years because of another force. Gravity. When the accreted asteroids become large enough, about the size of a large mountain, gravity joins in and greatly accelerates the process. That's the reason our rocky planets – Mercury, Venus, Earth and Mars – were formed over just a few million years.'

'So why didn't the asteroids in the asteroid belt coalesce into a planet?' asked Liz.

'That's a good question, Liz,' said Frank. 'The reason why they didn't is because the gas giant Jupiter disrupted the planet-forming process. Its strong gravity caused the asteroids to zoom off in different directions, colliding with each other and forming millions of smaller asteroids, the asteroid belt between Mars and Jupiter. Most asteroids remain in the asteroid belt but occasionally bits break off and fall to Earth. They're seen as flaming fireballs as they plunge through the Earth's atmosphere, burning up and hitting the Earth as meteorites.'

'So are all the asteroids in the asteroid belt small?' asked Liz.

'No, they're not,' replied Frank. 'That's a common misconception about the asteroid belt, that things are very small. Some of the biggest asteroids are really more correctly thought of as minor planets – they're several hundred miles across. For example, Vesta, the second largest asteroid in the belt at 326 miles across, has a mountain three times higher than Everest. It almost became a planet before Jupiter's massive gravity stunted its growth. Now, it's a miniature world.'

'You said that Vesta is the second largest asteroid in the asteroid belt,' said Viv. 'What's the largest?'

'Ceres,' replied Frank, 'but I'll come to that later.'

'This is all very interesting,' said Rupert, 'but I don't see how it's connected to the alien asteroid.'

'You will,' said Frank. 'Just bear with me a little longer.'

'Didn't we send a probe to the asteroid belt?' asked Liz.

'We did,' said Frank. 'The Dawn probe arrived at the asteroid belt in July 2011 and beamed back pictures of Vesta. That's how we know it has a mountain three times higher than Everest. The probe also discovered that Vesta has an iron core similar to Earth, showing that the Earth's core formed when the planet was still young. In fact, Vesta is very similar to the embryonic Earth in its first few million years.'

Continuing, he said, 'The asteroid belt is an ancient, violent and remote place located just 300 million miles from Earth. Unfortunately, not all the asteroids stay in place – they can roam all over the solar system. The moon's pockmarked, disfigured surface is evidence of that. It records a violent past of a massive, sustained bombardment, an intense rain of asteroids and debris from outer space. Millions of craters cover the moon's surface, including the largest one in the solar system, some 2,500 kilometres across, and it too is covered by thousands of smaller craters. Most of these were caused by a storm of asteroids that blasted the moon about four billion years ago, and if that happened to the moon, then it must have happened on Earth too. The Late Heavy Bombardment, as it was known, lasted for 200 million years. The impacts generated earthquakes bigger than any in recorded history, way off the Richter scale.'

'I still don't see where this is leading,' said Rupert, getting more and more frustrated.

Frank ignored the interruption and carried on, 'The asteroids not only brought destruction, they also brought materials – minerals, organic matter and ice. Lots of ice. Ice which melted on impact and became liquid water. Ceres, the solar system's largest asteroid, which comprises half the total mass of the entire asteroid belt, is composed mainly of ice. It has a rocky core surrounded by a large ice mantle. Compared to the Earth, Ceres is relatively small at 1,000 kilometres across, yet contains more water than all the fresh water on Earth. In fact, asteroids are the reason why the Earth has so much water. Why 70 per cent of our planet's surface is covered with water. It was the incessant bombardment of Earth four billion years ago that brought all the water. Not just the water in the oceans, but the water in the clouds, the rivers and the glaciers has all come from space.'

'Does Ceres have any liquid water?' asked Viv.

'That's what the Dawn probe is trying to find out,' replied Frank. 'Some scientists think there's an ocean of liquid water beneath the ice, formed by the hot inner core. Life as we know it depends on liquid water so, wherever there is liquid water, there may be life. Ceres may be home to primitive life forms flourishing in a sub-surface ocean.'

'So, if the asteroids brought water, they could also have brought primitive life to Earth?' said Liz.

'That's what some astronomers believe,' said Frank.

'In addition to water,' continued Frank, 'asteroids are rich in precious minerals. They could be mined for zinc, aluminium and platinum, even gold. Just one average-sized asteroid could contain minerals worth thousands of billions of dollars.'

'So that's why President Obama announced in 2010 that the Americans hope to send astronauts to an asteroid by 2025,' said Liz.

'I'm sure it's a major factor,' said Frank. 'The dream is that one day we could build cities on asteroids. Everything we need is there. Water, minerals, even oxygen and hydrogen from electrolysis of the water. Asteroids could be the stepping stones to outer space. And,' he continued, looking straight at Rupert, 'advanced civilisations may well use asteroid belts as bases to explore the Universe. Use them like we use service stations on motorways. Use them to replenish their supplies on their journey around the galaxy.'

'And you think that's what the aliens on the asteroid are doing?' said Rupert, 'using the resources on asteroid belts to explore the galaxy?'

'Yes, I do,' said Frank. 'I think it makes perfect sense. A mini world, a miniature planet, in a spheroid shape, the shape with the smallest surface area for any given volume and the reason why the stars, planets and moons are spheres, is ideal for interstellar exploration. There's no atmosphere to hinder its progress, it can rotate on its axis to simulate gravity, and house lots of scout ships to explore the planets. The asteroid could be completely artificial, built from scratch and assembled in space, or it could be a modified asteroid. For example, an asteroid that had a hollow interior.'

'But even if it travelled at 0.1c (ten per cent the speed of light), it would have taken 260,000 years to reach Earth, over a quarter of a million years,' said Rupert. 'And that's without any stops along the way,' he added hastily.

'That's true,' said Frank, 'but it probably doesn't matter. Those on board the asteroid will regard it as their home. Their planet. Whole generations will have lived and died on it. Only the first few generations will have remembered their original home. As far as the other generations are concerned, the asteroid is the only home they've ever known. In a way, they're like space-travelling gypsies.'

'But why are they doing it?' asked Rupert. 'For what purpose?'

'Ah, that's the 64,000 dollar question,' replied Frank. 'Why are we exploring space?'

'Out of curiosity,' said Liz. 'And to expand our knowledge. To satiate our thirst for what's out there.'

'Precisely,' said Viv. 'All of that and to see if we are alone.'

'Well, now we know we're not,' said Rupert. 'We know there's at least one other technologically advanced civilisation in the galaxy.'

'I still think they've come to conquer us and colonise the Earth,' said Liz.

'So do I,' said Rupert. 'I'd bet my bottom dollar on it.'

'Do you think they've left a dying planet?' asked Liz, 'and are looking for another suitable home, or are they just a warlike race of predators who destroy everything they encounter?'

'I'd like to think it's the former,' said Viv, 'but I fear it might be the latter.'

'If the asteroid didn't travel faster than light,' said Rupert, changing the subject, 'then why didn't we detect it earlier?'

'Because I think the aliens have developed some sort of "cloaking technology",' replied Frank, using Star Trek speak and winking at Liz, 'some means of making the asteroid invisible.'

'Then how come we managed to detect it?' said Rupert.

'To test our capabilities and response,' said Frank. 'I believe the aliens allowed the asteroid to become partly visible to see how technologically advanced we were, and now they know. Having witnessed our feeble attempt to divert the asteroid, they probably intend to eradicate us and colonise the Earth.'

The asteroid was humanity's nemesis. Its worst nightmare. It was like the Death Star in the Star Wars movies only infinitely more powerful and destructive.

'There must be something we can do,' thought Liz, thinking of Baby Blu and Charlotte. 'There must be something.'

# 31

# DESPERATION

Rob, Baby Blu and Charlotte were running out of what little supplies they had left. Even though they'd been very careful, their only fuel, wood, had shrunk from a bonfire-sized pile to just a small mound. The wood fire was central to their survival. It kept them alive. It provided light and heat; it melted snow to provide essential drinking water; it kept them warm; and it provided warm food from the few remaining tins in the larder.

The larder was almost bare. Fresh food was a distant memory. Tinned beans, tinned soups and the odd tin of corned beef was the order of the day. Gourmet dining it wasn't but it was better than the alternative – starvation and death.

Rob had set traps in the garden and, more recently, in the apartments, to try and snare any remaining wildlife. Birds were scarce but there was little meat on them anyway. He'd caught the odd squirrel but they too had become a rarity. He'd also caught a feral cat, and they'd even eaten a frozen grass snake! But it was the mammals that lived underground that survived the longest – rabbits, moles, mice and especially rats. It was these that provided the meat to supplement the tinned vegetables. As the dark freeze intensified, the rats had moved into the apartment block to take advantage of the plentiful supply of food on offer – dead humans. As these were consumed, even the rats had all but disappeared.

The garden where Rob set his traps resembled a sewage works, a frozen sewage works. It was stacked high with piles of frozen urine and faeces, piles of the bodily excrement from the denizens of the apartments, those still alive and those that had perished. The only consolation was that the freezing temperatures ensured there were no smells. Or disease.

The energy supplies had dwindled so much that each household was restricted to just 30 minutes of electricity per day. Gas and oil supplies had dried up long ago, and it wouldn't be long before the electricity supplies dried up too. Just a few weeks, or maybe months, at most.

To conserve their body heat, Rob, Baby Blu and Charlotte slept in a huddle wrapped in bundles of duvets and blankets, but even that didn't protect them completely from the freezing cold. The precious electricity was used to heat the oven, an oven containing pans of snow to produce water, a tin of beans and, if they were lucky, a skinned rat. The oven also contained a couple of large cobbles. The hot cobbles were wrapped in blankets to conserve their heat and placed in bed to help keep them warm. It was something that Baby Blu's parents had done, a trick that had been passed down from her grandparents, a trick that she had remembered. A trick to extract the maximum benefit from a heated oven. To waste nothing.

Rob and Baby Blu had discussed the future many times. The bleak future. Discussed what would happen when the food, or the drinking water, ran out. Or, if it ran out first, the precious wood needed to make the all important fires. What would they do? It was something they didn't want to think about, but something they couldn't avoid. They knew they'd have to confront it sooner or later.

They'd considered eating the dead people in the apartment block. Those who'd succumbed first – the elderly, the infirm and the sick – but decided against it. The very idea of consuming your fellow human beings was abhorrent to Baby Blu, especially after the rats had been at them. Even if they could have brought themselves to eat their neighbours, Rob worried that the rats might have infected the bodies with disease. Thankfully, Charlotte was still too young to comprehend any of this.

Another option, said Rob, was to eat him. For Baby Blu and Charlotte to eat parts of his body when the food ran out. He'd willingly sacrifice his body to let them live a little longer. First his fingers, then his toes, followed by his hands and feet. He could give them up and still live. Living without his limbs, his arms and legs, was a different matter. And he certainly couldn't live without his torso. But he didn't mind. He'd gladly sacrifice his entire body to give Baby Blu and Charlotte a few more weeks of life, enough maybe for the scientists to come up with an answer. It would be fresh meat free of disease. He deemed it better than all three of them dying needlessly.

Baby Blu was having none of it. She was adamant there was no way that she would eat her husband and Charlotte her daddy. It was out of the question. A non-starter. If they had to die, they would all die together. Die in a suicide pact. There was absolutely no way they would leave Charlotte, their beloved little daughter, alive by herself. No way at all.

Deep down, Baby Blu still had faith in the scientists. Still clung on to the faint hope that Liz and her colleagues might yet find a way to end the nightmare engulfing the planet. Might yet save them.

# 32

# OPTIONS

Panic engulfed the world. The few TV stations still functioning broadcast live pictures of the scout ships as they landed on the Earth. Live pictures of the geodesic-shaped machines and, two days later, live pictures of the aliens. Everyone, the politicians, the scientists, and the general populace, feared the worst. Feared an invasion of Earth and its subsequent colonisation by the aliens.

Top level emergency meetings were held by videoconference. This time round, in contrast to earlier meetings, there was less acrimony and more cooperation. There had to be. It was the last throw of the dice for planet Earth.

Their options were severely limited. The use of force was out of the question. Even the die hard hawks of the military conceded that. Any such attempt would be futile. Missiles or fighter jets would be intercepted and destroyed before they got anywhere near their target. The aliens had demonstrated their capabilities to do that already. No, it would have to be something more subtle, and more deadly, than simple military force. Something chemical. Or biological.

Several options were considered. Chemical options included the use of 'good' old-fashioned poisonous gases. Not chlorine or mustard gas (bis-$\beta$-chloroethyl thioether) used in World War I, but more sophisticated, more deadly, modern gases. The world had plenty of those.

Organophosphates were another option. First used by the Nazis in World War II, these nerve gases or neurotoxins act on the central nervous system and are lethal in minute doses. Modern versions immobilise and kill in minutes. Sadly, the world has plenty of these too.

A third option was to use the most deadly agent known, a strain of Botulinum toxin from Clostridium botulinum, a neurotoxin from the same stable as that used in Botox treatments. It's so deadly that just four kilograms is enough to wipe out the entire human population by respiratory failure. Just four thousand grams to wipe out seven billion people. No government admitted to possessing the agent, but such lack of admission counted for nothing in the murky, clandestine world of chemical and biological warfare.

Attacking the aliens with lethal chemical agents was fraught with difficulties. They couldn't attack the asteroid – they'd already tried that and failed. Their only option was to attack the aliens from the scout ships, a strategy which, even if successful, might provoke a massive retaliatory response from the aliens on the asteroid. Furthermore, killing one or two aliens from the scout ships in no way prevented other aliens, suitably protected aliens, from landing and colonising the Earth. And finally, such lethal chemical weapons didn't discriminate between aliens and Earth life. They'd kill Earth life too, including humans. So, just like military force, chemical weapons weren't the answer either. There was only one option left. It was time for the geneticists and molecular biologists to hold centre stage.

'We have to use something that's not only lethal to the aliens, but also prevents them from colonising the Earth,' said Professor Theodore Russell, one of the world's leading molecular biologists.

'Something that is specific to the aliens, which is lethal, and which doesn't damage life on Earth. And the only way to do that is to find some kind of microbial life, a virus or an archae "bacterium", to which they don't have any immunity.'

'Like the Earth bacteria that killed the Martians in HG Well's *War of the Worlds* novel,' gushed Liz, her voice sounding harsh and metallic on the videoconferencing link.

'Yes,' came the delayed reply, 'yes, a bit like that I suppose.'

'From what they've done so far,' continued Theodore, 'I think it's safe to say the aliens are a cold-loving species, a cold-loving species of advanced, intelligent life that seems to prefer a temperature of minus 60°C.'

'Why minus 60°C?' asked a voice from the meeting.

'Do you mean why do I think the aliens prefer to live at a temperature of minus 60°C, or why their bodies are suited, adapted, to a temperature of minus 60°C?'

'I really meant the former, but both I suppose,' replied the voice.

'I think minus 60°C is the temperature the aliens prefer because that's the temperature they've generated on Earth. They stopped expanding the array when the temperature dropped to minus 60°C, and its been stable at that temperature for weeks now. To answer the second part of your question is more difficult. Psychrophiles are known on Earth which thrive at different extremes of cold, from plus 15°C, which is hardly cold at all, down to minus 60°C, the current temperature of the Earth.'

'In that case, do you think the aliens have stabilised the temperature at minus 60°C to kill off all Earth life, rather than it being the temperature at which they live?' asked Frank, his voice too sounding harsh and metallic on the videoconferencing screen.

'That's a good point,' said the delayed reply from Theodore, 'but if their intention was to kill off all Earth life, I think they'd have dropped the temperature even further.'

Frank let it rest. He'd already had this discussion with his colleagues.

'We're pretty certain that the aliens are an advanced, intelligent form of psychrophile,' continued Theodore, 'but what we aren't certain of is whether they've evolved in the presence of light, or whether they live in total darkness. The asteroid always seems dark, but light was evident inside the scout ships. We'll have to pass on that one, at least for the time being.

'Right,' said Theodore, apparently relishing the challenge ahead, 'that's what we know, or think we know, about the aliens. The next step is to decide what type of microbial life to use against them; a virus, a bacterium or an archae "bacterium".'

'I think it has to be a psychrophile,' said Dr Janice Woodall, one of the UK's leading molecular biologists from Cambridge University, 'a psychrophilic archae "bacterium".'

'And, seeing we don't know whether the aliens live in the dark or in light of some kind, I think we should err on the side of caution and cover both bases,' said Professor Yamamoto Higura, a Japanese molecular biologist of some repute. 'We should use both types of psychrophile; those that have evolved and adapted to life in complete darkness – the chemoautotrophs – and those that evolved in the presence of light. For example, the eukaryotes that live by photosynthesis, such as the green snow algae.'

Following a short but lively discussion, it was agreed that using both types of psychrophile offered the greatest chance of success. They didn't know whether the aliens lived in the light or in the dark, so using both types increased their chances that the aliens wouldn't have immunity to one of them.

'That's all very well,' chimed a voice from the videoconferencing screen, 'but how do we acquire the samples? The conditions out there are atrocious.'

'Leave that to us,' said a commanding, authoritative voice. It was one of the military figures. 'We'll sort out something. But we need to know where to go.'

'Give us four hours,' said Theodore, 'to decide which psychrophiles to go for, and then we'll get back to you. Okay?'

The military figure nodded his assent.

Theodore surveyed the several videoconferencing screens before continuing. 'Okay, ladies and gentlemen, let's get cracking. Formulate your ideas in your own teams and then we'll reconvene in four hours time to thrash out the final solution. Thank you and good luck.'

Viv, Frank, Rupert, Liz and Zak joined Gregg and his fellow chemists, biologists and molecular biologists for the vital discussion. Although not specialists in the subjects themselves, they might, just might, be able to contribute on the more general aspects of the debate.

It didn't take the biologists and molecular biologists long to identify the best strains of both types of psychrophile, one that lived in darkness and one that lived in the presence of light, and the best locations in which to find them. That done, they turned their attention to resolving two other key issues. One, how to maximise the efficacy of the psychrophiles and two, how to deliver them.

'I suggest we start by looking at some of the world's superbugs, such as MRSA (Methicillin Resistant Staphylococcus Aureus),' said Dr Janice Woodall, 'and the work being done by Professor Todd Oakley and his team on bioluminescent bacteria. We...'

'Hang on a minute,' interrupted Rupert, 'aren't we jumping the gun here?'

His interruption created an uneasy silence. 'What do you mean?' came the acerbic response from an indignant Janice, clearly annoyed at being so rudely interrupted, especially by a non-specialist. 'What exactly do you mean by "jumping the gun?"'

'Well,' said Rupert, feeling distinctly uneasy at the way his comment had been received, and by the pairs of hostile eyes glaring in his direction, 'shouldn't we sort out the means of delivering the agents first? If we can't find a successful way to deliver them, then spending lots of time and effort maximising their efficacy is futile.'

Grudgingly, the biologists and molecular biologists conceded he'd made a valid point. 'I suppose you're right,' said Janice, who seemed to be leading the discussion. 'We'll address that issue first.'

'Biochemical weapons are usually delivered by missiles, which release their deadly cargo into the atmosphere over the intended target,' said Dr John Blackhouse, a biological warfare expert from Porton Down, 'but obviously that won't work here. The aliens would shoot them down before they reached their target.'

'Normal missiles, yes,' said Viv, 'but what about a Cruise-type missile, a ground-hugging missile? They might not detect that.'

'I think they would,' said John. 'We need to be smarter than that.'

'What about something smaller, like a drone?' said Frank. 'The Americans have some pretty sophisticated drones.'

'Good suggestion,' said John. 'Drones are much smaller than missiles and therefore less likely to be detected.'

'And they're much slower too,' said Rupert, 'making them more likely to be shot down.'

'But we're thinking along the right lines,' said Frank. 'I've read that the Americans have drones disguised as birds, even insects, that are pretty realistic.'

'That's the answer!' enthused John. 'We only need to deliver a tiny amount of the agent, so an insect is the perfect delivery vehicle. Something so small and so "natural" shouldn't attract their attention.'

'Right,' continued Janice, 'seeing that's sorted, let's carry on with finding ways to maximise the efficacy of the psychrophilic superbugs.'

Liz and her colleagues listened with increasing fascination as the biologists, molecular biologists and chemists discussed their ideas. Listened to their proposals to produce a highly resistant psychrophilic superbug with which to infect the aliens. They began by discussing the work of Todd Oakley and his fellow researchers at UC (University of California) Santa Barbara on bioluminescent squid.

'Some squids have a symbiotic relationship with "captured" bioluminescent bacteria,' said Janice. 'One, commonly called the Hawaiian Bobtail, uses bioluminescence to camouflage itself. Bioluminescent bacteria on the underbelly of the squid emit light to eliminate its shadow cast on the ocean floor by sunlight or moonlight and thereby conceal it from predators. The camouflage also helps it catch prey.'

'This is all very interesting,' said Rupert, 'but where exactly is it leading? I mean, what's it got to do with designing a psychrophilic superbug?'

Janice shot him a disdainful look then carried on. 'The point is, how do the bioluminescent bacteria know when to "switch on". It's no good if just one or two or even a few hundred switch on, they all have to switch on for them to have an appreciable effect. Thousands of them. All at once. But how do they do it? What "tells" thousands of individual bioluminescent bacteria to SWITCH ON NOW?' She paused, scanning the faces of those around her to gauge their reactions. They were absorbed, engrossed, in what she was saying, waiting eagerly for her to continue. 'The way they do it,' she continued, 'is by releasing a chemical messenger, a chemical that instructs them to emit light. A chemical trigger.'

'And has this chemical trigger been identified?' asked Frank.

'Yes, it has,' replied Janice. 'Identified and synthesised in the laboratory.'

'The relevance of all this to the task in hand still eludes me,' said Rupert, getting more and more frustrated.

'I'm coming to that,' said Janice, becoming irritated by Rupert's constant interruptions.

'Scientists reasoned that if bioluminescent bacteria release a chemical trigger to activate a response, then all bacteria might do the same, including pathogenic bacteria.'

'And do they?' asked Rupert with a trace of sarcasm in his voice.

'Yes, they do,' replied Janice forcefully. 'They all emit a chemical trigger to instruct other bacteria to perform some action. In the case of bioluminescent bacteria, it's to tell them to emit light. For pathogenic bacteria, it's to instruct them to release their toxins, the toxins that cause the disease.'

'So,' said Frank, thinking aloud, 'if that chemical messenger can be inhibited, nullified, then pathogenic bacteria become impotent. Harmless.'

'Precisely,' said Janice, 'and that's the reason why there's such a lot of research in that area.'

'But I still don't see the relevance of all this to the current problem,' reiterated a frustrated Rupert.

Janice shot the man with many questions a withering look. 'Not only do all bacteria release a chemical messenger,' she said loudly, 'but that chemical messenger is the same for every strain of bacteria studied so far. Hopefully, it'll be the same for psychrophilic bacteria too. So, if we use that chemical messenger in conjunction with the psychrophilic superbugs, it should really enhance their potency by triggering a massive release of toxins into the aliens at the same time. A massive dose that should prove fatal.'

'I see,' said Rupert. 'I'm sorry for doubting your intentions.'

'Apology accepted,' said Janice graciously.

'Is the chemical available?' asked Viv.

'The Americans have the most but we have a little too,' replied Janice.

'So, on the timescale we have available, it's only the Americans and ourselves who could launch biological attacks against the aliens using that chemical,' said Frank. 'The Americans in Alaska and ourselves in the Arctic.'

'I'm afraid so,' said Janice.

'Provided we have an insect drone,' said Viv.

'Oh, we've got some of those,' said John. 'Don't worry about that.'

'And provided we get samples of the psychrophiles,' said Frank.

'I'm sure the military will come up with a plan to do that,' said John confidently. The rest of them, however, weren't so sure.

'In that case,' said Janice, 'let's devise the best way to maximise the potency of the psychrophiles using the chemical trigger.'

Central to the ensuing discussion was whether the chemical trigger should be released into the atmosphere in the vicinity of the aliens at the same time as the psychrophiles, or whether it should be encapsulated to delay its release. After much debate, it was decided the best course of action was to delay the release of the chemical trigger by several hours, giving the psychrophiles time to spread throughout the alien's body. Once released, the chemical trigger would prompt the psychrophiles to simultaneously release billions of deadly toxins, deadly Earth toxins, which should prove fatal to the aliens.

It was a good plan, but would it work? Only time would tell. First, however, they needed samples of the psychrophiles.

# 33

# DRONES

Whilst awaiting the arrival of the psychrophile samples scientists around the globe deliberated on the best way to design and deliver the superbugs. In the UK and the USA, geneticists and molecular biologists focused on designing the superbugs, leaving the teams at the Simulation Chamber and especially the teams at the NASA/Johnson Space Center to concentrate on devising the best method of delivery. Rupert's advice hadn't gone unnoticed.

'What did you say?' said Carl, his harsh, metallic-sounding voice experiencing the usual transatlantic delay on the large video screen. 'I didn't quite catch all of it.'

'I said I thought we'd agreed that the best way to deliver the superbugs was by using a bird drone to release them in the vicinity of the aliens from the scout ships,' said Liz.

'There are problems with that,' said a military scientist from a second video screen, one linked to an underground bunker at a secret location near the Pentagon. 'We need a better way. One that is foolproof.'

'What problems?' asked Liz, hurt by his brusque comments.

'Well, for one thing, there are no birds in the Arctic winter, certainly not after the dark freeze of the last few months. If the aliens detected birds, they'd be suspicious and wouldn't hesitate to shoot them down. You saw what they did to the polar bear. We need to be cleverer than that. Remember, they are highly intelligent beings.'

Liz felt small, like a naughty schoolgirl who'd just been admonished by the headmaster.

'Not only that,' said Dr John Blackhouse, the warfare expert seconded from Porton Down to the Simulation Chamber, 'what if the aliens remain spacesuited? The superbugs would be ineffective. To do their job, they have to get inside the aliens' bodies.'

She felt even smaller after John's comments. 'I hadn't thought of that,' she said sheepishly.

'Well, we have,' said the military scientist in a confident, loud voice. 'We've thought about it a lot. An awful lot. And we've come up with a much better plan. This is our last chance to defeat the aliens. We have to get it right. It has to work.'

'And what is your much better plan?' asked Frank, irritated by the American's arrogance and his put down of Liz.

The military scientist paused before answering. 'Drone technology has advanced exponentially over the past decade,' he said. 'Almost everyone's aware of the plane-like drones being used in Afghanistan and Pakistan to hunt down and kill terrorists, but hardly anyone knows about the microscopic drones developed over the last few years. Insect drones that...'

'I'm aware of the Wasp class,' interjected Dr John Blackhouse, also irritated by the American's arrogance and his perceived ignorance of those he was addressing.

'Are those what you mean?' he said, more forcefully than intended.

'Many types of drones have been developed,' continued the military scientist, unperturbed by the interruption, 'but no, the Wasp class of drones are not what I meant. They are the size and shape of a bird. The insect drones I'm referring to are the size and shape of insects; wasps, bees and our latest drones, mosquitos.'

'You mean you've developed a drone the size of a mosquito?' gasped Liz, regaining her enthusiasm.

'Absolutely. It's almost indistinguishable from the real thing,' replied the military scientist with smug satisfaction.

'Wasn't there some controversy about that?' asked Frank, recalling a newspaper article he'd seen a few months ago. 'Didn't the American government fund the work on microscopic drones for use in urban areas, for domestic surveillance to keep tabs on people? A case of the Orwellian Big Brother syndrome gone mad.'

For the first time, the American military scientist looked uncomfortable. He glanced at his superior before continuing. 'You're right. Domestic surveillance was one possible use, a front presented to the public, but the main use was always a military one. The drone belongs to a class of Micro Air Vehicles or MAVs currently being developed for intelligence gathering and as a "swarm weapon" to launch *en masse* against enemy forces. The drones are equipped with a camera and a microphone and can be remotely controlled. They can land on a person's skin, take a sample of their DNA or inject a poison, and implant an RFID (Radio-Frequency Identification) tracking device. They can fly though an open window or attach themselves to your clothing to enter your home without you knowing anything about it. The only downside is their range; it's currently limited to several hundred metres.'

'I can see where you're going with this,' said Frank, as perceptive as ever.

'Can you?' replied the military scientist, intrigued to see if Frank could anticipate their plan. 'Please continue.'

'Well,' said Frank thoughtfully, 'from what you've said, I'd use a bird drone with a big range to transport the mosquito drones to within several hundred metres of the aliens, and then release them out of sight of the aliens.'

'Very good,' said the military scientist, clearly impressed with Frank's perceptiveness. 'And then what?'

'What do you mean, and then what?' asked Frank, perplexed by his question.

'And then what would happen next?' said the military scientist.

'The mosquito drones would fly the short distance to the aliens, land on their skin and inject the superbugs.'

'And…' said the military scientist.

'And hopefully they'd die,' said Frank, looking bemused.

'And the thousands, possibly millions, of aliens on board the asteroid. Would they sit back and do nothing? No, they'd retaliate by sending even more scout ships. Lots of them, this time with suitably protected aliens. We'd have achieved nothing except kill two aliens and arouse the anger of those on the asteroid. There's a better way than that.'

A silence permeated the room as people waited for him to continue.

'Just one, or maybe two, mosquito drones would land on the aliens' skin, obtain a sample of their DNA and return to the bird drone. They'd hardly feel anything, just a tiny pinprick. The bird drone would then return to base with their DNA samples, DNA samples that should really help our geneticists and molecular biologists design better superbugs.

'A few days, or weeks, later, after the superbugs have been finalised, a bird drone would unleash thousands of mosquito's loaded with the superbugs. Only one or two would land on the skin of the two aliens from the scout ships and inject the superbugs into their bodies. The rest would settle on their hair or their clothing, hopefully unnoticed or, preferably, secrete themselves inside the scout ship if the aliens left the hatch open. When the aliens return to the asteroid, the mosquito's would fly off and infect thousands of those on board. If, as expected, the superbugs are highly infectious, the disease should spread rapidly throughout the asteroid population.'

'How?' asked Frank. 'How would thousands of them just fly away and locate thousands of aliens? They can't be remotely controlled. Not on the asteroid. It's too far away.'

'You're right, they can't,' replied the military scientist. 'They'd locate their targets using heat-sensing devices, similar to how heat-sensing missiles lock on to their targets.'

'That's brilliant,' said Liz, clearly impressed.

'It is,' said Rupert, 'but it means the superbugs will have to be slow acting. They can't kill the aliens before they return to the asteroid.'

'That's correct,' said the military scientist. 'We know from previous visits that the aliens normally only stay for about two hours, and that it takes them about ten hours for the return journey to the asteroid, so the superbugs' effect would need to be delayed for at least twelve hours, possibly a little longer.'

'But how will we know if they've worked? 'asked Liz.

'If the asteroid leaves,' replied Viv. 'The aliens might be able to find a cure, an antidote, to the superbugs, but by then tens of thousands of them will have been killed.'

'More importantly,' said the military scientist, 'they'll know we have the technology to hurt them. Really hurt them. That should be enough to scare them off. To send them packing in search of an easier planet to colonise.'

'And if the asteroid remains?' asked Viv.

'If it remains,' answered the military scientist, 'then the Earth and everything on it is doomed.'

# 34

# SAMPLES

The military expeditions were successful. The dark-loving psychrophile identified by the scientists was obtained from ice-cores drilled at the Antarctic Vostock Station from a depth of 3,500 metres, close to the surface of the huge sub-glacial Lake Vostock. The light-loving psychrophile, a rare green snow algae, proved more difficult, but was eventually found in a remote region of the Arctic. As agreed beforehand, samples of each psychrophile were delivered to laboratories in Britain and the United States to form the basis of the superbugs.

With the first phase of the plan complete, it was time to implement the second phase – to obtain samples of DNA from the aliens.

During the past few weeks, visits from the scout ships had become more frequent. Not only that, both the number of ships and the number of aliens had also increased. Instead of just one ship with two aliens, there were now three ships and twenty aliens. And not just in Alaska and the Arctic, but also in the Antarctic, Siberia and the Himalayas. The aliens were beginning to make their move.

In Alaska, the aliens had started to construct buildings, geodesic-shaped buildings. Whether they were laboratories or accommodation blocks was unclear, but it unnerved them. Alien beings constructing buildings was the beginning of the end for the human race. It was the first step in the colonisation of planet Earth.

Although unnerving, the increase in the number of aliens visiting the Earth assisted their plan. Not at this stage – they only needed samples from one or two aliens – but later. Instead of infecting just four aliens (two in the Arctic and two in Alaska) with the superbugs, they now had the chance to infect ten times that number. The more they infected, the better. Perhaps the tide was beginning to turn in their favour.

The military were becoming increasingly frustrated by the lack of action. By the lack of a firm response. Any response. They wanted to launch Cruise missiles with conventional high explosive warheads to destroy the buildings before they became established. They argued the aliens wouldn't detect sophisticated ground-hugging missiles of a type they hadn't encountered before. Yes, they'd destroyed the ones sent to attack the asteroid, but those were in space and easy to detect. These were a different proposition altogether.

Up to a point, they were probably right. The aliens on the ground most likely wouldn't detect them but, as was pointed out in no uncertain terms, those on board the asteroid would. Would detect and destroy them, just as they'd destroyed the missiles aimed at the asteroid. Their plan was rejected. Overruled. But it left some of the hawks deeply unhappy. Unhappy and angry at the apparent impotence of the Earthlings.

The bird drones were ready to go. Two had been prepared in case one malfunctioned. They were white, ground hugging birds designed to blend in with the snow covered terrain with surface characteristics similar to those of a Stealth bomber to render them invisible to radar. Each bird drone contained several mosquito drones specially modified to extract samples of skin and blood from the aliens, samples from which they'd be able to obtain their genetic make-up. Their DNA.

Liz and her colleagues watched the screen as the two bird drones approached their target – the alien base camp in Alaska. Watched as they landed out of sight of the aliens, about 400 yards away. And watched as the mosquitos – about a dozen of them – emerged from the birds' mouths and flew towards their target.

Although the mosquitos were too small to be seen, especially in the Arctic gloom, their progress could be followed from their short range radio trackers. Everyone's eyes were fixed on the tiny white dots as they homed in on their target. Homed in on the aliens. They watched with bated breath as they approached the aliens, landed on their skin and then, a few moments later, returned safely to their mother birds. When the last mosquito entered its bird's mouth, the two birds took to the air to begin the return journey back to base with their precious cargo.

Liz and her colleagues were marvelling at the ingenuity and technical prowess of the Americans when the screen suddenly flashed red and the buzzer went off. What was it? What had triggered the alarm? Everyone was confused, And afraid. Very afraid. Had the aliens realised what had happened and were retaliating? It was pandemonium. Suddenly, a single word flashed on the screen in big red letters. MISSILE. Had the aliens launched a missile to destroy the American base where the birds were headed? For an instant, the screen went fuzzy as the cameras on the orbiting satellites switched their focus from the birds to the missile. As the image reappeared, the screen showed a Cruise missile skimming the ground. A Cruise missile heading straight for the alien base. Somehow, the military hawks had managed to launch a Cruise missile in direct violation of their orders.

'The bloody fools,' spat Viv. 'What the hell are they doing? They could bloody well ruin everything. It'll put the aliens on full alert. They'll almost certainly detect and destroy it.'

His words were prophetic. No sooner had they left his mouth when the missile exploded in a blinding flash of light. Just like the polar bear, it had probably been destroyed with a quantum ray.

'Let's hope they don't detect the birds,' said Frank, 'and shoot them down too. That would really piss me off.'

His colleagues were shocked. They'd never heard him use language like that before.

'I doubt they will,' said Viv. 'They're tiny compared to a missile and they're flying away from the aliens, not towards them.'

The aliens didn't detect them. Both bird drones returned safely to base with their precious cargo, samples of the aliens' DNA. Now, it was the job of the geneticists and molecular biologists to utilise that knowledge to design the superbugs.

# 35

# SUPERBUGS

Whilst waiting for the psychrophile samples from the expeditions, geneticists and molecular biologists around the world liaised via videoconferences on what modifications to make. On how to make the light-loving and dark-loving psychrophiles as potent as possible. Other teams worked on synthesising the chemical trigger. The chemical trigger that would instruct the psychrophiles to release their deadly toxins – to flood the aliens' bodies with a massive, lethal dose.

It had been established beforehand that the work would be done in the USA and the UK, partly because they had some of the best scientists, but mainly because they were the only two countries that possessed samples of the chemical trigger and the means of delivery – the mosquito drones.

Professor Theodore Russell, the world's foremost authority on genetics and molecular biology from Harvard University in Cambridge, Massachusetts, led the work. Discussions had shown they needed to genetically modify the genomes of the psychrophiles to produce the ideal superbug. Needed to incorporate artificial gene sequences to give them the characteristics they wanted. And to make them unlike anything the aliens would have encountered.

The ideal superbug would be extremely pathogenic, highly infectious and mutate rapidly, making it virtually impossible to find a cure. In combination with the chemical trigger, it should prove unstoppable, but only if the toxins were released at the right instant. For that to happen, the chemical trigger would have to be encapsulated.

The samples obtained from the aliens had caused them to make last minute modifications, but only minor modifications. The genetic make-up of the aliens was surprisingly similar to that of the Earth's primates. Like ours, their DNA was also built from four basic units. Not quite adenosine, cytosine, thymine and guanine (ACTG), but pretty close.

At first, they found it surprising that the aliens' genetic make-up was so similar to that on Earth but, the more they thought about it, the more sense it made. Life would only arise on planets having the right conditions, conditions similar to those on Earth. On planets in the so-called Goldilocks zone, where the temperature is neither too hot nor too cold. And on planets which possessed liquid water. On such planets, it was inevitable that chemical molecules would have formed that were the same or very similar to those on Earth. So it wasn't at all surprising that their DNA was similar to ours. Perhaps it was a universal trait. Perhaps all extraterrestrial life was based on Earth-like DNA. After all, the same chemical and physical laws operate throughout the entire Universe.

Theodore and his colleagues faced a delicate balancing act. On the one hand, the superbugs mustn't kill the aliens too quickly: they had to return to the asteroid. That meant a minimum 12 hour delay – two for their stay on Earth plus ten for their return journey to the asteroid. On the other hand, they had to take effect before the aliens had time to develop an antidote. They couldn't take too long to act. Furthermore, they had to allow sufficient time for the superbugs to spread and establish themselves throughout the aliens' bodies. That meant the superbugs acting somewhere between 12 and 24 hours. After some debate, they made an educated guess at 18 hours. That allowed the superbugs six hours to spread and establish themselves in the aliens' bodies. It was impossible to be more precise.

'But there's another problem too,' said Theodore to his senior colleague, Dr Martha Wannamaker, a renowned geneticist from Princeton University.

'I think I know what you're going to say,' said Martha. 'That we need two types of superbugs. One type to infect the aliens on the ground and one for those on the asteroid.'

'That's right,' said Theodore. 'We have to synchronise the effect of the superbugs. To have the best chance of success, they all have to act in unison. Act together. If they act on the 40 or so from the scout ships first, it'll give them plenty of time to find an antidote for those on board the asteroid. We need 40 superbugs that act in 18 hours and thousands that act in six hours. That way, they'll all take effect together, six hours after the aliens return to the asteroid.'

After days of feverish activity by geneticists and molecular biologists around the world, linked together by videoconference, both the dark-loving psychrophilic superbug and the light-loving psychrophilic superbug were finalised and produced. Forty to act in 18 hours and thousands to act in six hours. Deadly, highly infectious, rapidly mutating superbugs that would, hopefully, spread throughout the asteroid population like wildfire. Six hours after the aliens from the scout ships returned, deadly neurotoxins would flood the aliens' bodies. Paralysis and death should follow within minutes.

Not all the aliens would die – there were too many for that – but sufficient to make them have a rethink. To reassess their options. To make them depart.

As Theodore and his teams worked on the genetic modifications, they experienced a strange sensation. Powerful, vivid images flooded their brains, strange unworldly images. Images filled with profound, specific ideas. Out of this world ideas for the genomic structure of the superbugs. Structures that were completely different to those which Theodore and his colleagues had come up with. The images were so powerful that the novel structures had to be implemented. Had to be obeyed. It was as if they were in a hypnotic trance, being controlled by an invisible presence. It was unlike anything they'd ever experienced.

At first, Theodore and his colleagues kept the strange experience to themselves but, as soon as the work on the superbugs was complete, someone was bound to mention it. And they did. As soon as the first one mentioned it, the floodgates opened. It all came pouring out. Everyone involved wanted to talk about their weird 'supernatural' experience.

Listening to the account of their strange experience, Liz's thoughts flashed back to the metaphysical conversation she'd shared with Rupert. But only briefly. More urgent matters demanded her attention.

The completed superbugs, together with the encapsulated chemical trigger, were loaded into the mosquito drones, both in the USA and the UK, 40 with an 18 hour time delay to infect the aliens on the ground, and thousands with a six hour time delay to infect those on board the asteroid. Everything was ready. It was time to launch the attack.

A few hours later, dozens of the latest long range bird drones took off from the northern tip of Norway and the North West tip of the United States *en route* to the Arctic and Alaska respectively. They'd considered using much faster jet fighters or even guided missiles as the delivery vehicles, but dismissed the idea. They'd be detected and destroyed. Hours later, dozens of birds landed out of sight of the aliens in both the Arctic and Alaska and released their deadly payloads.

Thousands of mosquitos flew silently to their targets, to the twenty or so aliens at each site. Guided by remote control, 40 injected their deadly cargo into the aliens on the ground, whilst the remaining thousands slipped quietly and unnoticed into their scout ships. Unseen. Unheard. Waiting. Waiting to be transported back to the asteroid. Waiting for their chance to infect thousands more.

The Earthlings waited too. Waited to see if their plan would succeed. There was nothing more they could do.

# 36

# WHISPERS

The following 18 hours were the longest of their entire lives. Time seemed to slow down. To stand still. It was the longest day in planet Earth's history.

Everyone was nervous and fidgety. Although no one actually said it, they all knew this was their last chance. The last throw of the dice. Failure meant extinction.

To relieve the tension, people gathered in small groups to make small talk. They talked about anything other than what was happening. Anything to take their minds off the gravity of the situation. But the conversations were muted, subdued, almost whispered, as if they weren't meant to be heard. The final, faint words of a dying world.

As the day dragged on, people began to drift away from their small huddles to be alone, alone with their own thoughts. Liz was no exception. After enduring several hours of meaningless small talk, she excused herself to visit the toilet and grab some moments by herself. In the ladies, she thought about Baby Blu and Charlotte, about how they must be suffering, and burst into tears.

'Don't you think it strange what Theodore said?' remarked Frank.

'You mean the unworldly ideas that flooded his brain?' said Viv. 'Ideas on how to modify the DNA sequences of the psychrophiles?'

'Well, not just that but also how he and his colleagues apparently had no option but to implement them, as if they were being controlled. As if they were puppets dancing to the Puppet Master's tune.'

'It's probably a result of all the stress and pressure they've been under,' said Gregg. 'Stress can play strange tricks on the mind.'

'I disagree,' said Rupert. 'I don't think it's that at all.'

Viv, Frank, Zak and Gregg looked at him with surprise. For a moment, no one spoke, stunned by his unexpected remark. Gregg broke the silence. 'Why, what do you think it is, Rupert?'

Rupert looked uncomfortable before answering. 'I think a "Superintelligence" implanted the ideas into the brains of Theodore and his colleagues,' said Rupert, glancing at Frank, 'ideas to produce superbugs that would be effective against the aliens. Superbugs they couldn't counteract.'

Viv, Gregg and Zak looked at him in disbelief.

'A "Superintelligence". What the hell do you mean by that?' retorted Gregg.

'What extremely advanced civilisations could evolve into,' interjected Frank, trying to defuse the escalating tension developing between Rupert and Gregg. 'I overheard a discussion he had with Liz, a metaphysical discussion, whereby really advanced civilisations could discard their physical bodies and exist as pure energy. Pure thought. Millions of minds coalesced into one "Superintelligence" patrolling the Universe. $E = mc^2$ and all that.'

'Have you gone stark raving mad?' said Gregg. 'That's absolute, utter rubbish! I've never heard such bloody nonsense in all my life,' he spat.

'You should learn to open your mind to every possibility,' replied Rupert, remembering his closed mind mentality to Liz's ideas. 'You shouldn't dismiss anything that isn't impossible.'

'You're fucking deluded,' said Gregg angrily. 'All this stress has addled your fucking brain.'

'It's what Liz believes too,' said Rupert calmly. 'Is she "fucking deluded" too?'

'If she believes all that crap, yeah, she fucking well is,' retorted Gregg.

'I'm sorry you feel like that,' said Rupert, 'but we're entitled to our ideas.'

'Not fucking stupid ideas,' replied Gregg, going red in the face.

'Why do you think they "intervened" with the DNA sequences,' asked Viv, doing his bit to calm the situation. 'What was wrong with Theodore's ideas?'

'They must have known they wouldn't work. Wouldn't be effective. That the aliens would have been able to counteract them. So they intervened to design superbugs that would work. Superbugs the aliens couldn't counteract,' replied Rupert.

At that instant, Liz, who'd overheard the exchange between Rupert and Gregg on her way back from the toilet, made her decision. She knew immediately who she wanted to spend the rest of her life with.

# 37

# DECISION TIME

It was decision time for Baby Blu and Rob. Should they eat him alive, or should they all commit suicide and die together? Killing themselves was just about bearable, but the thought of having to kill their three-year-old child first, well, they didn't know if they could do that. To kill their only daughter. Their own flesh and blood. Someone they loved and cherished with all their heart. Someone who trusted them. Completely. Someone who loved them unconditionally. Someone who relied on them. How could they kill their only daughter? The very thought of it filled them with revulsion. It was abhorrent, an act that was against every mother and father's instinct. Against every natural law. Yet they had to make a decision. The food, water, wood, everything, had run out. There was nothing left. Nothing but despair and a slow, lingering death.

As he did every day, Rob went outside to dump their human waste into the garden and check the traps. As usual, they were empty. The rats had either got wise or they too had perished. But something was different. At first, he couldn't quite put his finger on what it was. Then it hit him. The 'day' wasn't as dark as previous days – it was a little lighter. He looked up at the sky and, for the first time in months, saw a glimmer of light filtering through the gloom. A few rays of sunlight struggling to reach the Earth. Was it real or was he hallucinating? Had the lack of food and drink affected his senses? Made him imagine things that weren't there? He rubbed his eyes and looked again at the sky. It was definitely lighter! He dropped the pan and dashed inside to tell Baby Blu. Perhaps there was a ray of hope after all. Perhaps they wouldn't have to make that awful decision.

# 38

# SUCCESS

IT MUST HAVE WORKED! Twenty-four hours after the attack, the aliens began dismantling the buildings at the base camps and returning them to the asteroid. At about the same time, the asteroid's fan-like array began to retract.

'We've done it!' exclaimed Viv triumphantly. 'We've bloody well done it. We've beaten the bastards.' Eyebrows were raised at his coarse, out of character language, but it was understandable given the circumstances.

'We have,' said Frank, staring intently at the video screens. 'We most certainly have. It looks like they're preparing to leave.'

They hugged each other like there was no tomorrow. Everyone hugged everyone else. They danced and jumped around the room like little children, shouting and singing at the top of their voices, behaviour most unbecoming of scientists. Viv unlocked the drawer in his desk, pulled out a bottle of champagne, shook it vigorously and popped the cork. Then, he sprayed all of them with some of France's finest. It was the kind of behaviour associated with the winning dressing room after a major cup final, or the podium of a Formula One race. Joy and celebration were the order of the day.

'I thought I'd never get to use this,' he said. 'I thought we'd had it.'

As the days went by, they watched teams of spacesuited aliens – they weren't taking any chances – dismantle the buildings and return them to the asteroid. Within a week, the buildings from all five base camps were back on board the asteroid, as were all the scout ships. The aliens had retreated to the relative safety of their starship.

As the fan-like array retracted, sunlight began to penetrate the darkness. For the first time in months, bright, warm, life-giving rays from our mother sun began to brighten the days, replacing the darkness and gloom of the dark freeze. Slowly, bit by bit, daylight began to return as more and more sunshine bathed the planet. And it began to warm up too.

With the fan almost completely retracted – it had taken far less time to retract the fan than it had to expand it – a strange thing happened. One of the hexagonal panels on the asteroid began to open, revealing a small aperture. A small aperture from which an object emerged.

'Isn't that the manned rocket?' said Frank, straining his eyes as he studied the image on the video screen. 'Can't we magnify it?'

Rupert twiddled some knobs to enlarge the image.

'IT IS!' exclaimed Viv. 'It's the manned rocket we sent with Bubba and Nikolov on board. It looks like they're sending it back to Earth.'

A few minutes later, the aperture closed and the asteroid departed. Everyone clapped and cheered as it receded into the distance, a dim star returning to the depths of outer space. Very soon, it was just a distant speck. Moments later, it disappeared from view completely.

Theodore couldn't get over his strange experience. He was convinced some 'supernatural force' implanted the DNA structures into his brain – they were so different, so radical, so... alien, they couldn't have come from a human brain. He thought their own ideas would have worked but obviously the 'supernatural force', or whatever it was, thought otherwise. Either way, it didn't matter. The superbugs worked and the aliens had gone.

The one person who wasn't surprised was Rupert. He was convinced that a 'Superintelligence' had directed the work of Theodore and his fellow geneticists and molecular biologists. A 'Superintelligence' that patrolled the Universe to ensure it behaved itself. To observe wherever life originated; to let it evolve in whatever direction evolution took it; to let it develop into intelligent life, hopefully into a technologically advanced, peaceful civilisation.

If a species developed nuclear technology and destroyed themselves, well, that was their own fault – they wouldn't interfere. However, under no circumstances would they allow a technically advanced civilisation from one world destroy a less technically advanced civilisation from another world. That was strictly forbidden. It was completely and utterly unacceptable. Against the laws of the Universe. THAT'S WHEN THEY INTERVENED.

Rupert believed it was them who designed the fatal gene sequences in the superbugs, the sequences that mystified Theodore and his colleagues. That it was them who tracked predatory civilisations to make sure they behaved themselves, and if they didn't... well, they'd intervene. In Rupert's eyes, they were THE GUARDIANS OF THE UNIVERSE.

# 39

# REUNION

Once the asteroid had departed, Liz dashed straight to Baby Blu's apartment near Chester – she had to know if they'd survived.

'Good luck,' said the army driver as she raced up the steps carrying a large bag. She stopped at the door and tried to open it. It was locked. She hammered frantically on the door, calling out her sister's name at the same time. Over and over. But no one answered. Just as she was beginning to despair, she heard footsteps. Faint at first but getting steadily louder. Someone was approaching the door. A few seconds later, she heard the unmistakable sound of a key entering a lock, followed by a click as the lock disengaged. She turned the handle and burst through the door like a whirlwind, almost knocking Rob off his feet.

She couldn't believe what met her eyes. The gaunt, thin 'stranger' stood before her was nothing more than skin and bone. A skeleton. He reminded her of her dad just before he died. If Rob looked like this, she feared the worst for Baby Blu and Charlotte. Especially little three-year-old Charlotte, her beloved niece.

'How's Baby Blu and Charlotte?' she blurted out, dreading the reply as soon as the words had left her mouth. 'Are they…'

'They're alive,' said Rob. 'I can't say they're fine because they aren't, but they're both still alive.'

'Thank God,' said Liz, tears streaming down her cheeks. 'Thank God for that.'

The sound of Liz's voice brought Baby Blu and Charlotte to the door. They were dirty, dishevelled and thin as rakes. Liz ran to meet them, scooped Charlotte into her arms and embraced her little sister. She sobbed uncontrollably, relieved that they were alive but shocked at their condition.

'Here,' she said, rummaging in her bag. 'I've brought you some food and drink. Take it, but don't eat and drink too much at once.'

Her advice fell on deaf ears. Baby Blu, Charlotte and Rob ate and drank as if their lives depended on it. They were absolutely famished. If it made them sick, then so be it. Their emaciated bodies craved food. And drink. They simply couldn't help it.

As Liz watched them gorge themselves, she heard footsteps. Baby Blu heard them too. 'Who's that?' she asked. 'Is it Gregg?'

Liz smiled and watched her sister's face as the door opened and a man strode into the room.

## 40

# A NEW BEGINNING

Gradually, the world began to return to some semblance of normality. The temperature had reached its seasonal average and the first green shoots were sprouting from the soil. Livestock had returned to the fields. Cows and sheep that had been deliberately kept alive, grazing on the green shoots of recovery. The countryside began to look a little like the England of old. But the dark freeze had exacted a terrible toll. Ninety-nine per cent of all cold-blooded life had been exterminated. Ninety-nine per cent of the ectotherms. Ninety-nine per cent of all reptilian life. Gone forever. Extinct.

The endotherms, the warm-blooded animals, fared better, but even these were decimated. In fact, much of the wildlife came close to extinction. Plants, animals, birds, fish, even insects. As usual, it was the microscopic life that fared best. The bacteria and viruses.

The dark freeze exacted a heavy toll on humans too. Half the world's population perished, some 3.5 billion people. Men, women, children and babies. Not surprisingly, Third World countries suffered most, countries in South America, Africa and Asia, although a billion people perished in the developed countries too. No country emerged unscathed.

The sunlight and rising temperatures were most welcome but they had an unwanted side effect – they melted the piles of human waste, the frozen piles of urine and excrement, causing foul smells and, worse still, disease. They were a breeding ground for pathogenic bacteria. The authorities did their best to remove them, but the diseases claimed many lives, especially those of the weak and vulnerable.

Of more concern were the decomposing bodies of the dead. The 3.5 billion dead humans, half the world's population. The stench of death was bad enough but it was the propensity for disease that worried the government. It might have been construed as callous, but in the UK the bodies were collected in huge, sealed trucks and dumped in massive lime pits. Hundreds of lime pits, each containing over ten thousand human bodies.

It took time but, slowly and surely, things began to return to some semblance of normality. Food crops were grown, livestock reared, families reunited.

The dark freeze had been horrific, yet some good emerged. It taught the citizens of planet Earth to cooperate more, to cease their petty feuding, to pull together for a brighter, better future. And, most importantly of all, it taught them to take nothing for granted.

# 41

# AN UNLIKELY COUPLING

'RUPERT!' What are you doing here?' said Baby Blu, startled by his appearance. 'Where's Gregg?' she asked, looking at Liz.

'Gregg and I have ended our relationship,' said Liz. 'It's unfortunate but we weren't really suited. Rupert's the one I love and want to spend the rest of my life with.'

'And Liz is the only one for me, the woman I want to share my life with,' said Rupert, putting his arm around her and pecking her gently on the cheek.

'Well, well,' said Rob, 'I never expected…'

Baby Blu's icy stare cut him off in mid-sentence.

'You make a lovely couple, don't they Rob?'

'They do,' said Rob, suitably chastised. 'They most certainly do.'

'We've got something to tell you,' said Liz excitedly, putting her arms around Rupert and shooting him a beaming smile. 'Haven't we Rupert.'

'We have,' replied Rupert, returning her smile and kissing her tenderly on the cheek.

'Oh, I think I know what you're going to say,' said Baby Blu, jumping up and down with delight. 'You're going to get married, aren't you,' she gushed.

'Yes, we are,' replied Liz. 'We are.'

# EPILOGUE

The asteroid had long since gone but one thought stuck in Liz's head. A thought that wouldn't go away. That haunted her. Gnawed at her. Why had the aliens returned the two astronauts? Why had they let Bubba and Nikolov return to Earth? It could have been an act of kindness, or mercy, but their previous behaviour hadn't suggested they possessed such traits. Or – and it was this that really bothered her – it could be something sinister. Had they tampered with the two astronauts? Genetically modified them? Altered them to produce offspring in their image? Human-alien offspring or, even worse, alien offspring. Super intelligent alien children who thrived in cold conditions. Children who would thrive and multiply in a climate of minus 60°C. Alien children who would grow into alien adults who would take over the planet. Try as she might, she just couldn't get the thoughts out of her head. She vowed there and then to ring Carl.

'Hi Carl. It's Liz here. I've been thinking about the two astronauts...'

# ACKNOWLEDGEMENTS

I would like to thank all the people who have helped make *The Dark Freeze* a better book. To my cousin, Brian, my niece Michelle Johnson, and my friends Sharon and Ian Taylor and Neville and Phyllis Jackson, for reading the entire manuscript and making valuable suggestions. And to my wife Vera, for her sufferance during its writing.

Special thanks go to my two sons, Andrew and Michael, and again to Sharon Taylor, not only for reading the manuscript but also for proof reading it, and to my nephew, Stuart Gent, for helping design the book's cover.

To all of you I offer my sincere thanks.